classic country house mystery – body in the library, closed circle of suspects, foul weather – all elevated by Banville's immaculate, penetrating prose.' Peter Swanson

SNOW

JOHN
BANVILLE

faber

First published in 2020
by Faber & Faber Limited
Bloomsbury House
74–77 Great Russell Street
London WC1B 3DA

This paperback edition published in 2021

Typeset by Faber & Faber Limited
Printed and bound by CPI Group (UK) Ltd, Croydon, CR0 4YY

A CIP record for this book
is available from the British Library

ISBN 978–0–571–36270–7

2 4 6 8 10 9 7 5 3 1

To John and Judith Hannan

WINTER, 1957

I'm a priest, for Christ's sake — how can this be happening to me?

He had noticed the empty socket where the light bulb was missing but had thought nothing of it. However, when he was halfway along the corridor, where the darkness was deepest, something seized him by the left shoulder, some sort of animal, it seemed, or a large heavy bird, that drove a single talon deep into the right side of his neck just above the rim of his collar. All he felt was the quick, stabbing blow, then his arm went numb all the way down to his fingertips.

Grunting, he stumbled away from his assailant. There was a taste at the back of his throat, of bile and whiskey mixed, and of something else, harsh and coppery, that was the taste of terror itself. A hot stickiness was spreading down his right side, and he wondered for a moment if the creature had vomited on him. He went on, reeling, and came to the landing, where a single lamp glowed. In the lamplight, the blood on his hands looked almost black.

His arm was still numb. He lurched to the head of the stairs. His head swam, and he was afraid he would fall, but with his left hand he clutched the banister and managed to negotiate his way down the sweeping curve of the staircase to the hall. There he stopped, swaying and panting, like a wounded bull. No sound now, only a dull slow drumming in his temples.

A door. He wrenched it open, desperate for sanctuary. His toecap caught the edge of a rug and he pitched headlong, slack and heavy, and, falling, struck his forehead on the parquet floor.

I

He lay still in the dimness. The wood, smelling of wax polish and old dust, was smooth and cool against his cheek.

The fan of light on the floor beyond his feet folded abruptly as someone came in and pushed the door shut. He flopped over on to his back. A creature, the same or another, leaned over him, breathing. Fingernails, or claws, he didn't know which, scrabbled at his lap. Sticky there, too, but not from blood. He saw the flash of the blade, felt it slice coldly, deeply, into his flesh.

He would have screamed, but his lungs failed him. No strength, any more. As he faded, so did the pain, until there was nothing except a steadily creeping cold. Confiteor Deo . . . *He released a rattling sigh, and a bubble of blood swelled between his parted lips, swelled and swelled, and burst with a little pop that sounded comical in the silence, although by now he was beyond hearing it.*

The last thing he saw, or seemed to see, was a faint flare of light that yellowed the darkness briefly.

'The body is in the library,' Colonel Osborne said. 'Come this way.'

Detective Inspector Strafford was accustomed to cold houses. He had spent his earliest years in a great gaunt mansion much like this one, then he had been sent away to school to a place that was even bigger and greyer and colder. He often marvelled at the extremes of discomfort and misery that children were expected to endure without the slightest squeak of protest or complaint. Now, as he followed Osborne across the broad hallway – time-polished flagstones, a set of antlers on a plaque, dim portraits of Osborne ancestors lining the walls on either side – it seemed to him the air was even icier here than it was outside. In a cavernous stone grate three sods of damp turf arranged in a tripod smouldered sullenly, giving out no detectable warmth.

It had snowed continuously for two days, and this morning everything appeared to stand in hushed amazement before the spectacle of such expanses of unbroken whiteness on all sides. People said it was unheard of, that they had never known weather like it, that it was the worst winter in living memory. But they said that every year when it snowed, and also in years when it didn't snow.

The library had the look of a place that no one had been in for a very long time, and today it wore a put-upon aspect, as though indignant that its solitude should be so suddenly and so rudely violated. The glass-fronted bookcases lining the walls stared before them coldly, and the books stood shoulder to shoulder in an attitude of mute resentment. The mullioned windows were set into deep granite embrasures, and snow-light glared through their numerous tiny leaded panes. Strafford had already cast a sceptical eye on the architecture of the place. Arts-and-Crafts fakery, he had thought straight off, with a mental sniff. He wasn't a snob, not exactly, only he liked things to be left as they were, and not got up as what they could never hope to be.

But then, what about himself? – was he entirely authentic? He hadn't missed the surprised glance with which Colonel Osborne, opening the front door, had scanned him from head to toe and back again. It was only a matter of time before he would be told, by Colonel Osborne or someone else in the house, that he didn't look much like a policeman. He was used to it. Most people meant it as a compliment, and he tried to take it in that spirit, though it always made him feel like a confidence trickster whose trick has been exposed.

What people meant was that he didn't look like an *Irish* policeman.

Detective Inspector Strafford, first name St John – 'It's pronounced Sinjun,' he would wearily explain – was thirty-five and looked ten years younger. He was tall and thin – 'gangly' was the word – with a sharp, narrow face, eyes that in certain lights showed as green, and hair of no particular colour, a lock of which had a tendency to fall across his forehead like a limp, gleaming wing, and which he would push back with a characteristic stiff gesture involving all four fingers of his left

4

hand. He wore a grey three-piece suit that, like all his clothes, appeared to be a size or more too big for him, a narrowly knotted wool tie, a fob watch on a chain – it had been his grandfather's – a grey gabardine trench coat and a grey wool scarf. He had taken off a soft black fedora and now held it by the brim at his side. His shoes were soaked from melted snow – he didn't seem to notice the puddles forming under him on the carpet.

There was not as much blood as there should have been, given the wounds that had been inflicted. When he looked more closely he saw that someone had mopped up most of it. The priest's body had been tampered with too. He lay on his back, hands joined on his breast. His legs were aligned neatly side by side. All that was lacking was a set of rosary beads twined around his knuckles.

Say nothing for now, Strafford told himself. There would be time enough for the awkward questions later on.

On the floor above the priest's head stood a tall brass candlestick. The candle in it had burned out completely and the wax had flowed all down the sides. It looked, bizarrely, like a frozen cascade of champagne.

'Damnedest thing, eh?' the Colonel said, touching it with the toe of his shoe. 'Gave me the shivers, I can tell you. As if there'd been a Black Mass, or something.'

'Umm.'

Strafford had never heard of the murder of a priest before, not in this country, or at least not since the days of the Civil War, which had ended while he was still a toddler. It would be a huge scandal, when the details got out, *if* they got out. He didn't want to think about that just yet.

'Lawless, that was his name, you say?'

Colonel Osborne, frowning down at the dead man, nodded. 'Father Tom Lawless, yes – or just Father Tom, which is what everyone called him. Very popular, in these parts. Quite the character.'

'A friend of the family, then?'

'Yes, a friend of the house. He often comes over – *came* over, I suppose I should say now – from his place up at Scallanstown. His horse is stabled here – I'm master of the Keelmore hounds, Father Tom never missed an outing. We were supposed to ride yesterday, but there was the snow. He called in anyway and stayed for dinner, and we gave him a bed for the night. I couldn't have let him go out again in that weather.' His eyes went back to the corpse. 'Though looking at him now, and what's become of the poor chap, I bitterly regret that I didn't send him home, snow or no snow. Who would do such a terrible thing to him I can't think.' He gave a slight cough, and waggled a finger embarrassedly in the direction of the dead man's crotch. 'I fastened up his trousers as best I could, for decency's sake.' So much for the integrity of the crime scene, Strafford thought, with a silent sigh. 'When you look you'll see that they – well, they gelded the poor chap. Barbarians.'

'"They"?' Strafford enquired, raising his eyebrows.

'They. He. I don't know. It's the kind of thing we used to see a lot of in the old days, when they were fighting for their so-called freedom and the countryside was thick with murdering ruffians of all sorts and hues. There must be a few of them still about, if this is anything to go by.'

'So you think the killer, or killers, got in from outside?'

'Well, for God's sake, man, you don't imagine anyone in the house would do a thing like this, do you?'

'A burglar, then? Any signs of forced entry – smashed window, broken door lock?'

'Can't say, haven't checked. Isn't that your job, searching for clues and so on?'

Colonel Osborne looked to be in his early fifties, lean and leathery, with a nail-brush moustache and sharp, ice-blue eyes. He was of middle height, and would have been taller if he hadn't been markedly bow-legged – the result, perhaps, Strafford thought sardonically, of all that riding to hounds – and he walked with a curious gait, at once rolling and rickety, like an orangutan that had something wrong with its knees. He wore highly polished brown brogues, cavalry twill trousers with a sharp crease, a tweed shooting jacket, checked shirt and a spotted bow tie in a subdued shade of blue. He smelled of soap and tobacco smoke and horses. He was balding on top, with a few strands of sandy hair heavily oiled and brushed fiercely away from the temples and meeting at the back of his skull in a sort of spiked ruffle, like the tip of the tail of an exotic bird.

He had seen action in the war as an officer with the Inniskilling Dragoons, did something noteworthy at Dunkirk and was awarded a medal for it.

Very much a type, was Colonel Osborne. A type that Strafford was thoroughly familiar with.

Odd, he thought, that a man should take the time to dress and groom himself so punctiliously while the body of a stabbed and castrated priest lay on the floor in his library. But of course the forms must be observed, whatever the

7

circumstances – afternoon tea had been taken every day, often outdoors, during the siege of Khartoum. That was the code of the Colonel's class, which was Strafford's class, too.

'Who found him?'

'My wife.'

'I see. Did she say if this is the way he was, lying like this, with his hands joined?'

'No. In fact, I tidied him up a bit.'

'I see.'

Bloody hell, he thought. *Bloody* hell.

'But I didn't join his hands – that must have been Mrs Duffy.' He shrugged. 'You know what they're like,' he added quietly, with a meaning look.

By 'they', Strafford knew, he meant Catholics, of course.

Now the Colonel produced a monogrammed silver cigarette case from the inside breast pocket of his jacket, pressed the catch with his thumb, opened the case flat on his palm and proffered two full neat rows of cigarettes, each row corralled behind an elastic strap. The brand was Senior Service, Strafford noted automatically. 'Care to smoke?'

'No, thanks,' Strafford said. He was still considering the corpse. Father Tom had been a big man, with burly shoulders and a barrel chest. There were woolly clumps of hair in his ears – priests, being wifeless, tended to neglect that kind of thing, Strafford reflected. Which reminded him – 'And where is she now,' he asked, 'your wife?'

'Eh?' Osborne stared at him for a second, twin tusks of cigarette smoke flaring from his nostrils. 'Oh, yes. She's upstairs, resting. I made her take some brandy and port. You can imagine the state she's in.'

'Of course.'

Strafford, batting his hat softly against his left thigh, looked about distractedly. Everything felt unreal, the big square room, the lofty bookcases, the fine but faded Turkey carpet, the furniture arranged just so, and the body, laid out so neatly, the eyes open and filmed over, gazing upwards vaguely, as if their owner were not dead but lost in puzzled speculation.

And then there was the man standing on the other side of the corpse, in his pressed slacks and checked cotton shirt and expertly knotted bow tie, with his military moustache and his cold eyes and a star of light from the window behind him twinkling on the slope of his taut, tanned scalp. It all seemed too theatrical, especially with that unnaturally brilliant white light pressing in from outdoors. It was too much like the last scene of a drawing-room melodrama, with the curtain about to come down and the audience getting ready to applaud.

What had gone on here last night, that had left this man dead and mutilated?

'You came down from Dublin?' Colonel Osborne enquired. 'Treacherous going, I imagine. The roads are like glass.' He paused, lifting one eyebrow and lowering the other. 'You drove alone?'

'They got me on the telephone, and I came across. I was visiting relatives down here.'

'Ah. I see. What was the name again? Stafford?'

'Strafford, with an *r*.'

'Sorry.'

'Don't worry, everyone makes the same mistake.'

Colonel Osborne was nodding, frowning, thinking. 'Strafford,' he murmured. 'Strafford.' He took a long draw from his cigarette. He was trying to place the name. The detective didn't offer to help him.

'There'll be more people arriving shortly,' he said. 'Guards, in uniform. A forensic team. And a photographer.'

Colonel Osborne stared in alarm. 'From the newspapers?'

'The photographer? No – one of ours. To make a photographic record of the – of the crime scene. You'll hardly notice him. But the story will probably be all over the papers, you know, and on the wireless, too. No stopping that.'

'No, I suppose not,' Colonel Osborne said gloomily.

'Of course, what exactly the story will *be* won't be our decision.'

'How's that?'

Strafford shrugged. 'I'm sure you know as well as I do that in this country, nothing gets into the papers that hasn't been – well, vetted.'

'Vetted? Who by?'

'The powers that be.' The detective gestured towards the corpse at their feet. 'It is a priest that was murdered, after all.'

Colonel Osborne nodded, making a sideways chewing motion with his lower jaw. 'They can vet away, as far as I'm concerned. The less of it that comes out, the better pleased I'll be.'

'Yes. You might be lucky.'

'Lucky?'

'It mightn't get out at all. I mean, the circumstances might be – glossed over, shall we say? It's not unheard of.'

The Colonel missed the irony of that last observation. The glossing over of scandals wasn't so much unheard of as the norm. He was gazing down at the corpse again. 'Awful business, though. God knows what the neighbours will say.'

Once more he eyed the detective with that quizzically one-sided look. 'Strafford,' he said. 'Funny, I thought I knew all the families in these parts.'

By which he meant, of course, all the Protestant families, as Strafford was well aware. Protestants made up five per cent of the population of the still relatively young Republic, and of this number only a fraction – 'Horse Protestants', as Catholic Ireland derisively called them – still managed to cling on to their estates and live more or less as they had done in the days before independence. It was hardly surprising, then, that they should all expect to know each other, or at least to know of each other, through an intricate network of relatives, in-laws, neighbours, as well as a cohort of ancient enemies.

In Strafford's case, however, it was apparent that Colonel Osborne was stumped. The detective, amused, decided to re-lent – what did it matter?

'Roslea,' he said, as if it were a password, which, when he came to think of it, it was. 'Over near Bunclody, that side of the county.'

'Ah, yes,' the Colonel said, frowning. 'Roslea House? I think I was in the place once, at a wedding or the like, years ago. Is that your—?'

'Yes. My family lives there still. That's to say, my father does. My mother died young, and I was an only child.' *An only child.* It always sounded strange, to his adult ears.

'Yes, yes,' Colonel Osborne mumbled, nodding. He had been only half listening. 'Yes indeed.'

Strafford could see the man was not impressed – there were no Osbornes anywhere near the parish of Roslea, and where there were no Osbornes there could be, for the Colonel, nothing else of much interest. Strafford imagined his father chuckling. His father derived a quiet amusement from the pretensions of his co-religionists and the elaborate rituals of class and privilege, or imagined privilege, by which they lived, or sought to live, in these straitened times.

Thinking of these things, Strafford was once more struck by the strangeness of this killing. How could it possibly have come about that a Catholic priest, 'a friend of the house', should be lying here dead in his own blood, in Ballyglass House, hereditary seat of the Osbornes, of the ancient barony of Scarawalsh, in the County of Wexford? What, indeed, would the neighbours say.

They heard a far-off knocking at the front door.

'That's probably Jenkins,' Strafford said. 'Detective Sergeant Jenkins, my second in command. They told me he was on his way.'

2

The first thing everyone noticed about Sergeant Jenkins was the flatness of his head. It looked as if the top of it had been sliced clean off, like the big end of a boiled egg. How, people wondered, was there room for a brain of any size at all in such a shallow space? He tried to hide the disfigurement by slathering his hair with Brylcreem and forcing it into a sort of bouffant style on top, but no one was fooled. The story was that the midwife had dropped him on his head when he was born, but it seemed too far-fetched to be true. Oddly, he never wore a hat, perhaps on the principle that a hat would flatten his carefully fluffed-up hair and spoil the attempted camouflage.

He was a young man, still in his twenties, serious in manner and dedicated to his job. He was bright, too, but not as bright as he believed himself to be, as Strafford often had cause to note, with a certain sympathy. When something was said that he didn't understand he would go silent and watchful, like a fox scenting the approaching hunt. He wasn't popular on the Force, which was reason enough for Strafford to like him. They were both outsiders, a thing that didn't trouble Strafford, or not much, though Jenkins hated being isolated.

When people told him teasingly, as for some reason it amused them to do, that what he needed was a girlfriend, he would scowl and his forehead would redden. It didn't help that his name was Ambrose, which was bad enough, but made worse by the fact that everyone, with the exception of himself, knew him as Ambie. Hard to seem a man of consequence, Strafford acknowledged sadly, when your skull was as flat as an upturned plate and your name was Ambie Jenkins.

He had come down by squad car, which had turned in the driveway and departed just as the three-man forensics team arrived in their black van. They'd greeted him, and the four of them had tramped up the front steps together, trailing plumes of breath-smoke in their wake.

Strafford and Jenkins greeted each other. They had worked together before. Strafford liked the younger man, but got back no more than a grudging respect. He supposed Jenkins held his religion against him, as did most of the Force. A Protestant and a Garda officer – it even sounded wrong.

The forensics team comprised Hendricks the photographer, a thick-set young man with horn-rimmed spectacles. Willoughby, the fingerprint expert, a notorious drinker. And their boss, the chain-smoker Harry Hall.

Strafford had worked with these three before. Privately, he knew them as Larry, Curly and Moe. They stood in the flagged hallway stamping the snow from their boots and blowing into their fists. Harry Hall, the butt of a cigarette stuck to his lower lip with a curved inch of ash clinging to the tip, eyed the antlers and the blackened portraits on the walls and gave one of his smoker's laughs.

'Jesus Christ, will you look at this place?' he wheezed. 'Next thing Poirot himself will appear on the scene.' He pronounced it *Pworrott*.

14

A couple of uniformed Guards had also arrived in a squad car, one tall and the other short, mouth-breathers, both of them, just out of the Garda training college at Templemore and trying to hide their inexperience and gaucheness behind defiant, chin-jutting stares. There wasn't really anything for them to do, so Jenkins told them to stand in the hall on either side of the front door and make sure no one entered or left without proper authorisation.

'What's proper author—?' the tall one began, but Jenkins fixed him with a dead-eyed look and he said no more. When Strafford had led Jenkins and the forensics boys off to the library, the tall Guard looked at the shorter one and whispered, 'Proper authorisation, what's that when it's at home?' And they both chuckled, in the cynical fashion they were trying to learn from the old hands on the Force.

Harry Hall took in the bookshelves, the marble fireplace, the mock-medieval furniture.

'It's a library,' he muttered incredulously to Hendricks. 'It's an actual fucking library, and there's a body in it!'

Forensics never gave their first attention to the corpse; it was an unofficial part of their professional code. Hendricks was at work, however, the flashbulbs of his Graflex popping and fizzing and leaving everyone in the room light-blind for a second or two after they had gone off.

'Come and have some tea,' Colonel Osborne said.

The invitation had been directed pointedly at Strafford alone, but Sergeant Jenkins either didn't notice or didn't care. He followed the two men as they went out of the room. They went along a dim hallway and entered the kitchen.

'Will they be all right in there?' Colonel Osborne asked of

Strafford, nodding back towards the library.

'They'll be very careful,' Strafford answered drily. 'They don't usually break things.'

'Oh, I didn't mean – that's to say, I just wondered—' He frowned. He was filling the kettle at the sink. Outside the window the bare black branches of the trees were laden along their tops with strips of snow that glistened like granulated sugar. 'It all seems a bad dream.'

'It usually feels like that. Violence always seems out of place, which is hardly surprising.'

'Have you seen much of it? Murder, that kind of thing?'

Strafford smiled mildly. 'There isn't any *other* kind of thing – murder is unique.'

'Yes, I see what you mean,' Osborne said, though it was obvious he didn't, quite.

He put the kettle on the stove, had to look for matches, found them at last. He opened cupboards and stared into them helplessly. It was plain he hadn't spent much time in the kitchen over the years. He took three mugs from a shelf. Two of them had cracks down the sides, like fine black hairs. He set them on the table.

'What time was the body found—?' Jenkins began, but stopped when he noticed the other two men looking past him. He turned.

A woman had come in, without making a sound.

She stood in a low doorway leading off to another part of the house, with one hand folded tensely over the other at the level of her waist. She was tall – she had to stoop a little in the doorway – and markedly slender, and her skin was pinkly pale, the colour of skimmed milk into which had been mixed a single drop of blood. Her face was like that of a Madonna by one of the lesser Old Masters, with dark eyes and a long sharp nose with a little bump at the tip. She wore a beige cardigan and a calf-length grey skirt that hung a little crookedly on her hips, which were no broader than a boy's.

She wasn't beautiful, Strafford thought, but all the same something in her frail, melancholy looks pressed a bell deep within him that made a soundless, sad little *ping*.

'Ah, there you are, my dear,' Colonel Osborne said. 'I thought you were sleeping.'

'I heard voices,' the woman said, glancing from Strafford to Jenkins and back again with expressionless eyes.

'This is my wife,' Osborne said. 'Sylvia, this is Inspector Strafford. And—?'

'Jenkins,' the policeman said, with heavy emphasis, and the trace of a resentful scowl. He didn't understand why people couldn't remember his name – it wasn't as if he was called Jones, or Smith, or something equally common. 'Detective Sergeant Jenkins.'

Sylvia Osborne gave the men no greeting, only came forward from the doorway, chafing her hands against each other. She had an appearance of being so cold, it seemed she might never have been warm in her life. Strafford was frowning. He had thought at first she must be Osborne's daughter, or a niece, perhaps, but not, certainly not, his wife – she looked to Strafford to be at least twenty, if not twenty-five, years younger than her husband. In which case, he thought, she had to be a second wife, since there were grown children. He wondered what had become of the first Mrs Osborne.

The kettle on the stove sent up a shrill whistle.

'I met someone on the stairs,' Mrs Osborne said, 'some man. Who is he?'

'Probably one of mine,' Strafford answered.

She watched as her husband poured boiling water into a big china teapot.

'Where's Sadie?' she asked.

'I sent her to her sister's.' Osborne glanced at Strafford. 'Housekeeper. Mrs Duffy.'

'Why did you do that?' his wife asked in a bewildered tone, wrinkling her pale forehead. All her movements were slow and effortfully deliberate, as if she were wading under water.

'You know what a gossip she is,' Osborne said, avoiding her eye, and then murmured in an undertone, 'not that her sister isn't one, too.'

Mrs Osborne glanced aside, putting a hand to her cheek.

'I don't understand it,' she said faintly. 'How could he have got into the library, when he fell down the staircase?'

Again Osborne glanced at Strafford, with an almost imperceptible quick little shake of the head.

'I imagine that's what Inspector Strafford's man is trying to discover,' he said to his wife, over-loudly, then softened his tone. 'Will you have some tea, my dear?'

She shook her head, and, still with that dazed expression, turned and wandered out through the doorway she had entered by, her hands still clasped at her waist and her elbows pressed against her sides, as if she were in danger of collapsing and had to hold herself upright.

'She thinks it was an accident,' Osborne said quietly, when she had gone. 'Didn't see any point in enlightening her – she'll know the truth soon enough.'

He handed round the mugs of tea, keeping the uncracked one for himself.

'Did anyone hear anything in the night?' Sergeant Jenkins asked.

Colonel Osborne looked at him with some displeasure. He was surprised, it seemed, that a fellow who was clearly from the lower ranks should think he had the right to speak without first asking permission of a senior officer.

'Well, certainly I heard nothing,' he said shortly. 'Dominic might have, I suppose. My son, Dominic, that is.'

'What about the others in the house?' Jenkins persisted.

'No one heard anything, so far as I know,' the Colonel replied stiffly, peering into his mug.

'And where is he now, your son?' Strafford asked.

'He took the dog for a walk,' Osborne said. His expression suggested that even to him it sounded incongruous, to say the least. Here a dead man, there a dog in need of walking.

'How many people were in the house last night?' Strafford asked.

Osborne turned his eyes upwards, moving his lips as he counted silently.

'Five,' he said, 'including Father Tom. And there was the housekeeper, of course. She has a place' – he nodded towards the floor – 'downstairs.'

'So, that's you and your wife, your son, and Father Lawless.'

'That's right.'

'Four, by my reckoning. You said there were five, not counting the housekeeper?'

'And my daughter, did I not mention her? Lettie.' Something passed fleetingly over his face, like the shadow of a cloud skimming across a hillside on a windy day. 'I doubt she heard anything. She's a deep sleeper. In fact, all she seems to do is sleep. She's seventeen,' he added, as if this explained not only the girl's sleeping habits but a great deal else besides.

'Where is she now?' Strafford asked.

Colonel Osborne took a sip from his mug and made a wry face, whether at the taste of the tea – it was so strong it was almost black – or at the thought of his daughter, Strafford couldn't decide. He laid his two palms flat before him on the table and pushed himself to his feet.

'I'd like to see the room where Father Lawless slept last night,' he said.

Jenkins too was standing now. Colonel Osborne remained seated, looking up at them, and his hitherto brisk and sceptical manner faltered for a moment, and for the first time he seemed uncertain, and vulnerable, and afraid.

'It's like a bad dream,' he said again. He gazed almost pleadingly at the two men standing over him. 'I suppose that will pass. I suppose it will soon start to seem all too real.'

3

Colonel Osborne ushered the detectives out of the kitchen. Harry Hall appeared, lighting a cigarette inside the shelter of a cupped hand.

'Have a word?' he said to Strafford.

The detective looked at him and tried not to let his antipathy show. Not that it mattered – the two men disliked each other, for no particular reason, and didn't let it interfere with their work. They really didn't care enough about each other to fight. All the same, the tension between them was palpable, and Colonel Osborne frowned, glancing from Harry Hall to Strafford, and from Strafford to Jenkins, with a look of puzzled enquiry.

'A word?' Strafford said.

Harry Hall said nothing more, only turned and walked out of the room. Strafford hesitated a moment, then followed.

In the library, Hendricks was fitting a new roll of film into his camera, while Willoughby, wearing a pair of rubber gloves, was kneeling by the door and listlessly dusting the knob with a soft sable brush. Harry Hall sucked worriedly at his cigarette.

'This is a weird one,' he said in an undertone.

'Would you say so? – I was beginning to think something of the sort myself,' Strafford answered. Harry Hall only shrugged. It always puzzled Strafford that his irony so often went unnoticed.

'He was stabbed upstairs and made it down here somehow,' Harry Hall was saying. 'I suppose he was trying to get away from whoever it was that attacked him. My guess is he got in here and fell – he'd already lost a bucket of blood – and that he was lying here when his tackle was cut off, balls, prick, the whole shebang. Which we didn't find, by the way. Someone must have kept it for a souvenir. Clean cut, with a razor-sharp knife. A professional job, by the look of it.'

He made a hissing sound as he drew on his cigarette, and turned to look at the corpse. Strafford was wondering absently how it could be that someone, anyone, should have notched up a sufficient number of castrations to be considered a professional. Were there professional castrators, outside the realm of animal breeding?

'As you can see,' Harry Hall went on, 'someone tidied him up. The blood was swabbed from the floor, but not till after it was dry.' He snickered. 'Some job that must have been.'

'And when would the job have been done?'

The big man shrugged. He was bored, not only with this case, but with his work in general. He had seven years to go before retirement. 'First thing this morning, probably,' he said, 'given that the blood was dry. The stair carpet was washed too – the stains are still in it.'

They stood in silence for some moments, gazing at the body. Hendricks was sitting on the arm of a high-backed chair with his camera on his lap. His work here was done, and he was taking a break before moving upstairs to start shooting there. Of the three of them, Hendricks gave the impression of being the keenest at his job, while in fact, as Strafford knew, he was the laziest of the lot.

Willoughby was still kneeling by the door, still dusting away. He, like the other two, knew the crime scene had been thoroughly compromised, and that their work would surely prove a waste of time. Not that it mattered to him.

'The housekeeper,' Strafford said, brushing that wing of hair away from his eyes, 'she'll be the one who cleared up, or did her best to, at any rate.'

Harry Hall nodded. 'On orders from Colonel Bogey, I presume?'

'Osborne, you mean?' Strafford said, with the ghost of a smile. 'Probably. Old soldiers don't like the sight of blood, so I'm told. Brings back too many memories, or something of the sort.'

They were silent again, then Harry Hall came a step closer to the detective and lowered his voice still further. 'Listen, Strafford, this is not good, this thing. A dead priest in a houseful of Prods? What are the papers going to say?'

'Probably the same thing as the neighbours,' Strafford answered absently.

'Neighbours?'

'What? Oh, the Colonel is worried there'll be a scandal.'

Harry Hall again gave a small, sour laugh.

'I'd say there's a fair possibility of that, all right,' he said.

'Oh, I wouldn't be so sure,' Strafford murmured.

They stood there, Harry Hall working at the last of his cigarette and Strafford stroking his lean jaw thoughtfully. Then he walked over to Willoughby. 'Anything?'

Willoughby rose from his knees in weary stages, grimacing. 'This back of mine,' he gasped, 'it's killing me.' There were beads of sweat on his forehead and on his upper lip. It was nearly noon, and he was badly in need of a drink. 'There's prints, of course,' he said, 'four or five different sets, one of them bloody, which I suppose it's safe to say would be the reverend father's.' He lifted his lip at one side in what was meant to be a grin but looked more like a snarl. 'Must have been one strong boyo, to get himself from the landing down to here.'

'Maybe he was carried.'

Willoughby shrugged. He was as bored as the other two. They were, all three of them, bored and cold and eager to get the hell out of this big chilly gloomy bloody place and head back as fast as their black van would carry them, and the snow would permit, to their cosy quarters in Pearse Street. They were Dubliners – being in the country gave them the jitters.

'What about the candlestick?' Strafford asked.

'What about it?'

'Any prints on it?'

'Haven't tested it yet. I had a quick look – seems to have been wiped clean.'

'This is going to be heap big trouble,' said Harry Hall, slowly shaking his head from side to side. 'A lot of fingers could get badly burned here.'

Strafford looked at the nicotine stains on the big man's meaty hands.

'Did someone call for an ambulance?' he asked.

'It's on the way from the County Hospital,' Harry Hall answered. 'Though when it'll get here is anybody's guess, in this weather.'

'It's only snow, for God's sake,' Strafford said with a flash of irritation. 'Why must everybody keep going on about it?'

Harry Hall and Willoughby exchanged a look. Even the

mildest outburst by Strafford was taken as another sign of his aristocratic aloofness and general disdain for the people it was his distasteful duty to have to work with. His nickname, he knew, was Lord Snooty, after a character in one of the school-boy comics. He wouldn't have cared about any of this, if it weren't that his reputation as a toff added to the difficulties of his job.

'Anyway,' Harry Hall said, 'we're done here.'

'Right,' Strafford responded. 'Thanks. I know there wasn't much you could do, given the—'

'We done all we could,' Harry Hall cut in heavily, narrowing his eyes. 'I hope that's what you're going to put in your report.'

Strafford was tired of these Three Stooges, and was as eager to be shot of them as they were to be gone.

'Has Doctor Quirke been informed there'll be a corpse on the way up to him?'

Doctor Quirke had recently been appointed State Pathologist.

Harry Hall looked at Willoughby and smirked.

'He's away,' Harry Hall said.

'Oh? Away where?'

'He's on his honeymoon!' Hendricks said. 'Woo-hoo!'

And he let off a flashbulb, just for the hell of it.

4

Strafford wandered about in the downstairs rooms for a while, getting his bearings. This was what he always did at the start of an investigation. He needed to fix in his mind the geography of the place where the crime had been committed. It was a matter of noting the details of the situation and arriving at a point of view. Then he could incorporate himself into the scene, like a cut-out cardboard figure in a stage designer's maquette, not moving but himself being moved. The notion of being at once a part of the action and above it appealed to him, he wasn't sure why. *Playing at God,* his girlfriend, Marguerite – his former girlfriend, rather – would have said, with one of her sour looks. Marguerite was a person of few words. Her face said more than any words would have expressed. She should have been a mime artist, Strafford often thought, not without a flare of malice, sharp and brief as a match flame.

There were two drawing rooms, one to the right and one to the left of the front door. Only the one on the left showed signs of being lived in. A log fire was burning in the grate, and there were books and newspapers scattered about, and cups and saucers and glasses on a low table, and someone's tartan scarf was draped over the back of an armchair. How familiar it all was to him, the shabby furniture and the vague clutter, and that faint smell of must and damp that all old houses give off. It was in rooms like this that he had spent his childhood years. Old impressions had a way of holding fast.

He went and stood in the bay of a big window that looked out on bare trees and the snow-covered lawn and the curve of the rutted drive leading down to the main road. There was a hill in the distance, capped with snow. It looked unreally neat and picturesque, like a decorative scene on a Christmas cake. The hill must be Mount Leinster, he thought. Behind it the sky was heavy with purplish, leaden clouds – more snow was on the way.

Strafford tapped the nails of two fingers against his front teeth, a thing he did when he was distracted, or deep in thought, or both.

Harry Hall was right, this case was a weird one. It had the potential to land him in a great deal of trouble, if he didn't take the greatest care and handle it just the right way.

What that way was, or indeed what exactly the trouble that menaced him might be, he couldn't say, yet. But priests just didn't get murdered in this country, and certainly not in places like Ballyglass House. The Catholic Church – the powers that be, in other words – would shoulder its way in and take over. There would be a cover-up, some plausible lie would be peddled to the public. The only question was how deeply the facts could be buried. The violent death of a priest wasn't a thing to be ignored entirely, like the packing off of a troublesome youth to an industrial school, or the consignment of a pregnant girl to a convent laundry.

Yes, a weird one. He knew very well that was why Hackett – Detective Chief Superintendent Hackett, his senior officer in Dublin – had put him in charge of the case. 'You know the lie of the land down there,' Hackett had said on the telephone that morning. 'You speak their lingo, they'll talk to you. Good luck.'

In this case he was going to need more than luck, which was a thing he didn't believe in, anyway. You make your own luck, or it's made for you, by accident.

Something now, some ancient instinct, told him he was not alone, that he was being observed. Cautiously he turned his head and scanned the room. And then he saw her. She must have been there when he came in. In these old houses you only had to keep still and stay quiet in order to fade into the background, like a lizard on a stone wall.

She was curled up under a brown blanket on an old sofa in front of the fire, with her knees drawn up to her chest and arms wrapped around her shins. Her wide eyes seemed enormous – how had it taken him so long to feel, in that fabled spot between his shoulder blades, the force of their scrutiny?

'Hello,' he said. 'Sorry, I didn't see you there.'

'I know. I was watching you.'

All he could see of her were her face and her forearms, since the rest of her was hidden under the blanket. She had a broad brow and a sharp chin, and those eyes that seemed as big as a lemur's. Her wiry hair surrounded her face in a mass of unruly and, by the look of them, not particularly clean curls.

'Isn't it disgusting,' she said, 'how your thumb gets all white and shrivelled when you suck on it?'

Strafford smiled. 'Do you suck your thumb?'

'Only when I'm thinking.' She held up her hand for him to see. 'Look at that – it's as if I'd just been dragged out of the sea.'

'You must be Lettie,' he said.

'And who are you? No, let me guess. You're the detective.'

'That's right. Detective Inspector Strafford.'

'You don't look much like a—' She stopped, seeing his already wearying expression. 'I suppose people are always telling you you don't look like a policeman. You don't sound like one, either, with that accent. What's your name?'

'Strafford.'

'I mean your first name.'

'It's St John, actually.'

The girl laughed.

'St John! That's almost as bad as mine. They call me Lettie, but I'm Lettice, really, believe it or not. Imagine giving a child a name like Lettice. It's after my grandmother, but all the same.'

She was watching him closely, her eyes wrinkled in sly amusement, as if she expected him at any moment to perform some wonderful trick, to stand on his head, say, or levitate. He remembered, from his own youth, how a new face in the house always seemed a promise of change and excitement – or of change, anyway, since excitement was a thing so rarely experienced in their kind of household, hers, and his of old, as to seem the stuff of extravagant fantasy.

'Do you like to watch people?' he asked.

'Yes. It's amazing what they get up to when they think there's no one looking. Thin ones always pick their noses.'

'I hope I didn't, before I noticed you.'

'You probably would have, given time.' She paused, fiddling with a knot in the blanket. 'It's really thrilling, isn't it? – a body in the library! Have you solved it yet? Will you be calling us all together at dinner time to explain the plot and reveal the killer's name? My money's on the White Mouse.'

'The—?'

'My stepmother. Sylvia, queen of the headhunters. Have you met her? You might have, but not noticed, since she's practically transparent.'

She threw the blanket aside, rose from the sofa, stood on tiptoe and clasped her hands together high above her head, stretching and grunting. She was tall, lean, dark of complexion, and slightly bow-legged – her father's daughter. She was not at all pretty, in any conventional sense of the word, and she knew it, but her knowing it, evident in her clownishly slouchy demeanour, gave to her, paradoxically, a certain sulky allure. She was wearing jodhpurs and a black velvet riding jacket.

'Off for a gallop, are you?' Strafford enquired.

The girl let her arms fall to her sides. 'What?' She glanced down at herself. 'Oh, the outfit. No, I don't care for horses – smelly brutes, and liable to bolt, or bite, or both. I just like the get-up. Very slim-making, and comfy, too. These used to be my mother's – my real mother, that is, who died – though I had to have them taken in quite a bit. She was a big girl.'

'Your father thought you were still asleep.'

'Oh, he gets up at sparrow fart himself and thinks anyone who doesn't is' – here she fell into a startlingly convincing impersonation of Colonel Osborne – '*a damned layabout, don't-ye-know*. Honestly, he's such an old fraud.'

She picked up the blanket, draped it over her shoulders and stood beside him at the window. They both looked out at the snowbound landscape.

'My God,' she said, 'the frozen bloody wastes. Oh and look,

they've cut down more trees in the copse.' She turned to Strafford. 'You know, of course, we're as poor as church mice? – half the timber is gone, and the roof is going to cave in any day. It's the House of Usher.' Struck, she paused, wrinkling her nose. 'I wonder why church mice should be thought of as poor? And how could a mouse be rich, anyway?' She drew the blanket close about her. 'I'm so *cold*!' She gave him another sidelong, playful glance. 'But of course, females are always cold, aren't they, in their extremities. That's what men are for, to warm us up.'

A shadow moved in the window and Strafford turned from the girl in time to see a hulking boy in rubber boots and a leather jacket walking past, doing a sort of clumsy goose-step in the deep snow. He had freckles and a thick shock of tangled hair, so darkly, deeply red it was almost the colour of bronze. The sleeves of his jacket were too short, and his exposed wrists gleamed more whitely than the white snow all about him.

'Is that your brother?' Strafford asked.

The girl gave a shriek of laughter.

'Oh, that's priceless!' she cried, shaking her head and making the dark curls bounce, her laugh turning into a gurgle. 'I can't wait to tell Dominic you thought Fonsey was him. He'll probably take a horse whip to you, or something – he has an awful temper.'

The boy was out of sight by now.

'Who's Fonsey?' Strafford asked.

'Him' – she pointed – 'the stable boy, I suppose you'd call him. He looks after the horses, or he's supposed to. He's part horse himself, I believe. What do you call those creatures there used to be in ancient Greece?'

32

'Centaurs?'

'That's it. That's Fonsey.' She gave another hiccup of laughter deep in her throat. 'The centaur of Ballyglass House. He's a bit loony' – she put a finger to her temple and made a screwing motion with it – 'so watch out. My name for him is Caliban.'

She was looking at Strafford again, with those enormous grey eyes, clasping the blanket to her throat as if it were a cloak.

'St John,' she said thoughtfully. 'I've never met a St John before.'

Strafford was batting his fedora against his thigh again. It was another of his habits, another of his tics, of which there were many. Marguerite used to say they drove her mad.

'You'll have to excuse me,' he said. 'I've some things to do.'

'Hunting for clues, I suppose? Sniffing cigarette butts and peering at fingerprints through a magnifying glass?'

He began to turn away, then paused.

'How well did you know Father Lawless?' he asked.

The girl shrugged. 'How *well* did I know him? I don't know that I knew him at all. He was always hanging around, if that's what you mean. Everyone thought he was a card. I never took much notice of him. There was something oogey about him.'

'"Oogey"?'

'Oh, you know. Not at all pious or preachy, took a drink, life and soul of the party, all that kind of thing, but at the same time always on the lookout, always watching—'

'The way you do?'

She narrowed her lips into a line. 'No, not the way I do. Like a Peeping Tom – *that* kind of oogey.'

'And what do you think happened to him?'

'"Happened to him"? You mean, who stabbed him in the neck and cut his goolies off? How should I know? Maybe it wasn't the White Mouse. Maybe she and the Man of the Cloth were getting up to monkey business together and Daddy knocked him off in a jealous rage.' She put on her father's voice again, jutting out her lower lip. *Damned cheek of the feller, comin' in here and havin' at my missus!*

Strafford could not help but smile.

'I don't suppose you heard anything in the night?' he asked.

'You mean, did I hear His Reverence getting it in the neck? 'Fraid not. I sleep like a log – anyone will tell you that. The only thing I ever hear is the Ballyglass ghost rattling his chains and moaning. You know the place is haunted, I suppose?'

He smiled again.

'I've got to go,' he said. 'I'm sure I'll see you again before I leave.'

'Yes, in the dining room, no doubt, for cocktails at eight. *Murder at the Mansion*, and all that. I can't wait.' He was already moving away from her, laughing softly now. 'I shall wear an evening gown and a feather boa,' she called after him. 'And I'll have a dagger in the top of my stocking!'

5

The forensics team had gone off in their van, leaving a disdainful whiff of exhaust fumes in the front hall. Strafford went to the foot of the staircase and leaned over, with his hands braced on his knees, to examine the carpet. Yes, there were pinkish stains in the pile, all the way up. They were very faint. The housekeeper had done her best, but as he told himself, blood is thicker than soap and water. He grinned. *Soap and water*. He rather liked that.

He climbed the staircase, smacking a palm softly on the banister rail as he went. He was trying to imagine the priest reeling down these stairs with blood pumping out of the severed artery in his neck. Unless he had seen or at least heard his assailant coming, he must have been amazed. Who would dare to kill a priest? Yet someone had.

Crossing the landing, he stepped into the short enclosed passageway that led along to the next, long corridor and the bedrooms giving off it. In the carpet here also there was the trace of a bloodstain, this one large and circular. So this was the spot where he had been stabbed. It had been done from behind, surely, since he was a big man and would have defended himself against an attacker coming at him directly with knife in hand.

Did that mean it was someone who had been in one of the bedrooms, waiting for him to pass by? – or was there another way to get in here, another entrance from outside? These old houses were always confusing, from the piecemeal alterations that had been made to them over the years.

He walked on, and sure enough, here was a French window and outside it an ancient spiral staircase made of iron and painted black, and rusted in places to a filigree as delicate as lace. He examined the window catch. It hadn't been forced. From the look of it, the window hadn't been opened in years.

He heard voices from an open doorway behind him. He went into the room and found Jenkins and Colonel Osborne standing by a rumpled bed. The room was small and the bed was big, and the mattress had a hollow down the middle of it. The only other furniture was a chest of drawers and a rush-seated chair. The priest's cassock hung on the back of the door, like the flayed black pelt of some large, smooth-skinned animal.

'Anything here?' Strafford asked.

Jenkins shook his head. 'He got up at some point in the night – Harry Hall puts the time of death between three and four a.m. – dressed himself, even put his clerical collar on, left the room, and didn't come back.'

'Why would he have put on his collar if he was only going to the lavatory?'

'WC's in the other direction, down at the end of the corridor,' Colonel Osborne said, pointing with a thumb.

'Then what do you think he was doing?' Strafford asked.

'Can't say,' Osborne replied. 'Might have been going down for another nip of Bushmills. I gave him a nightcap to take up here with him when he was turning in.'

Strafford looked around. 'Where's the glass?'

'Didn't see it,' Jenkins said. 'He would have taken it with him, if he was going down for another, then dropped it maybe when he was attacked.'

Strafford still hadn't taken off his trench coat, and he was holding his hat in his left hand. He looked about the low, cramped room once more, then walked out.

On the landing, Colonel Osborne sidled up to him and spoke out of the corner of his mouth. 'Care to stay for lunch?' he muttered. 'Mrs Duffy is on her way back from her sister's, she'll fix up something for us.'

Strafford glanced over his shoulder at Jenkins, who was just then coming out of the bedroom behind them. 'Does that include my colleague?'

Osborne looked uncomfortable. 'Well, I thought your chap might shift for himself. There's the Sheaf, down the road. Decent enough place, I'm told. Sandwiches, soup. They might even rise to a plate of stew.'

'Is that the Sheaf of Barley? That's where I'll be staying tonight.'

'Oh, but we could have offered you a billet here.'

Strafford smiled at him blandly. 'Two billets, I take it you mean.'

'Eh?'

'One for me and one for Sergeant Jenkins.'

The older man sighed irritably. 'Have it your own way,' he said shortly. 'Tell Mr Reck – he's the landlord at the Sheaf – that you've come from here. He'll look after you. But you will have lunch with us, yes?' He cast a dark glance in Jenkins's direction. 'The two of you.'

'Thank you,' Strafford said. 'Very kind.'

Here again was the shadowy passageway between two corridors where the priest had been stabbed. Strafford stopped and peered about in the gloom. 'We need to find that whiskey glass,' he said. 'If he was carrying it and dropped it, it must be here.' He turned to Sergeant Jenkins. 'Get those two galoots you have guarding the front door on to it, it'll keep them from falling asleep. The glass probably rolled under something.'

'Right.'

Strafford looked upwards. 'Is there usually a bulb there?' he asked, pointing to an empty socket, which was set inside a shade hardly bigger than a teacup and made of what might have been human skin, stretched and dried and translucent.

Colonel Osborne examined the socket. 'Should be a bulb, yes, of course there should. Didn't notice it was missing.'

'Someone removed it, then?' Strafford asked.

'Must have, since it's not there.'

Strafford turned to Sergeant Jenkins. 'Tell those two to look for a bulb, as well as the glass.' He gazed up at the empty socket again and put a finger and thumb to his chin. 'So it was planned,' he murmured.

'What's that?' Osborne asked sharply.

Strafford turned to him. 'The murder. It must have been premeditated. That should make things a little easier.'

'Should it?' The Colonel looked baffled.

'A person acting on impulse can be lucky. He'll strike out without thinking, and afterwards everything looks natural, because it is. But a plan always has something wrong with it. There's always a flaw. Our job is to find it.'

There was a commotion below, shouts, and a dog yelping. A draught of cold air came sweeping up the stairs, followed by the sound of the front door slamming. 'Hold on to him, for God's sake!' someone bellowed angrily. 'Mrs Duffy will have a fit if he puts muddy paw marks on the carpets.'

Strafford and the two men with him leaned over the banister and peered down into the front hall. The stable boy, Fonsey, was there, with his mop of red hair and his leather jacket. He was struggling to restrain a large and very wet black Labrador retriever by jerking violently at its leash. At the door, taking off a pair of leather gauntlets, was a young man in a checked overcoat and a hat with a feather in the band. His wellington boots were muddy, and stuck with dabs of melting snow. A long staff with a shepherd's crook was leaning against the hall table. He removed his hat and gave it a vigorous shake. It was his petulantly commanding voice they had heard.

'My son,' Colonel Osborne said to Strafford, and then called out, 'Dominic, the police are here!'

The young man looked up.

'Oh, hullo,' he called.

At sight of the Colonel, Fonsey let go of the dog and lumbered hurriedly to the front door and was gone. The dog, suddenly losing interest in being excited, splayed its large paws and shook itself thoroughly, throwing off a spray of snow-water in all directions.

Colonel Osborne led the way down the staircase. 'Dominic,' he said, 'this is Detective Inspector Strafford, and – and his assistant.'

'Jenkins,' the sergeant growled, spacing out the syllables. 'De-tec-tive Ser-geant *Jen-kins*.'

'Sorry, yes, that's right,' Colonel Osborne said, colouring a little. 'Jenkins.'

Dominic Osborne was classically handsome, with a long straight jaw, a slightly cruel-looking mouth and his father's flinty blue eyes. He glanced from one to the other of the two detectives, and a corner of his mouth twitched, as if he were seeing something funny.

'The long arm of the law,' he said with arch sarcasm. 'Who'd have thought it, here in Ballyglass House?'

Strafford studied the young man with interest. He wasn't as cool as he was pretending to be, and his voice was strained behind its languid tone.

The dog was sniffing at Strafford's shoes.

'Come along,' said the Colonel to the two detectives, rubbing his hands. 'Let's see if that lunch is ready.'

Strafford leaned down and scratched the dog behind its ear. The animal wagged its tail and let its tongue hang out in a friendly grin. Strafford smiled. He had always liked dogs.

From the start there had been something odd about this case, in a way he had never encountered before. Something had been niggling at him, and suddenly now he realised what it was. No one was crying.

6

The ambulance was still on its way from Wexford General Hospital when Strafford was called to the telephone to be told by his boss, Chief Superintendent Hackett, to cancel it.

'We're sending down a wagon from here,' Hackett said above the crackling on the line – he might have been speaking from outer space, so poor was the connection and so distorted the sound of his voice. 'I want the body brought to Dublin.' Strafford made no reply to this. He knew from the Chief's tone that the makings of a cover-up were already being put in place, like the props on a stage set. Strafford wasn't the only one to see himself in the role of stage designer. There were others, more determined and far more skilled than he at painting fake scenery and making silent alterations to the plot. 'Are you there?' Hackett barked irritably. 'Did you hear what I said?'

'Yes, I heard.'

'And?'

'It's too late to cancel the ambulance, it will be here any minute.'

'Well, send it back! I told you, the corpse is to come up here.' There was another pause. Strafford could sense Hackett's irritation rising. 'There's no point in standing there with your trap shut,' the Chief Superintendent growled. 'I can hear you doing it.'

'Doing what?'

'Saying nothing! You know damn well this thing will have to be handled with kid gloves.' There was a sigh, heavy and tired. 'The palace has spoken to the Commissioner. Officially, so far as we're concerned, the priest's death was an accident. And by *we* I mean *you*, Strafford.'

The palace was the residence of the Archbishop of Dublin, John Charles McQuaid, the most powerful churchman in the country. The Garda Commissioner, Jack Phelan, was a prominent member of the Knights of St Patrick. So there it was – the Church had stepped in. If His Grace Doctor McQuaid said Father Lawless had stabbed himself in the neck by accident and thereafter had cut off his own genitals, then that's what had happened, so far as the public at large would be permitted to know.

'For how long?' Strafford asked.

'For how long what?' Hackett snapped back. He was tense. Hackett wasn't often tense. Jack Phelan must have laid it on with a vengeance.

'How long are we expected to keep up the pretence that this priest was stabbed by accident? It's rather a lot to ask people to believe.'

Hackett sighed again. When there was a lapse like this on the line, if Strafford listened hard he could hear, behind the electronic crackles, a sort of distant warbling. It always fascinated him, this eerie, cacophonous music, and gave him a shiver, too. It was as if the hosts of the dead were singing to him out of the ether.

'We "keep up the pretence"' – it amused Hackett to mimic Strafford's accent and his finical turns of phrase – 'for as long as it bloody well takes.'

Strafford tapped two fingernails against his front teeth.

'What was that?' Hackett asked suspiciously.

'What was what?'

'Sounded like somebody knocking coconut shells together.'

Strafford laughed soundlessly.

'I'm going to send Jenkins back with the corpse,' he said. 'He can give you a preliminary report.'

'Oh, going it alone, are we? Gideon of the Yard solves the case single-handed.'

It was never clear to Strafford which the Chief resented more, his deputy's Protestant pedigree or his preference for doing things in his own way.

'Do you want me to write up a report now,' Strafford asked, 'or will I leave it to Jenkins to give it to you in his own words? There's not much to report on, as yet.'

Hackett didn't reply, but asked a question instead. 'Tell me, Strafford, what do you think?' He sounded worried – as worried, Strafford told himself, as only a diktat from the palace could make him.

'I don't know what I think,' Strafford said. 'I told you,' he continued, 'I've next to nothing to go on, yet' – adding, perfunctorily – 'sir.'

He was cold, standing with the phone receiver clammy in his hand and a draught from under the front door curling round his ankles.

'You must have some sort of an idea of what happened,' Hackett persisted, making no effort to hide the irritation in his voice.

'Colonel Osborne believes the killing was done by someone from outside – he insists there must have been a break-in.'

43

'And was there?'

'I don't think so. Harry Hall had a good look round before he left, and so did I, and neither of us found any sign of a forced entry.'

'So it was someone in the house, then?'

'It must have been, as far as I can see. That's the assumption I'm going on.'

'How many people were there last night?'

'Five, six, including the dead man and the housekeeper. There's a scullery maid who comes in, but she lives locally and would've gone home. It's always possible someone had a key to the front door – any footprints outside would have been obliterated by this morning.' He winced. His boss didn't care for big words.

'Christ almighty,' Hackett muttered, with an angry sigh. 'There's going to be some stink over this, you know that?'

'Pretty whiffy already, wouldn't you say?' Strafford suggested.

'What are they like, the family?' Hackett asked.

'It's a bit public, where I'm speaking from,' Strafford said, loudening his voice. 'Jenkins will fill you in.'

Hackett was thinking again. Strafford could picture him clearly, leaning back in his swivel chair in his tiny, wedge-shaped office, with his feet on his desk and the chimney pots of Pearse Street dimly visible through the room's single, small square window, the panes of which would be hazed over with frost, except for a clear oval in the centre of each pane. He would be wearing his blue suit, shiny with age, and the greasy tie that Strafford was convinced he never unknotted, only loosened at night and pulled over his head. There would be the same years-old calendar on the wall, and the same dark-brown stain where someone had flattened a bluebottle uncountable summers ago.

'It's a queer bloody business,' the Chief said now, ruminatively.

'Queer, certainly.'

'Anyway, keep me up to date. And Strafford—'

'Yes, sir?'

'Remember, they may be the gentry, but one of them did for that priest.'

'I'll keep it in mind, sir.'

Hackett hung up.

It was only when he returned to the kitchen that Strafford realised just how cold it had been in the hall. Here, the range was lit and the air hummed with heat, and there was a smell of roasting meat. Colonel Osborne was sitting at the table, drumming his fingers on the wood, while Sergeant Jenkins stood leaning against the sink with his arms folded tightly across his chest and all three buttons of his jacket fastened. Jenkins was a stickler for what he considered good form. Strafford had the feeling the two men hadn't exchanged a word since he had been called away to the phone.

'That was Hackett,' he said, addressing Jenkins. 'There's an ambulance on the way from Dublin.'

'But what about—?'

'The one on the way from Wexford we're to send back.'

The two men looked stonily at each other for a moment. They had both known this case would be complicated, but they hadn't expected the machinery to have had so many spanners tossed into it so soon.

Outside the window above the sink, a robin alighted on the sill and regarded Strafford with an eye like a shiny black bead. The sky was a mass of swollen, bruise-coloured cloud hanging so low it seemed it must be resting on the roof.

'Lunch is on the way,' Colonel Osborne said, in an absent-minded tone, looking at nothing in particular. He drummed his fingers again. Strafford wished he would stop. It was a sound that always grated on his nerves.

Mrs Duffy had returned from her sister's, and now she bustled in from the pantry. She too, like everybody else Strafford had so far encountered at Ballyglass House, had the look of a character actor hired that morning, and fitted the part altogether too convincingly. She was short and dumpy, with blue eyes and plump pink cheeks and steel-grey hair gathered in a bun low at the back of her neck. She wore a black skirt and a spotless white apron and fur-lined black bootees. She began to lay out plates and knives and forks on the table. Osborne, rising from his chair, introduced her to Strafford and Sergeant Jenkins. She blushed, and for a moment it seemed she might be about to curtsey, but if so she stopped herself, and turned instead and went to the range and gave the firebox a vigorous riddle. Her broad back expressed a deep and general disapproval.

'Sit down, gentlemen, do,' Osborne said. 'We don't stand on ceremony here.'

They heard the front doorbell ring.

'That will be the ambulance from Wexford,' Strafford said. He glanced at Jenkins. 'Do you mind? Tell them we're sorry, but they won't be needed.'

Jenkins went out. Osborne had fixed Strafford with a shrewdly searching eye.

'What's up?' he asked. 'Why are they sending down a second ambulance – why won't this one do?'

'I imagine it's a question of expediency,' Strafford said coolly. 'The sooner the post-mortem is done, the better.'

Osborne nodded, but his look was sceptical.

'I imagine your chief is a worried man,' he said.

'He's concerned, certainly,' Strafford responded, blank-eyed.

He sat down at the table. Mrs Duffy came forward bearing a large steaming earthenware bowl, holding the hot sides of it with the aid of a tea towel. She set the bowl on the table between the two men.

'Will I serve, Colonel,' she asked, 'or will you help your-selves?' She turned to Strafford. 'I hope you like steak-and-kidney pudding, sir?'

'Oh, yes, certainly,' Strafford said, and swallowed hard.

'Just the thing for a cold day like this,' the housekeeper said, folding her plump hands under her bosom. She glared at the detective, as if daring him to contradict her as to the compat-ibility of pudding and weather.

'Yes, thank you, Sadie,' Colonel Osborne said pointedly, and the woman waddled back to the pantry with an offend-ed air. The Colonel gave Strafford an apologetic frown. 'She will rattle on, if you give her the chance.' He ladled food on to Strafford's plate. 'Reheated from yesterday, I'm afraid,' he said.

Strafford smiled weakly. 'Oh, I always think steak-and-kidney pud is better the second day, don't you?' He felt noble and brave. He could not understand how the kidneys of a cow had come to be regarded as food fit for human consumption.

Sergeant Jenkins returned, and shut the door behind him. Osborne frowned – clearly it still irked him to have to entertain someone from the 'other ranks' at his table – but he managed a friendly enough tone. 'Come, Sergeant, sit down and have some of this excellent pie. The boiled eggs are small, as you see – they're pullets' eggs. Sadie's – Mrs Duffy's – husband rears them. In my opinion, the pullet produces a far finer and tastier egg than the larger varieties.'

Pullets' eggs, and a dead body in the library. Life is strange, Strafford thought, but a policeman's life is stranger than most.

Jenkins was hungry, Strafford could see, yet he held back from starting until the other two had taken up their knives and forks. His mother would have taught him to wait and watch. Choosing your cutlery was always a perilous business when you were dining among the gentry.

'I imagine the driver wasn't too pleased to be sent away again,' Strafford said, 'after coming all the way out here through snow and ice.'

Jenkins gave him a look.

'I told them they weren't needed, and they left,' he said. 'I didn't notice whether they were displeased or not.'

The three men ate in silence for a time, then Strafford put down his knife and fork.

'I have to ask you, Colonel Osborne,' he said, frowning, 'to give me an exact account of the morning's events, insofar as you can.'

Osborne, chewing on a gristly knob of kidney, looked at him with raised eyebrows. He swallowed the piece of meat more or less whole. 'Do we have to go into all that at the table?' Strafford didn't reply, only went on looking at him with a neutral gaze. He sighed. 'It was my wife's screaming that woke me,' he said. 'I thought she must have fallen, or bumped into something and injured herself.'

'Why was she in the library?' Strafford asked.

'Eh?'

'What was she doing in the library in the middle of the night?'

'Oh, she wanders about the place at all hours,' Osborne said, in a tone dismissive of the ways of women in general, and of his wife in particular.

'Is she an insomniac? – has she trouble sleeping?'

'I know what an insomniac is!' Osborne snapped. 'And yes, she is. Always has been. I've learned to live with it.'

But has *she*? Strafford wondered. It was not a question, he imagined, that her husband often posed to himself. Osborne's second marriage seemed to have gone thoroughly stale. How long, the detective wondered, had the ageing soldier been married to his so much younger wife, the woman her step-daughter had nicknamed the White Mouse – aptly, Strafford thought, from what he had seen of her in her brief appearance earlier.

'So what did you do?'

Osborne shrugged. 'I put on a dressing gown and slippers and went down to look for her. I'd been deeply asleep, so my mind was a bit fuddled, I imagine. Found her in the hall, sitting on the floor, moaning. Couldn't get a word of sense out of her, except that she kept pointing to the door to the library. I went in and – and found him.'

'Was the light on?' Strafford asked. Osborne looked at him,

not understanding. 'In the library,' Strafford said, 'was the light switched on?'

'Can't say. Must have been – I remember being able to see clearly what was what – a shock, I can tell you. But maybe I switched it on myself, I don't know. Why do you ask?'

'No reason. I'm just trying to picture the scene – it helps.'

'Well, there was blood all over the place, of course – huge pool of it on the floor underneath him.'

'What way was he lying?' Sergeant Jenkins asked. 'I mean, was he lying on his back?'

'Yes.'

'And did you – did you interfere with his clothing in any way?'

Osborne glowered at him, and addressed Strafford. 'Of course I did. I had to have a look, to see what had happened to him. Then I spotted the blood on his trousers, and the – the wound, there.' He stopped for a moment, then went on. 'I was in the war, I'm no stranger to violence, but I can tell you I damn near vomited at the sight of what they'd done to him.' He again made that angry, sideways chewing motion with his lower jaw. 'Bastards – forgive my French.'

Strafford picked over the mess of food before him, pretending to be eating it but in reality distributing it around the plate, as he had learned to do as a child. The dish itself he had always found peculiarly disgusting, but somehow the pullets' eggs, hardly bigger than marbles, added to the awfulness.

'Did you call the Guards right away?' he asked.

'Yes, I phoned the barracks in Ballyglass, looking for Radford – Garda Sergeant Radford. He has the 'flu.'

Strafford stared. 'The 'flu?'

'Yes. His wife came to the phone, said he was very sick and that she had no intention of getting him out of bed in this weather – I thought her tone distinctly rude, I must say. Mind you, they lost a son not long ago. If it hadn't been for that I'd have given her a proper wigging, I can tell you. She spoke to Radford, and came back and said he'd told her to tell me to get on to the Garda barracks in Wexford. I called 999 instead and they put me on to your people.'

'My people? In Pearse Street?'

'I suppose it was Pearse Street. Somewhere in Dublin, anyway.'

'And who did you speak to there?'

'Some desk-wallah or other.' Osborne, suddenly angry, threw down his knife, which skittered off the table and fell to the flagstone floor with a jarring clatter. 'For God's sake, what does it matter who I spoke to?'

'Colonel Osborne, a murder has taken place in your house,' Strafford said, keeping his voice low and his tone mild. 'It's my task to investigate the crime, and to find out who committed it. As you'll understand, that means I need to know everything that's knowable about the events of last night.' He paused. 'Can you remember anything of what your wife said when you found her in the hall, after she had discovered Father Lawless's body?'

The housekeeper, having heard the knife falling on the flagstone floor, came hurrying from the pantry with a replacement. Colonel Osborne snatched it out of her hand, without giving her a glance, and banged it down on the table beside his plate. Mrs Duffy sniffed, and went back to the pantry.

'I told you,' the Colonel said to Strafford, 'she wasn't making sense – she was hysterical. What would you expect?'

'I shall have to speak to her, of course,' Strafford said. 'Indeed, I'll have to speak to everyone who was in the house last night. Perhaps I should start with Mrs Osborne?' The Colonel, whose forehead had turned dark red under his leathery tan, was struggling to rein in his temper.

'You'll understand, Colonel, as a former officer, the importance of detail, of thoroughness. Often people have seen or heard things they don't realise the significance of – that's where I come in. It's part of my training to hear the – the nuances, shall we say.'

He could feel Jenkins's eye fixed on him incredulously. No doubt he was reflecting on the fact that the training he himself had received had been of a more rudimentary variety, from people who probably wouldn't know the meaning of the word nuance.

Colonel Osborne was attacking his food again, vexedly, jabbing with his knife and fork as if they had once been weapons. Strafford assumed the man had things he would rather not disclose – hadn't everyone? – and that it would be no easy job to prise them out of him.

The doorbell rang again. Colonel Osborne leaned far back on his chair, craning to see out of the window above the sink. 'It's the second ambulance,' he said.

Jenkins put down his cutlery. Unlike his boss, he was partial to steak-and-kidney pie – his mother used to make it for him when he was a boy – pullets' eggs or no pullets' eggs. He rose from the table, with the pained look of a man sorely put upon.

Strafford laid a hand on his arm. 'Tell those two rookies they can go, will you, Sergeant? There's no point in keeping them hanging around here.'

When Jenkins had gone, Strafford leaned forward and set his elbows on the table.

'Now, Colonel,' he said, 'let's go over it once more, shall we?'

7

'You must be the brother-in-law,' the man said, stopping in the hallway, and added jovially, 'I thought you weren't allowed in the house.'

He was a big, florid-faced fellow in his thirties, with wavy fair hair and strikingly large dark eyes. He wore a three-piece tweed suit, the colour and texture of porridge, with brown suede shoes, and sported a red silk handkerchief in his breast pocket. He was carrying a camel-hair overcoat and a brown felt hat. He had come in from outside but his shoes were dry, Strafford noted, so he must have worn galoshes.

Strafford, exiting the kitchen and still holding a napkin, had recognised at once yet another type familiar to him from of old. Here, to the life, was the very model of a rural professional – solicitor? doctor? successful vet? – breezy, off-hand, self-consciously charming, proud of his reputation but a bit of a rake, and behind it all as watchful as a weasel. He smelled strongly of expensive hair oil.

'Name's Hafner, by the way,' the large man said, 'Doctor Hafner. Also known as the Kraut, especially if you've been listening to Lettie.'

'I'm Inspector Strafford.'

'Are you, now,' Hafner said, lifting an eyebrow. 'Sorry. I took you for the other fellow.'

For the moment, Strafford put aside the question of the

precise identity of the 'other fellow'. Brother-in-law, the man had said, so the Colonel's brother, then, it must be, or Mrs Osborne's.

The light in Hafner's dark eyes grew more intense. They hadn't shaken hands. 'And what are you an inspector of, may one ask?'

'I'm a detective.'

'Oh? What's up? Someone steal the silver?'

'There's been an incident,' Strafford answered. He looked at the black bag at the doctor's feet. 'Are you making a house call, or just visiting?'

'Bit of both. What sort of incident?'

'Fatal.'

'Someone's dead? Good Christ – not the old boy?'

'Colonel Osborne? No. A priest, name of Lawless.'

This time, both of Hafner's eyebrows shot so high they almost touched his hairline. 'Father Tom? No!'

'Well, yes, I'm afraid so.'

'What happened?'

'Maybe you should see Colonel Osborne. Will you follow me?'

'Jesus,' Hafner said under his breath. 'So they did for the padre at last.'

'Do you look after the health of all the family?' Strafford asked the doctor.

'I suppose I do,' Hafner said, 'though I never thought of it in those terms.' He brought out a packet of Gold Flake and a Zippo lighter. 'Care for a fag?'

'No, thanks,' Strafford said. 'I don't smoke.'

'Wise man.'

56

Strafford opened the drawing-room door.

'Good, she's gone,' he said.

'Who?'

'Lettice.'

'Lettice? You mean Lettie? Is that her name, Lettice? I never knew.' He laughed. 'Imagine calling a child Lettice!'

'Yes, that's what she said.'

The fire had died down, and the room was appreciably chillier than it had been earlier. Strafford took the poker to the embers and placed two logs on top of them. A swirl of smoke filled his nostrils, making him cough.

'So what happened to Tom the Boy?' Hafner asked. 'Father Lawless, that is – I suppose I'd better start showing a bit of respect.'

Strafford didn't answer directly. He was watching the smoking logs, his eyes still watering a little. 'It struck me, what you said in the hall.'

'What did I say?' Hafner enquired.

'"So they did for him at last." What did you mean?'

'Nothing. It was a joke – poor taste, I'll grant you, in the circumstances.'

'You must have meant something. Wasn't Father Lawless popular in the house? He was a frequent visitor, I know that. Kept his horse stabled here, even stayed over, sometimes – he stayed last night, in fact, because of the snow.'

Hafner came to the fireplace and he too stood looking at the logs in the hearth, which by now had begun to flame, un-willingly, as it seemed, giving off as yet no perceptible heat.

'Oh, he was always welcome here, right enough. You know how the Prods like to keep a tame priest about the place—'

He stopped, and glanced quickly sideways at Strafford. 'Oh, God, I suppose you're one, are you?'

'Yes, I'm Protestant, if that's what you mean. Church of Ireland, that is.'

'Put my foot in it again, so. Will it do any good if I say I'm sorry?'

'No need to apologise at all,' Strafford said. 'I don't mind.' He gave one of the logs a push with the toe of his shoe. 'You said you were "supposed to be" the family doctor here. Care to elaborate?'

Hafner produced a throaty little laugh. 'I can see a fellow would want to watch his words around you,' he said. 'What I meant is that I mainly look after Mrs O.'

'Why? – is she ill?'

Hafner drew deep on his cigarette. 'No, no. Only delicate, you know – highly strung. Her nerves—' He let his voice trail off.

'She's quite a bit younger than Colonel Osborne.'

'She is that, yes.'

They were silent. The matter of the Osbornes' marriage and its likely intricacies hung in the chill air between them, though closed for the moment to further interrogation.

'Tell me about Father Lawless,' Strafford said.

'I will, if you tell me first what happened to him. That damned horse of his throw him? It's a mad brute.'

One of the burning logs crackled and spat.

'Your patient, Mrs Osborne, found him this morning, in the library.'

'Heart? He was a terrible man for the bottle, and' – he held up his cigarette – 'the fags.'

'More a – a haemorrhage, you might say. The body has been taken to Dublin, where they'll do a post-mortem first thing in the morning.'

Sergeant Jenkins had gone off in the ambulance, sitting in front, wedged in the bench seat with the driver and his assistant, having baulked at travelling in the back with the corpse. Strafford had conferred with him on what to report to Chief Superintendent Hackett when he got to Dublin, and had told him to come back first thing tomorrow with the Chief's instructions.

By rights, Hackett should have come down to Ballyglass himself, but he had let it be known that he had no intention of doing so, using the weather, of all implausible things, as an excuse. Strafford knew perfectly well that his wily boss's real reason for staying away was a prudent determination not to put himself directly on the scene of a scandalous and potentially explosive case. Strafford didn't mind being left to get on with things on his own. On the contrary, he was quietly gratified to find himself in sole charge, at least for the present.

'It was bound to be something like that, sooner or later,' Hafner said, with professional cheeriness. 'Father Tom lived hard, despite the dog collar. He was always being hauled up in front of the Hierarchy and ordered to mend his ways. I believe the Archbishop himself had to speak to him more than once – he has a house down here, you know, over on the coast.'

'Who?'

'The Archbishop.'

'Doctor McQuaid, you mean?'

Hafner chuckled. 'There's only one Archbishop – only one that counts, at any rate. Dirty your bib and he'll be down on you like a ton of bricks, whether you're Catholic, Protestant, Gentile or Jew. Runs a tight outfit, does His Grace, without regard for creed, race or colour – no matter who you are, you're still liable to get it in the neck.'

'So I'm told.'

'Your crowd have it easy, believe me. He's wary of the Prods, but if you're a Catholic and in a position of any consequence, the reverend Doctor only has to lift his little finger and your career goes up in smoke – or into the flames of hellfire, and *then* up in smoke. And it doesn't just apply to priests. Anyone who gets a belt of the crozier is done for, as far as holy Ireland is concerned. This can't be news to you, even if you are a swaddler.'

It was a long time, as long ago as his schooldays, since Strafford had heard himself and his co-religionists referred to by that derogatory term, the origin of which he had never been able to discover.

'You sound as if you're speaking from experience,' he said.

Hafner shook his head, with a sort of scowling smile. 'I've always minded my Ps and Qs. The Church keeps a sharp eye on the medical profession – the mother and her child and all that, you know, the basis of the Christian family. Have to look after that, above all.' He was silent for a moment, brooding. 'I met him one time, the Archbishop.' He turned to Strafford. 'Frosty bugger, I can tell you. Ever see him in the flesh? Has this long thin face, bloodless and white, as if he'd been living in the dark for years. And the eyes! "I hear you are a regular visitor over at Ballyglass House, Doctor," he says to me, in that slow soft voice he has. "And are there not enough Catholic families in the parish for you to be attending to, at all?"

Believe me, I wondered on the spot if I should start packing my medical bag and looking for a practice over the water. Not that I've done a damn thing to merit his ire, other than my job.'

Strafford nodded. He didn't care for this fellow, with his gruff jollity and his man-of-the-world patter. But then, there weren't a great many people whom Strafford did care for.

'You said you thought I might be someone's brother-in-law,' he murmured. 'Who is that?'

Hafner pursed his lips and whistled silently, to show how impressed he was. 'You don't forget a thing, do you. What did you say your name was?'

'Strafford.'

'Stafford?'

'No – Strafford.'

'Ah, sorry. Well, I thought you might be the infamous Freddie Harbison, her ladyship's brother, whose name is never mentioned within these walls. He's always broke, and hangs around looking for whatever there is to be picked up. He's the black sheep of the Harbisons of Harbison Hall – every family has one.'

'What did he do, to earn such a bad reputation?'

'Oh, there are all kinds of stories about him. Dodgy business ventures, a little light pilfering, the darling daughter of this or that Big House put in the family way – you know the kind of thing. It could all be just tittle-tattle, of course. One of the chief pleasures of rural life is denigrating your neighbours and stabbing your betters in the back.'

Strafford took down from the mantelpiece a framed photograph, somewhat faded, showing a younger and sleeker

Colonel Osborne, wearing baggy linen slacks and a cricket jumper, standing on the lawn in front of Ballyglass House, smiling down, with somewhat stiff parental fondness, at a boy of twelve or so and a younger girl, playing together, the girl sprawled in a miniature wheelbarrow that the boy was pushing over the grass. Behind them, on the steps of the house, there was visible a vague, dim female figure. She was dressed in a pale calf-length summer gown. Her left hand was lifted, not in greeting, it seemed, but rather in warning, and although her face was blurred by the shadow of a beech tree, her stance made her seem alarmed, or angry, or both. It was a strange scene, Strafford thought. It looked staged, somehow, a tableau, the significance and meaning of which had faded, just as had the photograph itself. Only one of the woman's feet was visible, in an old-fashioned shoe with a sharply pointed toe, resting so lightly on the step that she seemed about to launch herself out upon the air, like a gossamer-gowned figure in a Pre-Raphaelite painting.

'The first Mrs Osborne?' Strafford asked, turning the photograph for Hafner to see.

'I suppose so,' the doctor said, peering at the woman's shadowy form. 'She was a bit before my time.'

'She died, I take it?'

'Yes, she died. Fell down the stairs out there, broke her back.' He saw Strafford's look of surprise. 'Didn't you know? Tragic thing. She survived for a few days, I believe, then gave up the ghost.' He peered more closely at the photograph, frowning. 'By the way she's standing there, posed like that, she does look breakable, doesn't she.'

8

Doctor Hafner shared a few more scraps of general gossip – Strafford knew the man would be far too careful to give away family secrets, if he were privy to them, which, being a doctor, he surely was – and went off into the house in search of his patient.

Strafford remained by the fireplace. He had a way, when he was trying to sort out the facts of a case, of lapsing into a sort of dull half-trance. Afterwards, when he had come back to himself, he would hardly be able to remember what direction his thoughts had taken, or what the result of them had been. All that was left behind was a vague, fizzing glow, like that of a light bulb that's about to burn out. He had to suppose that, when he was lost to himself in this way, he must have got somewhere, must have made some sort of progress, even if he didn't know where the somewhere was, or even what progress would consist in. It was as if he had fallen briefly asleep and dropped at once into the midst of a powerful and deeply revelatory dream, all the details of which turned transparent the instant he woke up, though the sense, the afterglow, of their significance remained.

He went out to the hall and tried on a number of the pairs of wellington boots standing under the coat rack, until he found a pair that fitted him at least approximately. Then he put on his coat and hat and knotted his scarf at his throat and stepped out into the cold white glare of the winter afternoon.

The snow had stopped, but from the big-bellied look of the sky it was certain that there was more to come.

He walked around by the side of the house, pausing now and then to get his bearings. The place in general was seriously in need of repair and renovation. The frames of the big windows were decayed and their putty was crumbling, and there were cracks running up the walls where growths of buddleia had lodged, their branches leafless now. When he looked up, craning his neck, he saw how the gutters sagged, and the way the protruding edges of roof slates had been splintered and left jagged by countless winter storms. A warm wave of nostalgia washed over him. Only someone who had been born and brought up in a place like this, as he had, could know the particular, piercing fondness he felt before the sad spectacle of so much decay and decrepitude. Helpless nostalgia was the curse of his steadily dwindling caste.

He came to the fire escape that he had seen earlier, through the other side of the French window on the first floor. Down here, the rust damage was much worse than it was higher up, and he was surprised the thing was still standing. The snow was undisturbed around the base of it. No one had climbed these steps recently – no one, he felt sure, had climbed them in a very long time. Heaven help anyone on the upper floors caught unawares by fire. He had a special fear of being trapped in a burning building – what a way to die that would be!

Now, for the second time that day, he sensed that he was being watched. He turned his head this way and that, squinting against the blinding glare of the pristine white lawn stretching away to the edge of a dense wood. He wondered if this was the copse Lettie had pointed out to him earlier, from the drawing-room window, where the timber had been felled. But no, it was too extensive to be called a copse. The black-branched trees seemed to press forward with desperate eagerness, as though they might at any moment break through the barbed-wire fence that was its border and make their determined way, hobbling along with their roots dragging, across the open expanse before them, to crowd about the house and thrash their limbs furiously against its defenceless walls. As a countryman, Strafford had a healthy respect for Mother Nature, but he had never been able quite to love her. Even in adolescence, when he read Keats and Wordsworth and became a pantheist, he had preferred to watch the grand old lady's cavortings from a safe distance. Nowadays, he saw behind the birdsong and the blossom only the endless and bloody struggle for dominance and survival. As Superintendent Hackett liked to say, doing his horny-handed son-of-the-soil routine, when you spent your day dealing with criminals, it was hard at night to love the little foxes.

By now he was convinced he wasn't alone out here, but his eyes were still dazzled by the contrast between the snowy lawn and the dimness of the trees beyond, and he could see no one. Then something moved, in a way that no wind-blown branch or bird-disturbed tangle of twigs would move. He put up a hand to shade his eyes, and made out what seemed to be a face, although at such a distance it was no more than a pale smudge against the darker background of the trees. But yes, it was a face, surrounded by what looked like a rusted halo of hair. Then suddenly it was gone, as if it had never been there. Was it a person he had seen, or only a trick of the snow-light reflected against the mud-brown depths of the trees?

He felt all at once both exposed and isolated. Who was the watcher, himself or the one who had been there and then vanished?

He set off across the lawn. The snow was deep, and each footprint he left behind him was filled at once with a wedge of shadow. When he came to the spot at the perimeter of the wood where he had seen, or imagined he had seen, the figure watching him, he found a stand of bracken had been trodden on and crushed. He clambered over the barbed wire and pushed forward into the trees.

It was sheltered in here, and there were only scant patches of snow on the ground, too few and too scattered to register the trail of whoever it was had gone before him. There were no pathways, yet instinct guided him onwards, deeper and deeper into the wood. The tips of twigs whipped at him, and immense arcs of bramble reached out their thorned antennae and snagged his coat and the legs of his trousers. He pushed on, not to be daunted. He was nothing but a hunter now, his nerves stretched, his mind empty, his breathing shallow and the blood fairly racing in his veins. He felt the thrill of being afraid. The watched watcher, the hunted hunter.

He spotted something glinting darkly on a leaf, and reached down a fingertip and touched it. Blood, and it was fresh.

On through the sullenly resistant trees he pushed, watching out for more droplets of blood, and finding them.

After a little way he stopped. He seemed to have registered the sound before he heard it. Ahead of him, someone was chopping something, not wood, but something like it. He stood and listened, taking in distractedly the smells around him, the sharp scent of pine, the soft brown savour of loam. He went forward again, more cautiously, thrusting branches out of his way and ducking to avoid the briars. He might have been the hero in a fairy tale, hacking his way towards the enchanted castle in the magically still and frozen forest.

Briar rose – *Rosa rubiginosa.* From where had he dredged that up? It fascinated him, the things his mind knew without knowing it knew them.

He was cold by now, seriously cold. His trench coat was absurdly inadequate out here. Shivers ran through him, and he had to grit his teeth to keep them from chattering. One of the borrowed wellington boots, the left one, must have a split in it, for he could feel an icy wetness seeping into the heel of his sock. He felt ridiculous. It was as if he had been lured into the wood only to be laughed at and made mock of.

The ground sloped suddenly, and he almost slipped on the half-frozen mush of sodden leaves underfoot. He paused to listen. All he could hear was his own laboured breathing. The chopping sound ahead had stopped. He went on again, down the slope, skidding and sliding, grabbing at low-hanging leafless branches to keep himself upright. At last he came to the deep heart of the wood. Here, a kind of twilight reigned. He could feel his heart pounding in its cage. Think no thought, he told himself, merely be, like an animal. His years as a policeman had taught him to be not fearless, only to disregard the fact of being afraid.

The gloom began to lighten, and in a moment he came to the edge of a clearing, a sort of hollow basin at the very bottom of the wood. A carpet of snow had settled here unhindered, on this open ground.

In the middle of the clearing there sat, or rather squatted, an ancient caravan, painted green, with an impossibly narrow door and a low rectangular window at the back. Strafford experienced a faint shock of recognition. His father had acquired one just like it, when one summer he conceived the idea of taking the family on a touring holiday to France. Nothing had come of this plan, of course, and the thing had been left to rot in the stable yard, canted forward dejectedly and resting on the tip of its tow bar. This one was wheel-less, its paint was peeling, and the back window was webbed over with the grime of years. How it had got here, so deep into the wood, he couldn't think. At one corner of its rounded roof a tall metal chimney stuck up, crooked and comical, like a battered stovepipe hat, chugging out sluggish puffs of dirty-grey smoke.

A sawn-off block of railway sleeper was set as a step in front of the door.

On the ground, to the left, there was a circular, ragged bloodstain, some three feet in diameter. The fresh blood, so stark against the snow, put Strafford in mind of something that it took him some moments to identify. It was the Wicked Stepmother's blood-red, flesh-white, irresistible apple. He did not think it would be a sleeping beauty, reclining on her virgin couch, that he would find here today.

He stepped out of the shelter of the trees and crossed the clearing. The soles of his rubber boots squeaked in the snow. The sound, impossible to suppress, would alert whoever might be inside the caravan to his approach.

The door was fitted with an old car-door handle, pitted and scratched. Strafford lifted a hand and made a knuckle, but before he had a chance to knock, suddenly the door was flung open, with such force that he had to step back smartly on to the snow to avoid being struck.

A figure loomed bear-like before him. It was a figure he recognised. Big shoulders, broad brow, red hair the colour of bronze in the light of the doorway. Fonsey, the feral boy, in dungarees, hobnailed boots, a soiled woollen vest and the leather jacket with the moth-eaten fur collar.

It took Strafford a moment to recover. He introduced himself by his surname only. Young men of the likes of Fonsey were leery of policemen. Strafford glanced at the bloodstain on the ground. 'Been hunting, have you?'

'I have permission,' Fonsey said. 'I wasn't poaching.'

'I didn't say you were poaching,' the detective answered. 'It was just' – he glanced again at the stain in the snow – 'with so much blood, it must be some big beast you caught.' He moved forward and set one foot on the makeshift step. 'Look, do you mind if I come in for a minute? It's cold out here.'

He could see Fonsey calculating how unwise it would be to refuse him entry, and deciding it was better not to find out. He was young, probably no more than eighteen or nineteen, suspicious, and vulnerable despite his bulk. He was missing a front tooth. The rectangular gap looked very stark and black, like the mouth of a deep cave seen from the far side of a valley. It was, Strafford thought, the most unnerving thing about him.

The caravan inside smelled of paraffin and candle grease and rancid meat, of sweat and smoke and dirty socks. Under the window, on a table there – it was hardly more than a Formica-covered shelf, hinged to the wall and braced on two front legs – a skinned and spatchcocked rabbit was laid out on a sheet of butcher's paper, ready to be cooked.

'Not so big a beast after all,' Strafford observed. Fonsey gazed at him, frowning, not understanding. Strafford smiled. 'I'm interrupting your dinner.'

'I only lit the stove a minute ago,' Fonsey answered. The missing tooth gave him a faint, whistling lisp. He nodded towards a pot-bellied stove, behind the sooty window of which a weak flame was sputtering. A few cut lengths of wood had been set leaning in a circle against its bulbous sides. 'I'm waiting for the sticks to dry out.'

He had shut the caravan door, and now in the enclosed space the foetid odours pressed in on Strafford. He tried to breathe through his mouth, but still the smells were there.

He took in the place at a glance. Everything seemed to have been whittled down in order to fit in the confined space. There were two narrow bunks, facing each other on either side of the rear window, a tall, shallow cabinet of shinily veneered wood, and a pair of ancient bentwood chairs. At the front end of the room there was a sort of cramped little kitchen. On a small table with long legs stood a miniature cooker connected by a rubber tube to a yellow gas canister underneath the table. There was a sink, and a draining board with hooks above it on which to hang cups and a few cooking utensils.

Strafford felt the hulking boy watching him, and heard him breathing. He turned to him, taking in more fully the bagginess of the dungarees and the stains of various hues on his vest, and a pang of pity ran through him like a tiny quick electric charge. Fonsey. From Alphonsus, that would be. He looked like a big baffled child, a waif lost down here in the

70

depths of the wood. How had he come to this, living alone in this desolate place?

And the parents who had burdened him with that ridiculous name – Alphonsus! – what had become of them?

'You heard what happened at the house?' Strafford asked. 'You know a priest was killed?'

Fonsey nodded. His eyes were a soiled shade of yellowish green, with incongruously long lashes, curving upwards, like a girl's. On his broad forehead there was an angry rash of pimples, and there was a running sore at one side of his lower lip that he kept picking at. To the other smells he added his own raw tang, a blend of leather, hay, horse-dust and swarming hormones.

His hands were huge, and redly raw from the cold – he had just come in from butchering the rabbit. Would they be capable, those hands, of stabbing a man in the neck and mutilating him where he fell? But hands are only hands, Strafford reflected. Would Fonsey himself have it in him to murder a priest?

A draught from somewhere brought a particularly gamey whiff from the table where the rabbit lay in a small, purplish heap.

'Tell me, Fonsey,' Strafford said, in a conversational tone, 'where were you last night?' He glanced about again, in a purposely distracted manner. 'Were you here? Did you sleep here?'

'I'm always here,' Fonsey answered simply. 'Where else would I be?'

'So this is your home, is it? What about your family, where do they live?'

'Have none,' the boy said, without emphasis, stating the bleak, bald fact for what it was.

He had suffered in his life, that much was clear. Strafford could sense the boy's dull, abiding anguish. It was almost a smell, like the thick, flesh-warm stink of the meat on the table.

'Are you from the town?' Strafford asked. Fonsey looked blank again. 'I mean, were you born here, in Ballyglass?'

The boy turned his face away and muttered something under his breath.

'What was that?' Strafford was keeping up a friendly, soothing tone.

'I said, I don't know where I'm from.'

There was nothing to say to that.

Strafford had assumed at first that the boy must be mentally slow. He saw now, however, that despite his shambling gait and hulking frame – he was built top-heavy, like a buffalo, and was so tall he had to bend his head to fit under the low ceiling of the caravan – he was deceptively alert, with even a glint of cunning. He was a creature in hiding, hoping the hounds might eventually pass by and go in search of likelier game.

Strafford held out his hands to the stove. It was giving off only the faintest glimmer of warmth.

'Did you know Father Lawless?' he asked casually. 'Father Tom – did you know him?'

Fonsey shrugged. 'I'd see him around the place. He have a horse here. Mister Sugar. Great bloody beast' – he pronounced it *baste* – 'seventeen hands, with a mad eye on him.'

'Did you look after him? – Mr Sugar?'

'I look after them all, all the mounts. That's my job.'

Strafford nodded. He could feel the boy willing him to be gone.

'So you didn't have much to do with the priest,' he said, 'with Father Lawless, other than to look after his horse. Did he talk to you, at all?'

Fonsey frowned, and his eyes went vague, as if it were a trick question. He touched a fingertip to the sore on his mouth. 'How do you mean, talk?'

'Well, you know – did he chat to you, did you talk together about horses, and so on?'

The boy slowly shook his great round head, with its broad brow and its tangle of matted curls. His hair, in the dimness of the caravan, had deepened in colour, and gleamed like burnt toffee now.

'Chat?' he said, as if it were a new and novel word. 'No, he didn't chat to me.'

'Because, you know, he had a reputation for being very – well, very outgoing and friendly.'

There was a pause, then Fonsey gave a low snicker, pursing his glistening pink lips and touching his finger again to the weeping cold sore on his lip.

'Ah, sure, they're all that,' he said. 'The priests are all friendly.'

And he laughed.

9

The way was steeper on this side of the clearing. Fonsey had pointed him in this direction, saying it would lead him straight to the road to Ballyglass House. He clambered awkwardly up the slope, driving the heels of his boots deep into the leaf mould for traction, afraid he might take a fall. He pictured himself sprawled deep in a patch of brambles with a broken ankle, calling for help in a voice becoming ever feebler, as the winter twilight turned to night and darkness settled over him and he froze to death.

When he got to the road at last, he realised he didn't know in which direction to turn for Ballyglass House, and stood looking vaguely this way and that, then shrugged and set off to the right.

Frozen grass crackled under his boots. A hunched crow, perched on a high branch, eyed him as he went past and opened wide its black beak and cawed at him.

The road was little used. He had gone what he thought must be at least a quarter of a mile when a cattle lorry came rattling up behind him, and he stopped and stood well in from the verge to let it pass. The driver, seated high up behind the spattered windscreen, sounded his horn at him in cheerful derision.

He walked on. He was cold to the bone. He felt a surge of anger, tinged with self-pity. He should have listened to his father and gone for the law. He would be a successful barrister by now, with a wig and a gown and a starched white collar, strutting about the Four Courts, discussing briefs and exchanging gossip about his clients, and drinking port of an evening in the warmth of a Dublin pub all mahogany and brass and black-and-white tiles. Yes, that was the life he had spurned, and now here he was, trudging along a country byroad in the cutting air of a winter's eve, sullen and solitary and furious at everything, himself especially.

Now he heard a second vehicle approaching behind him, and he stepped back to allow it to pass. It was an old grey two-door Ford van. High and squat, with its humped back and long, bulbous front grille and staring headlamps set atop broad grey mudguards, it bore a striking resemblance to a moose. Stencilled in large black lettering on the side of the vehicle was the legend:

JEREMIAH RECK
FAMILY BUTCHER
QUALITY MEATS

Instead of passing him by, the van drew to a rattling stop. The driver was a big soft-faced man of sixty or so, with oiled hair brushed sleekly back from a high, smooth forehead. He had glossy brown eyes, the lids of which drooped at the corners – Einstein's eyes, Strafford thought, at once mournful and merry. This could only be Mr Jeremiah Reck himself. He leaned across the bench seat and pushed open the passenger door.

'Get in, get in, my man,' he said, with a lordly flourish. 'Who do you think you are, Scott of the Antarctic?'

Strafford did as he was bade and climbed up on to the seat. A blast of hot dry air from the heater blew in his face, and at once his sinuses began to sting.

The driver had turned sideways the better to study his passenger, and now he put out a hand. 'I am Reck,' he said. 'And who might you be, my pale friend, if you don't mind my asking?'

'My name is Strafford.'

'Strafford with an *r*?'

'That's right.'

'Ah. Then I believe we're to have the pleasure, nay, the honour, of your company, tonight.'

'Oh, yes?' Strafford said, not understanding.

'At the Sheaf of Barley. I am *that* Reck.'

'But your sign says—?'

'Yes, I'm that Reck also. Butcher, grocer, publican *and* guesthouse-keeper. A man of parts, you might say, and you'd be right.' He joggled the gearstick and released the clutch, the wheels spun on the icy road and then caught hold, and the van leaped forward with a lurch. 'May I ask, Mr Strafford, what you're doing out here on these wild ways on such a day as this? Where were you coming from?'

'I was down in the woods.'

Reck nodded. He had the softly breathing demeanour of certain large slow men who live in contentment with themselves and the world. So great was his girth that the bulge of his lower belly was wedged under the steering wheel. Strafford leaned back on the creaky leather seat. His toes, blown upon by the lower part of the labouring heater, were beginning to warm up.

'Down in the woods, eh?' Reck said thoughtfully, and hummed a snatch of the tune of 'The Teddy Bears' Picnic' – 'dum-t'dum t'dittity-dum' – and then made a whistling sound by sucking air in through his front teeth. 'Having a word with the Horrible Boy, were we?'

'The—?'

'Fonsey the Fierce.'

'Yes, I was, as a matter of fact. *Is* he fierce?'

'I should say so. He's our Gargantua, or do I mean Pantagruel? It's many years since I read that book. I know him as the Horrible Boy. It's a term of affection, you understand.'

'What's his other name? – or has he got one?'

'Indeed he has. Welch, he is called. You would pronounce it *Walsh*, but down here, in the County of the Uncouth, we say Welch. His mother was one Kitty Welch – or Walsh, if you insist.'

'Does she still live here, in Ballyglass?'

'No. She's off in England somewhere. Manchester, I believe.'

'And his father?'

Reck produced a ripe, rumbling chuckle.

'Well now,' he said, 'our Fonsey, you see, is another instance of that rare phenomenon, the immaculate conception. Rare, I say, but the Star of Bethlehem does put in uncommonly frequent appearances over this fertile land of ours, as I'm sure you're well aware.'

He paused, and made that sucking sound with his teeth again. It was a kind of whistling in reverse.

'Kitty put him in an orphanage before she went off – she was criticised for it in the town, but what choice had she?

78

– and when he was old enough to use his fists, he became obstreperous and was packed off to a penitential colony in the west, a place called Carricklea, known and feared by all youthful delinquents – no doubt you've heard of it? When he came out, years later, the Lady Reck and myself looked after him for a while. I took him on as an apprentice at the butchering, but he hadn't the stomach for it. He didn't like poleaxing poor dumb creatures, any more than I do, but I operate on the principle that if you're prepared to eat them, you must be prepared to murder them. Anyway, came a day and our Fonsey was gone from us at the Sheaf, and the next we heard of him he was living in a caravan down in Ballyglass Wood, minding the horses for Their Worships up at the House. He does the odd delivery for me still.' He paused again, shaking his large smooth globular head. 'Poor Fonsey, he lives a hard life, and deserved better.'

'Why did he leave?' Strafford asked.

'Why did he leave Mrs Reck and myself? Who can say? The ways of the wild are not our ways, and Fonsey is the wilderness itself. The Lord only knows what they did to him at Carricklea. He wouldn't say, and I stopped asking. The scars showed, however, physical and spiritual.'

Through a rent in the clouds low in the western sky the setting sun appeared, shedding a dark-gold glare. Reck asked:

'Would it be indiscreet to enquire what business it was you were conducting with young Fonsey, down in the woods?'

'Oh, I talk to a great many people. It's what detectives do. Dull work.'

'So you weren't following a "definite line of inquiry", as they say in the papers?'

'No, no. There are no such lines, as yet.'

Rounding a bend, they almost ran into a flock of sheep, tended by a boy in a coat that was far too big for him and belted at the waist with a twist of yellow binder twine. Reck stopped the van and the two men sat stranded amid a moving sea of dirty grey fleece. Strafford idly studied the milling animals, admiring their long aristocratic heads and the neat little hoofs, like carved nuggets of coal, on which they trotted so daintily. He was struck too by their protuberant and intelligent-seeming shiny black eyes, expressive of stoical resignation tinged with the incurable shame of their plight, avatars of an ancient race, being herded ignominiously along a country road by a snot-nosed brat with a stick.

'An interesting creature, the sheep,' Jeremiah Reck observed. '"Their cry has not changed since Arcady" – I think I have that right. May I enquire, sir, if you are a bookish man?'

'I read when I have time.'

'Ah, but you should make time. The book is one of our great inventions as a species.' The sheep passed on, and the butcher engaged the gears. 'You're not a native of these parts yourself,' he said. It was not a question.

'No, but not far off – Roslea.'

'Over beyond New Ross? Well, at least you're a Wexford man.'

Strafford smiled to himself, amused by that 'at least'.

They drove on. Strafford found soothing the sound of the van's tyres sizzling in the slush.

'I take it you've heard of the death of Father Lawless,' he said.

'Oh, I did, I did. News travels fast, round these parts. What happened to the poor fellow, at all?'

'Well, he died.'

'That's what you might call an unforthcoming answer,' Reck said, '—if it is an answer at all.' He whistled for a while through his teeth. It was a thing that could become annoying, over time. Strafford felt he should sympathise with Mrs Reck. 'They're saying he fell down the stairs in the middle of the night,' the butcher went on, 'but if I were asked, I'd guess there was more to it than that.'

'Oh, yes?'

'Yes. For instance, I wouldn't think the authorities up in Dublin would send down a detective inspector to investigate an accident, now, would they? They'd have left it to the local man.'

'Sergeant – Rochford, is it?'

'Radford.' Reck chuckled. 'Our bold Dan the Man, Sheriff of Deadwood Gulch.'

'I haven't met him,' Strafford said, looking out at the snow-clad trees passing by the window. 'He's been unwell, it seems.'

'Unwell?' Reck pursed his lips. 'Is that so? Hmm.'

Strafford had already guessed the nature of Radford's un-wellness.

'The 'flu, I'm told,' he said.

'Ah. The 'flu. It's going round – Mrs Reck had it, but is recovered. I've so far been spared, myself.' He paused, doing his whistle. 'You know the Radfords lost a son?'

'Lost?'

'He drowned. Only a young fellow.'

Strafford turned to look out of the window again. A dead son, a father left to his sorrow.

'Very sad,' he said.

Reck's whistle, he thought, was the sound of a singing kettle coming to the boil.

'So Fonsey's father is an unknown quantity,' he said. 'Is that the case?'

'Well, Kitty Welch is bound to know, but she's not saying. For my part, I have my suspicions, but I keep them to myself. Poor Kitty wasn't a bad girl, only a little skittish, when the moon was full. You would have to forgive her – though not many did, in this parish.' He sighed. 'People can be very censorious, don't you find?'

They rounded the bend, and there was Ballyglass House, looming out of the frozen mist off at the end of the winding drive, its chimneys smoking like a battery of cannons.

Reck drew the van to a halt. The lights were on in the downstairs windows of the house, for the winter afternoon was dying fast in the western sky, where more snow clouds were massing.

'Will you care to dine with us, later?' Reck asked, in his amiably rounded tones.

'I hope so.'

'I shall convey that information to M'Lady Reck. Something modest but nutritious, yes? And tell me now, is there anything you will not eat?'

'I don't think so.'

'I confess to an aversion to the brassicas, myself, and in particular' – he sank his voice to a shuddering whisper – 'the Brussels sprout.'

'Oh, I'll eat anything,' Strafford said.

'Within reason?'

'Within reason. Maybe I could telephone you to let you know when I'll be with you?'

Reck nodded absently, peering through the windscreen at the house.

'A remarkable family, the Osbornes,' he said, 'remarkable in many ways. You'll have met the second Mrs Osborne?' He paused, still gazing up at the house, nodding slowly and doing his indrawn whistle. 'And you'll know the first one died in similar circumstances to Father Tom?' He turned a lively eye on Strafford. 'I fear that staircase must be jinxed.'

'Thank you for the lift,' Strafford said, opening the door. 'I'll walk from here. And I'll see you later. If I'm going to be late I'll be sure to telephone. If I *am* late, will you leave out a key?'

'Oh, don't worry about that, I'll be at my post. The true landlord never sleeps.' He watched Strafford as he stepped out on to the mixture of mud and snow in the gateway. 'You know,' he said, 'I don't believe the Horrible Boy, fearsome as he is, would have it in him to murder a priest, him that couldn't choke a chicken without shedding a tear.'

10

The house was set on a rise, and as he approached it along the drive it seemed to loom out over him and open its mock-Palladian wings as if to enfold him in its sombre embrace. He wasn't so fanciful as to take inanimate objects for anything other than they were. No house was haunted, no ghosts walked. Yet not a full day had passed since a man had died here, stabbed in the neck and mutilated and left to lie in a mess of his own blood and breathe his last. Surely such a violent act should leave something behind, a trace, a tremor in the air, like the hum that lingers when a bell stops tolling?

He clung to the belief that death was more than mere extinction. His grandfather had been a bishop. The genes will out.

A bat flitted above him, its wings feathering the encroaching dark.

He tried to feel how it would have felt, to be stabbed and slashed, to fall and bleed and die. When he was young and still a trainee in Templemore, he had imagined that as a policeman he would be granted a special kind of knowledge. He would learn things that other people didn't know, things of life and, far more significantly, things of death, and dying. A foolish expectation, of course – to live was to live, to die was to die. It was what everyone did. What was there for a detective to detect that other people weren't privy to?

Yes, he had been deluded in believing that at Templemore he would be received into a secret brotherhood, would be introduced, like an alchemist of old, to a body of arcane and secret knowledge. He had thought he would be not as others were, groping their way purblind through the world, dulled against everything except the simplest affects, the ordinary urges. He would be among the elect, above the world and its trivial doings. A fantasy, of course. And yet.

He had no one, no wife, no children, no lover – no friends, even. Nor had he a family, to speak of – a few cousins he occasionally saw, and an uncle in South Africa who used to send a card every Christmas but then had stopped, having died, probably. There was his father, of course. He thought of him, however, not as a separate entity, but as in some way a part of himself, the tree of which he was an offshoot, and which he would soon overshadow and, in time, outgrow.

None of this troubled him, or not seriously. He didn't really know himself, and didn't care to. His life was a state of peculiar calm, of tranquil equilibrium. His strongest drive was curiosity, the simple wish to know, to be let in on what was hidden from others. Everything to him had the aspect of a cipher. Life was a mundane mystery, the clues to the solving of which were strewn all about, concealed or, far more fascinatingly, hidden in plain view, for all to see but for him alone to recognise.

The dullest object could, for him, flare into sudden significance, could throb in the sudden awareness of itself. There *were* clues, and he was their detector.

It was this train of thought that somehow brought up the image of Geoffrey Osborne's pale, etiolated wife. He saw her again, saw her, here in the cold blue air of evening, as she had appeared that morning in the kitchen doorway. Standing there, she had seemed not so much present, but to tremble, rather, on the brink of being. As he walked now, stumbling clumsily in someone else's leaky wellingtons, he found himself saying her name aloud, breathing it out on breaths that billowed like wafts of ectoplasm – *Sylvia*. It seemed an invocation. A summoning of sorts.

What was this sensation that was flooding through him, wholly novel and yet somehow familiar? Surely he wasn't falling in love, with a woman he had seen for no more than a moment? Love? That would knock him clean off his plinth.

The actual Mrs Osborne, when he encountered her again, was nothing like the daemonic figure of his fevered imaginings in the darkness of the driveway.

He pulled the rope that worked the doorbell. Mrs Duffy, when she opened the door, gave him an odd look that seemed to him at once complicitous and cautionary. Mrs Osborne, she said, had been asking for him. This made him frown. He didn't like coincidences – she had been asking for him while he was thinking of her – and he felt a stirring of unease.

He found the lady herself in a little parlour off the main hall. It seemed to be her private domain, and all her own work. There was a preponderance of chintz and faded silk, and a liberal strewing of cushions and an array of brass pots and crystal vases. Miniature china figurines stood about in attentive poses, got up in capes and crinolines and knee breeches and cocked hats. The overall effect was uncanny, and faintly comical.

Mrs Osborne was seated on a small, high sofa upholstered in yellow satin. Her dress of dark-blue chiffon had a deep collar, a tight waist, and a wide skirt that fanned out symmetrically on either side of her, arranged just so, its pleats suggestive of the half-shell on which Botticelli's Venus skims. She wore a string of pearls about her pale neck, and an emerald brooch in the shape of a scarab was pinned to the front of her dress. A small table before her was laid for afternoon tea. There were jugs, silver cruets, bone china cups, little knives, little forks, little spoons. Slices of assorted cakes were arranged on delicate little plates.

Strafford took all this in at a glance, and his heart sank. A star of reflected light on the cheek of the teapot seemed to wink at him in spiteful mirth. He felt a flush of embarrassment at the memory of the gusty emotions he had entertained out on the drive. Love me, love my knick-knacks.

'There you are!' Mrs Osborne exclaimed, her smile showing off two rows of small, even teeth, the top front two of which were lightly flecked with lipstick. She was as frothy and frilled as the gewgaws crowding all round her, and her eyes sparkled and her cheek was flushed. Strafford's heart plunged a fathom deeper still.

Mrs Osborne patted the place beside her on the sofa, inviting him to sit. He pretended not to notice. Instead, he fetched a chair, set it down in front of the tea table and sat stolidly upon it. His hostess frowned briefly, displeased by this rebuff, but then managed again a brilliant yet decidedly cockeyed smile. 'Yes, of course,' she murmured, 'of course – this way we can see each other's eyes. *Much* more friendly.'

She seemed to him more than a little mad.

Her hair, which had hung limp and lank that morning, was done up now in an elaborate eighteenth-century style. A thick braid was set tiara-like above her forehead, and at the sides there were bunches of curls that covered her ears. The heel of Strafford's sock inside his shoe was still wet. The wetness was warm now, and this was worse than when it had been cold. He wished he could be outside again, in the night's dank darkness. He would like to have been anywhere that was not this make-believe room, with its crowding trinkets and trifles. He felt like the White Rabbit.

'Shall I be mummy?' Mrs Osborne asked, and without waiting for him to reply set about pouring the tea. 'One lump or two?'

'No sugar, thank you.'

'Milk?'

'No, thanks.'

'Ah. You prefer it black. Good, so do I. Here you are.'

The cup, when she passed it to him, rattled very slightly in its saucer. He balanced it on his knee, the tea untasted. 'Mrs Osborne,' he said, 'I have to talk to you about last night.'

'Last night?'

'Yes. Or this morning, that is – I mean, when you found Father Lawless. Your husband said you couldn't sleep and—'

'Oh,' she exclaimed, with a tinkle of rueful merriment, 'I never sleep!'

'I'm sorry to hear that.' Strafford paused a moment, licking his lips, then pressed on again. 'But last night, in particular, I understand you were very – very restless, and that's why you came downstairs. Will you tell me what happened, exactly?'

'What happened?' She gazed at him in seeming bafflement. 'What do you mean, what happened?'

'I mean, when you found Father Lawless,' he said patiently. 'I wonder, did you switch on the light?'

'The light?'

'Yes, the electric light.' He pointed to the light fixture above his head. It had a pink shade, with roses painted on it. 'Did you switch it on, when you went into the library?'

'Why do you ask?'

'Because I'm wondering how clear a view you had of the body – Father Lawless's body.'

'I don't understand,' she murmured, frowning, and casting this way and that, as if searching for enlightenment from the wallpaper, or one of her china figurines.

Strafford sighed.

'Mrs Osborne, you came downstairs at some time in the early hours of this morning and found Father Lawless in the library. Isn't that so? And he was dead. Do you remember that? – do you remember finding him? Had you turned the light on? Did you see how he had died? Did you see the blood?'

She sat motionless, in silence, still scanning the room in perplexity. 'I suppose I must have,' she said uncertainly, in a faint, faraway voice. 'If there was blood, I mean, I must have seen it' – she turned suddenly and stared at him – 'mustn't I?'

'That's what I'm asking you,' he said. He felt as if he were trying to unwrap some delicately breakable thing from fold upon fold of unexpectedly resistant tissue paper. '*Can* you remember?'

She shook her head from side to side, like an uncomprehending child, still staring at him. Then she stirred herself and sat up very straight, setting her shoulders back and blinking, as though she had just woken from a trance. 'Would you like some cake?' she asked, setting her brilliant smile in place again, like a carnival mask. 'Mrs Duffy baked it – I asked her specially.' Her look darkened, and she sank abruptly into a sulk. 'I'm sure it's very nice,' she said petulantly. 'Mrs Duffy's cakes are always very nice. She's famous for her nice cakes, Mrs Duffy is – everyone talks about them – the whole county talks about them, Mrs Duffy's cakes!'

Fat iridescent tears welled in her eyes and sat trembling on the lower lids, but did not fall. Strafford, steadying his cup and saucer with one hand, extended the other across the table, and the woman before him lifted up her own hand, with a child's solemn tentativeness, and placed it in his. He felt the chill of her palm, felt the small thin bones beneath the skin. Her knuckles were blue. Neither of them spoke, but sat gazing at each other in a shared, bewildered helplessness.

The door opened, with what to Strafford seemed a bang, and Colonel Osborne came bustling in.

'Ah, here you are!' he said, beaming at his wife. 'I was looking for you everywhere.' He paused, staring at the two of them staring back at him, one holding the other's hand. 'Is everything – is everything all right?' he asked, bewildered himself now.

Strafford let go of Mrs Osborne's hand and rose from the chair. He was about to say something, he wasn't sure what, but Mrs Osborne cut him off. 'Oh for Christ's sake,' she snapped, in a new, hard voice, 'why can't you all leave me alone!' Then she jumped up from the sofa, brushing away the unshed tears with the heels of her hands, and pushed past her husband and was gone.

'I'm sorry—' Strafford began, at the same moment that Colonel Osborne groaned, 'Oh Lord!'

11

It was stingingly cold, but she didn't care. She had been making her way down the hillside through the trees when, just in time, she caught sight of Strafford, stepping out of the caravan and starting up through the trees in her direction.

She moved sideways, away from the path – it was her path, she had been making it for months, no one else walked on it or even knew it was there – and hid herself among a stand of birches. Her duffel coat was the same colour as her surroundings, and she hoped it would camouflage her. But what if he had spied her already? What if he had been specially trained in looking for people in hiding? He seemed to her a hopeless sort of detective, but appearances could be deceptive, as she very well knew.

If he did spot her, though, crouching here among the trees, what would she say, what excuse would she come up with for hiding from him? She could say her father had sent her with a message for Fonsey, something about the horses, and that she had got a fright when she saw a figure in black boots and a slouch hat climbing towards her up the hillside. But he wouldn't believe it, she knew he wouldn't.

Yet why was she hiding from him, anyway? Why shouldn't she be out walking in the woods? She had more right to be there than he did.

All the same, she would have turned and run back up the

hill to the road, except that it was too late now, he was already halfway up the slope. He wouldn't find the path, though, her path, but she could see he was going to pass very close to where she crouched among the pale slim trunks of the birches, hardly daring to breathe.

Was it fright or excitement that was making her heart beat so fast? Both, she supposed. Because she was excited, she was frightened, though in a pleasurable sort of way, thinking how maybe he'd spot her, and come over, and – and what?

Maybe that was it. Maybe she wanted to be caught, maybe she longed to be caught, not just here and now, on this snowy hillside, but always, and everywhere. Sometimes, when she was little, Dominic would let her play hide-and-go-seek with him and his friends, and when the game had started and she had hidden herself inside a wardrobe, behind a rack of her mother's dresses that smelled of sweat and stale scent, or was lying under the bed in the back bedroom, breathing in dust and trying not to sneeze, she would feel a sort of thick hot surge of something rising inside her – it was a bit like that heaving sensation you have when you're just about to vomit – and she wouldn't know whether she was afraid of being discovered in her hiding place, or hoping to be caught and dragged out in shame for everyone to see.

Once, one of the bigger boys, Jimmy Waldron was his name – she could still see him as he was then, with his buck teeth and greasy hair – had pounced on her where she had tucked herself behind the open door of the upstairs lavatory. Instead of shouting out to the others that he had found her, he had pushed her back into the lavatory and locked the door and put his hand up her dress and tried to kiss her, and wouldn't let her go, until in the end she bit him on the lip and made it bleed.

Strafford was level with her now, and so close, not more than five or six yards away, that she could hear him panting from the effort of scrambling up the steep, slippery slope. What if she were to spring out at him, like an animal, all fangs and claws? That would ruffle his composure, make him take notice of her, oh, yes. But she didn't move, and held her breath and let him go past.

She watched him until he had reached the crest of the hill and she couldn't see him any more. She heard a lorry going past, up there. Serve him right if he got knocked down.

He was dreadfully stuck-up, as bad as the chinless wonders at hunt balls who never asked her to dance because they were afraid of her, or her father's so-called horsey friends, who stood about with sherry glasses in their hands and smiled at her in that stupid, glassy-eyed way that they did. Half of them couldn't even remember her name. He wasn't as bad as her stepmother's family, though, the Harbisons, who thought they were God's gift to the county, and out of snobbery had let their dotty daughter marry her poor father and make his life a misery.

All the same, the detective was good-looking, in a scrawny sort of way – how *could* he be so thin? – and he had nice hands, she had noticed them, the nails clean and neatly clipped. She had a phobia about nails, the way they kept growing, like hair, growing and growing, even after you were dead, so someone had once told her. Imagine being stretched out six feet un-der the ground in the black-dark, your skull swathed in hanks of hair like steel wool, and your skeleton fingers clasped on your skeleton breast with inches of stuff as brittle and shiny as mother-of-pearl sticking out of the tips of them.

She left the shelter of the trees and went down the slope. She took her time, going carefully. She couldn't afford to slip and land on her backside in the half-frozen muck, for the skirt she was wearing wasn't her own. When she was sure Doctor Hafner – the Kraut – had left, she had gone into the bedroom where the White Mouse lay passed out on the bed, and had taken one of her tweed skirts and a heavy jumper out of the wardrobe, and brought them to her room and put them on.

She liked to wear her stepmother's things, she wasn't sure why, except that it gave her a sort of shivery feeling that she darkly enjoyed.

Now she paused in the trees at the edge of the clearing and took off her knickers – it wasn't easy, because of her riding boots – and put them in the pocket of her stepmother's skirt. The air, cool as silk, caressed her thighs. It didn't make her feel chilled at all – quite the opposite, in fact. She smiled. Oh, she was a bold girl, she knew she was, and gloried in it.

Here was the caravan, with Strafford's footprints leading away from it, and the big circular bloodstain in the trampled snow.

At the door she hesitated. Even still, after all this time, she hadn't been able to work out a form of etiquette to deal with these – whatever they were – she couldn't even think what word to use to describe what she was doing when she came down into the wood like this. Visits? It sounded ridiculously formal, and when she tried it out she heard it in exactly the prissy, strangulated way – '*vsts*' – that the White Mouse would say it, when she was doing her Queen Lizzie act and putting on that tiny clipped voice that made her sound just like a mouse squeaking. What about 'trysts'? No, that sounded like '*vsts*', only stupider.

Anyway, what did it matter? In her own mind, she wasn't really here. It was strange – how could one be in a place and at the same time not?

She lived in her own mind, that was the fact of the matter. Once, on a bright-green summer morning sparkling with dew – she remembered it so clearly – she had disturbed a spider's web that was strung between two heads of cabbage in the kitchen garden, and all the baby spiders had suddenly run out along the threads in all directions, there must have been hundreds of them, thousands, even. That was how it was with her, she was the spider sitting at the centre of the web, and all the little black things scurrying away from her were images of herself escaping into the world.

She gave the door a perfunctory knock – he could be up to anything, in there, the dirty brute – and entered through the narrow doorway.

When she was a child and her mother read *The Wind in the Willows* to her at bedtime, she had always been on the side of the weasels and the stoats.

Fonsey was squatting on his haunches in front of the stove, feeding it with lengths of cut branches.

'That wood is green,' Lettie said. 'How do you expect to get the thing going with green wood? You're such an ass.' He didn't even turn to look at her. The collar of his leather jacket was turned up, and he was wearing tennis shoes without laces – the boots he had just taken off stood beside the stove, agape like giant mouths and with their tongues hanging out. She could smell him from where she stood. 'And you stink like a polecat.' He mumbled something. 'What?' she said sharply. 'What did you say?'

'I said, how do you know what a polecat smells like?'

'Well, at least I know what a polecat *is*' – she didn't, in fact – 'which you don't.'

He stood up. She was always surprised by the size of him. In the impossibly narrow confines of the caravan he looked even bigger than he was. Getting to his feet like that, in his lumbering way, rolling his huge head on its short thick neck, he might have been some huge wild thing surging up out of its hiding place in a hole in the ground.

At these moments, when she came to the heart of the wood and climbed into his smelly lair, she knew she should be afraid of him, but she wasn't. It was he who was afraid of her, she knew he was. He was twice, three times as strong as she was, he could break her wrist, or her arm – he could break her neck – with one twist of those butcher's hands of his, yet of the two of them, she was the one in control. How could that be? Men, all men, in her experience of them, went in fear of women, though her experience in this area, as even she had to admit, wasn't what could be called wide-ranging.

Just then she caught sight of the eviscerated rabbit on the table. 'What's that disgusting thing?'

'My dinner.' He took down a blackened frying pan from its hook above the sink and set it atop the stove. 'Want some?'

'You won't get that thing hot enough with that—'

'—green wood. I know.'

98

'So what will you do, eat it raw? I can just see you, munching on a slab of it with blood dribbling down your chin. You're half animal yourself.'

He looked at her. She met his look with one of her own. Those awful pimples, she said to herself – how could she bear to come close to him, with those things all over his forehead?

'Did you bring any fags?' he asked.

From the pocket of her duffel coat she took a flat silver cigarette case and clicked it open. The case was one of numerous items she had borrowed from her stepmother, without asking, and had kept it. The cigarettes were Churchman's. She usually brought Senior Service, a fistful of which she would scoop out of one of the boxes of two hundred that her father ordered fortnightly from Fox's of College Green. The Churchman's she had pinched from Father Lawless. He wouldn't miss them. 'I got this, too,' she said, bringing out from an inside pocket a naggin bottle of Cork Dry Gin. She laughed. 'We can have a cocktail party.'

Fonsey did his crooked smile, showing the gap in his front teeth. 'Are you going to take off your coat?' he asked softly. When they were together like this, in the wood, he could make even the simplest question sound suggestive.

'Do you know how cold it is in here?' she demanded indignantly. 'Why don't you take off your coat, or whatever that thing is called that you're wearing?' He had told her his jacket was made from horse-hide, and that it had been worn by a Spitfire pilot in the war, who was killed. She didn't believe it, of course, except the bit about the horse-hide, for the thing reeked of the knacker's yard. Was it true, she wondered, what Dominic had once told her, that dog dirt was used in the process of tanning leather? The world was horrible in so many ways.

She was tearing the seal from the gin bottle with her fingernails. He watched her happily, picking absent-mindedly at the sore on his lip.

'That detective was here,' he said. 'Stafford, or whatever his name is.'

'I know. I saw him going up the hill. That rabbit really stinks, by the way. I can smell it from here.'

'Smells like you,' Fonsey said with a sly grin, pressing the tip of his tongue through the gap in his front teeth.

'You're disgusting.'

They sat down on the bunks, facing each other, leaning their backs against the walls of the caravan. They had lit their cigarettes, and now Lettie uncorked the gin. She held up the little bottle before her, frowning. 'How are we going to drink this?'

'Share and share alike.'

'You mean, the two of us drink from the same bottle? Not on your life – and certainly not with that revolting sore on your mouth. Find me a glass.'

He went and opened the cupboard and came back with a grimy tumbler. 'It's filthy!' she cried. 'Don't you ever clean anything?'

She took hold of a length of the hem of her skirt and ran it vigorously around the inside of the glass. Fonsey threw himself down on the bunk again, supporting himself on an elbow. Lettie's right leg was raised, and he could see all the way to the top of her stocking and the suspender button holding it taut.

'You have nice legs,' he said.

'Yes, nice and bandy, thanks to dear Papa.'

'I like them.'

'You'd like anything.'

She poured half the gin into the glass and handed him the bottle. 'Chin-chin.' She took a sip and grimaced. 'I hate the taste of this stuff, I don't know why I drink it.'

'Because it makes you feel better.'

'Maybe it makes you feel better. It makes me feel as if I've swallowed a dose of paraquat.'

'Then don't drink it. Give it to me.'

'Oh, shut up,' she said, feeling listless suddenly, and turned her face away from him. She took another drink, and another puff from her cigarette. She hadn't learned to inhale yet. A good smoke was wasted on her, Fonsey always said. She was studying the latening light in the dirty back window. 'What did you say to Sherlock Holmes?' she asked.

'Who?'

'The detective, remember? He was here? Or has he slipped out of your mighty brain already?'

'Did he see you?'

'Of course he didn't! I hid.' She paused. 'What did he ask you?'

'Nothing. He wanted to know where I was last night.'

'And what did you say?' She watched him over the rim of the glass.

'What do you think I said?'

She nodded, thinking. 'He's not as much of a duffer as he looks.'

'How do you know?'

'I just do.' She had drawn up both knees, and Fonsey's

gaze was fixed on the pale undersides of her legs, which now she parted a little, pretending not to notice she was doing it. He stared, and she laughed. 'Have a good look, why don't you?' she said, and took another, longer drink from the grimy glass.

He glanced up at her face, then fixed his humid gaze again on what she was revealing to him. She held out the last of her cigarette. 'Get rid of this, will you?'

He crushed the butt into a saucer on the draining board, beside the smouldering remains of his own cigarette.

'That pan is burning,' she said. 'There's smoke coming off it, look.'

He reached over and lifted the pan from the heat and dropped it on the floor with a clang.

'And the stove is smoking too. We'll be suffocated.'

'I got it going, anyway,' he said, 'even if the wood was green.'

'Oh, yes, you're a genius.'

She had relaxed her thighs completely now, allowing them to fall slackly apart. The wings of her duffel coat were pushed back, and her skirt had ridden up to her hips. Fonsey's brow was flushed, the pimples on it fairly glowing, and she could hear him breathing, not fast, but deeply, slowly. It seemed a kind of soft moaning. She thought of Strafford passing by her on the hillside, and of the sound of him panting, quick and hoarse.

Fonsey had taken on a strained look, almost as if he were in pain.

'Kneel down,' she commanded in a low voice, a little hoarse herself now. 'Come on, down on your knees, oaf.'

Oaf. It was a word she had come across recently, in some book or other. She had known it already, it was a common word, but this time she had taken special note of it, and remembered it. She liked it. Oaf.

Fonsey heaved himself from the bunk and sank on to his knees in front of her. It wasn't easy, there was hardly room for him, so narrow was the space between the bunks. She looked down at him as he thrashed about. She put one hand on top of his head, and dipped three fingers of the other into her glass and smeared the gin between her thighs. The alcohol stung her, but she didn't care. She didn't care about the sore on his lip, either. She didn't care about anything. 'Drink it,' she commanded, her voice thickening. 'Go on, lap – lap it up.'

He lowered his face past her knees and burrowed deep down between her thighs, like a terrier, she thought, digging in a foxhole. His hair was hot and ticklish against her skin. It was like being licked by an animal. She lifted languid eyes again to the twilight in the window. *Oaf*, she thought. *Lap. Lap my lap*. Lap my lap! She would have laughed, if she hadn't been so close to coming. Star-like lights popped and fizzled in front of her eyes, and she thought of those cartoon creatures, Tom the Cat, was it, and that rabbit, what was he called? When they got hit on the head, stars whirled above them in circles, like Catherine wheels. Bugs Bunny, that was it! She could smell the rabbit on the table. He had said it smelled like her. Maybe it did? Lap, oaf, lap. Stars. His tongue was rough, a cat's tongue. Tom the Cat, Tom cat, tomcat. Fizzles, fizzles. Fizzle.

Now Fonsey withdrew his head from between her thighs, and she leaned back, sighing, and drank the last few drops of gin in her glass. She often thought this was the best part of it all, these few lazy moments after it was over and her mind went fuzzy in that lovely way and she didn't have to think about anything at all. Fonsey, her poor oaf, her poor wild man of the woods, knelt with his shoulders slumped against her knees, his great shaggy head resting on her thigh. They never kissed, she wouldn't allow it, she wouldn't ever allow it, even if he hadn't got a sore on his mouth and pimples on his forehead and the taste of her on his lips. She just didn't want to kiss him. She didn't want to kiss anyone.

She put a hand against his shoulder and pushed him away. 'Now you,' she said.

He fumbled with the front of his dungarees, undoing the clasps and pulling it down, and she twined her legs around his neck, crossing her ankles at the back. She didn't watch him, hunched over himself there, trembling and grunting. She never wanted to watch, it was too ugly, that big purplish thing sticking up, the top of it like a helmet, and his fist pumping in that awful spasmodic way – he might as well be milking a cow. At the end he made a surprisingly soft little mewling sound, like the sound a child would make in its sleep. Her legs were still around his neck, and he let his head slump sideways and forward and glued his mouth to the soft cool pearl-grey flesh behind her knee. It looked so strange, that big head with its mass of greasy red curls, propped there between her knees, like a severed head on a platter.

He began to say something but she stopped him. 'Don't!' she said in a fierce whisper, grabbing him by one ear and twisting it hard. 'Don't start with the love business. You don't love me and I don't love you. Nobody loves anybody. Right?

Got that?' He mumbled something, trying to nod, and she let go of his ear, which glowed bright red.

She wasn't sure where the stuff he had pumped out of himself had gone to – it had spilled on the floor, she supposed, or splattered against the side of the bunk. On one of their afternoons together she had taken up a drop of it on her finger and tasted it, just the tiniest taste, with the very tip of her tongue, out of curiosity. It had a strange flavour, like salt and sawdust soaked in milk.

Imagine having globs of that goo inside you, sticky and hot, and those tiny little tadpoles squirming out of it and racing each other up along your tubes.

She had never let anyone do it to her, though more than a few had tried, including Jimmy Waldron, at a party at the Athertons' the previous Christmas. He was grown up now and studying to be a teacher or something, and played rugby. He seemed to have forgotten having trapped her in the lavatory, that day long ago when they were children. But she had remembered. Oh, yes, she had remembered. He had to be taken home from the Athertons', after being sick on the floor in the conservatory when she drove her knee with all her strength into his crotch. Maybe that would teach him to keep his hands out of places where they weren't wanted.

Fonsey had done up his dungarees and hauled himself back to the other bunk, and he leaned there now on his elbow again, looking at her with a half-witted grin. She pushed the heavy stuff of the skirt down over her knees. A pity she couldn't let the White Rabbit know what her stepdaughter had got up to in it just a minute ago. Next time maybe she'd make Fonsey shoot his stuff all over the front of it, then she could hang it back in the wardrobe and give the bitch something to wonder about.

'When are you going back to school?' Fonsey asked, lighting up another cigarette.

'I'm not,' she answered.

'Oh? Why not?'

'I'm just not, that's all.'

'Your Da will have something to say about that.'

'Yes, well, my "Da" can say what he likes.'

She had been a boarder for four years at a school in South Wales, a ghastly dump outside a town with a name she had never learned to pronounce properly, since it had about twelve consonants in it and hardly any vowels. She had told no one except Dominic that she wouldn't be going back after the Christmas holidays, and she hadn't told him why. The fact was, she had been expelled – Matron had caught her with a fellow, a townie, at the back gate one night, she with his thing in her hand – it reminded her of the rubber grip on the handlebar of a bike – and he with a hot paw halfway up her gymslip.

She might have got away with it, except that it was one more, and the most serious, in the long list of her depravities, so-called. She hadn't enjoyed the interview with Miss Twyford-Healy, the headmistress, but that was a small price to pay for the gift of freedom that had so suddenly been bestowed on her. Tee-Hee, which was what everyone called Miss Twyford-Healy, had written to her father, saying his daughter wouldn't be allowed to return after the Christmas break. She had managed to intercept the letter, though – so many mornings she had spent crouched on the landing, chilled to the bone in her nightdress, while she watched through the banisters for the post to come – and now she lay for what seemed hours in bed, sleepless, every night, wondering what exactly to say to her father, when the time came for her to go back to school and she had to tell him she'd been given the boot.

Funny, with so much on her mind, how something as trivial as being kicked out of school weighed so heavily on her thoughts. There was no accounting for herself, that was a fact.

12

Strafford found Dominic Osborne in the drawing room. Ballyglass was built on generous Victorian lines, and must have boasted twenty-five or thirty rooms, but over the years the family had hollowed out of it a compact bourgeois dwelling, consisting of little more than the kitchen, the dining room, one halfway habitable drawing room, three bedrooms, one bathroom, and a separate, undependable lavatory, while the rest of the place was allowed to sink into a state of timeless fixity, like the unvisited rooms in a museum where were kept the exhibits no one cared to look at any more. Strafford's father had effected an even more radical reduction of Roslea House, and these days hardly ventured beyond what used to be his study but which gradually he had transformed into an all-purpose bolthole, installing in it a double bed, the one he and his wife had slept in during the years of their brief marriage, a gas burner, a paraffin stove, as well as a number of decorated chamber pots, part of a collection assembled by a forgotten forebear.

It was dark by now. The curtains had been drawn and the electric lamps switched on. The Osborne heir was settled in a deep armchair by the fire, with a tray with tea things on a small table beside him, and a medical textbook open on his lap – he was a second-year medical student at Trinity College in Dublin. The Labrador that earlier had shaken itself and sprayed the hall with drops of melted snow was stretched out at the young man's feet, as fat and torpid as a seal. The fire was burning busily, and the air was heavy with the scent of flaming birch logs.

Looking up as Strafford entered, the young man frowned. The dog too lifted its big square head.

'Ah, I've been looking for you,' Strafford said. 'Not disturbing you, I hope?'

Dominic shut the book and put it on the floor beside his chair. 'I'm not disturbed. I suppose you want to – what do they say? – to grill me about Father Tom?'

'Well, grill is hardly the word,' Strafford answered. 'That's only in the pictures.'

'A light roasting, then?'

Strafford smiled. He approached the fire and held his hands out to the flames. 'That's only what the big boys do to the little boys at boarding school.'

'I won't be of any help to you,' Dominic said coldly. 'I heard nothing of what happened in the night. I'm a deep sleeper.'

'Yes, so is everyone else in the house, it seems, except your mother' – the young man stared – 'sorry, I mean your step-mother.'

'Yes, she creeps about a lot, in the wee hours.'

'I don't sleep well myself, usually, so I sympathise with her.'

'I'm sure she'd be very gratified to know that,' Dominic said, with pointed sarcasm.

Seen close to, he was not as convincingly handsome as he had appeared when Strafford had looked down on him that morning from the banisters at the top of what everyone in the house referred to as the back stairs. He was good-looking, certainly, with that straight jaw and his father's chill blue eyes, but there was something uncertain about him, something incomplete and evasive. What was he, twenty, twenty-one? Trinity had given him a swagger that still wasn't quite convincing, and possibly never would be. No, he was not quite the thing, this young man.

He was dressed like his father, indeed markedly so, in tweed jacket, cavalry twill trousers, checked shirt and spotted bow tie. The toecaps of his shoes gleamed in the firelight like chestnuts fresh out of their husks. Any day now, if he hadn't already done so, he would take to pipe-smoking, and getting drunk with the chaps from the rugby club on Saturday nights. He would drive a two-seater, and talk disparagingly of girls, and shoot crows in the copse, wherever it was, and plight his half-hearted troth to some landed family's horsey daughter. None of that would entirely convince, either. In Dominic Osborne, something, some undefinable finish, would always be lacking. There would always be something amiss.

On the other hand, he was a medical student, Strafford reminded himself, and as such he would know just where the jugular was. Could it have been a scalpel that did for the Reverend Thomas J. Lawless?

'Mind if I sit down?' Strafford asked of the young man, and without waiting for an answer settled himself in an armchair on the other side of the hearth. 'It's proving to be a long day.'

'Is it? Not for Father Tom, it's not.'

'Well, no.' A log fell silently asunder in the fireplace, producing a burst of sparks. 'I suppose you've known him most of your life, yes?'

Dominic gave a languid shrug. 'I wouldn't say that. I'm not sure I knew him at all, really. He was always round the place, of course.'

'"Round the place"?'

'Daddy – my father – liked him, or liked him being here, anyway. He was company, I suppose. They had interests in common – huntin' and shootin', all that.'

'Not to your taste, that kind of thing?'

'Is it to yours?'

'I live in the city now. Not much opportunity.'

'Maybe not for hunting, but for shooting, surely? You are a detective, after all.'

Strafford smiled. 'Unarmed.'

'Hmm.'

The log in the fireplace shifted again, putting on another little fireworks display. Strafford thought of the frost-bound world beyond the house, of the snow-covered fields and the bare black trees, all suspended in a vast and frozen silence. And then, of course, he thought of death.

'Did you know your mother?' he asked.

'What?' Dominic stared at him again. 'Did I know her? Of course I knew her.'

'What age were you when—?'

'I was twelve. You're aware that she fell down the back stairs, the same one that—?'

'Yes—' He had been about to remark on the coincidence, but stopped himself. It would hardly be in good taste.

The young man turned away and gazed into the fire. The dog at his feet had fallen heavily asleep, and began to twitch and whimper. Strafford was always struck by the fact that dogs should dream. How could they, since they were supposed to have no memory?

'I was the one who found her,' the young man said, still facing the fire. The leaping flames were reflected in the pupils of his eyes, making them appear deep black. 'It was night that time, too, with everyone asleep.'

'But not you.'

'What?'

'You must have been awake. You heard her fall.'

'Yes, I heard her.' He shifted in the chair abruptly and looked directly at the detective. 'Are you going to ask how it was, then, that I didn't hear the priest when he went tumbling down the same stairs, while I was in the same bed as that other night long ago?'

'No.' Strafford sighed. The fire was making him feel drowsy. 'Anyway,' he said, 'I don't believe he fell.'

'Oh?'

'He was still on his feet, until he made it into the library.'

'A different sound entirely, then,' Dominic said. He closed his eyes and leaned his head against the back of his chair. When he spoke again his voice resonated strangely, as if it were coming up out of some deep, echoing chamber.

'We were on a train once,' he said, 'years ago, in France, the four of us, my mother and father, my sister and me. It was one of those new diesel ones, very fast – an express, I suppose – travelling from Paris all the way down to the south. We were approaching Lyons, I think it was Lyons, when we hit something on the line. It made an extraordinary noise, a sort of clattering all along beneath the carriages. I thought we'd run into a level crossing, and that it was the noise of the wooden gate splintering and the broken bits tumbling under the wheels. The driver must have taken his foot off the – what do you call it, the dead man's brake? – because after the collision we just coasted for, oh, it must have been a mile or two, going more and more slowly, until finally we drifted to a stop. I shall never forget the silence that fell then. It was almost as ominous as the sound of whatever it was that had broken up underneath us.'

He rose from the chair and fed another log into the flames. He remained there, with his hands in the pockets of his jacket, gazing down into the fire, remembering.

'We had to wait for hours until another train came and collected us and took us on to Nice. Next day it was in the papers – two girls in a town the train was passing through had made a suicide pact and stepped out in front of the speeding engine. It was their bones that we'd heard, breaking up and spinning along the track, under the wheels.'

He stopped, and sat down again, and leaned his head back against the chair once more, and once more closed his eyes. 'It's a thing I'll never forget. I can hear it still, the sound of those bones, rattling along the track like skittles.'

The dreaming dog was giving sharp little high-pitched barks and fluttering its lips like a horse in a lather.

'I'm sorry,' Strafford said.

'For what? – for the girls who killed themselves, or for my mother?' He leaned an arm down and patted the sleeping dog's fat flank. Strafford watched him.

'Were you close, you and your mother?' he asked.

The young man gave an ugly little laugh. 'Haven't you read Freud? Aren't all sons close to their mothers?'

'Not all of them. Not always.'

'What about you, have you got one? – a mother, I mean.' Dominic leaned forward with his fingers laced together in his lap, studying the detective. 'I suspect you lost yours early too, like me. Am I right?'

Strafford nodded. 'Yes. Cancer. I was younger than you – I was nine.'

They fell silent. They were both gazing into the fire now. Strafford thought of his mother. Strangely, he didn't think of her very often, not as often, certainly, as he thought of his father. But then, his father was still living, and the living require more thought.

She had died, his mother, at this time of the year, in a downstairs room, much like this one, where a sofa had been turned into a makeshift bed for her. She would watch the birds outside on the lawn for hours on end, the thrushes and blackbirds and robins. The magpies in particular fascinated her, with their strange, clicking cries. She would smile and declare that they were all greedy beggars, the robins especially. 'Imagine being a worm,' she would say, in her reedy voice – the cancer was eating steadily into her oesophagus – and shake her head in sympathy for all weak and crawling creatures.

Strafford remembered the smell of medicine in the room, and the stifling warmth, all the windows shut and the air as dense and cloying as wetted cotton wool. She used to have him bring her the brandy decanter from the sideboard in the dining room, wrapped in a newspaper. By that stage she was allowed all the brandy she could drink, though it pleased her to pretend it was their secret, hers and his.

He sat upright in the chair, pushing these recollections to the side of his mind. How they cling, he thought, the dead.

'Tell me about last night, will you?' he asked, clearing his throat.

Dominic shrugged. 'What is there to tell you? I'm sure by now you've heard everything there is to hear.'

'Oh, I'm sure I haven't. Anyway, I'd like to know your version.'

After a pause, the young man spoke.

'I came down from Dublin on the afternoon train. Matty had borrowed the Recks' van to collect me from the station—'

'Matty?'

'Sorry. Matty Moran. He works, if that's the word, at the Sheaf of Barley. My father borrows him now and then, to trim the hedges, keep the rats down – odd jobs. If you're staying at the Sheaf you're bound to run across him, since he as good as lives in the bar there. That will be a treat for you.' He suddenly made a jester's unfunny face, drawing his mouth down at the corners. 'Matty is a Ballyglass "character", I'm afraid. One of many.'

'Was Father Lawless here when you arrived?'

'Yes, he'd come over for lunch, I believe, and then couldn't get back, because of the weather.'

'Did he spend a lot of time here? – generally, I mean.'

'Well, we stable his horse for him—'

'Yes, I know,' Strafford said, interrupting, trying not to sound impatient. He always found it a tedious business, extracting information from those too dim or distracted to offer it unprompted. Only the guilty were garrulous. 'So he was here quite frequently, yes?'

'Yes, I suppose he was a bit of a fixture. Why? Is that significant?'

'I don't know.'

'He liked it here. Why wouldn't he? Free bed and board, civilised people to talk to, if you don't count my sister. I don't think he should ever have become a priest. He wasn't suited to it.'

It was said with amused disparagement. What had this young man made of the priest who shouldn't have been a priest? So many questions to be asked, so many stones to be turned, in search of what might wriggle out from under them.

They were silent for a while, listening to the hiss and crackle of the fire. It was Dominic who spoke.

'Your job,' he said. 'I'm curious. It must be like trying to assemble a particularly intricate jigsaw puzzle, putting the pieces together, looking for a pattern, and so on?'

'I suppose so, in a way,' Strafford replied. 'The trouble is, the pieces don't stay still. They tend to move around, making patterns of their own, or what seem to be patterns. Everything is deceptive. You think you have the measure of things, and then it all shifts. In fact, it's more like watching a play, one in which the plot keeps changing—'

He stopped, and with his fingernails tapped a rapid tattoo against his front teeth. Yes, he thought, yes, that was what had been nagging at him, from the moment he had first arrived at Ballyglass House. Everyone seemed to be in costume, seemed to be dressed for a part. They were like a cast of actors milling about in the wings, waiting to go on. There was Colonel Osborne – he must have spent an hour in front of the looking-glass, rigging himself out as what he was or what he wished to seem to be – country squire, hero of Dunkirk, handsome still despite his years, wielder of a straight bat, blunt, bluff and safely dim. And here was his son, got up to look as much like him as could be managed, in tweed and twill, brown brogues and checked shirt, with his hair slicked back military fashion. There was Lettie, too, when Strafford had first encountered her, togged out in jodhpurs and riding jacket despite the fact she never got on a horse. And there was Mrs Osborne, who so far had played at least two roles, first as the madwoman in the attic, and then, in that absurd tea party charade, as a pert young royal, with Queen Elizabeth pearls and her blue frock and clipped vowels.

Why, even apple-cheeked Mrs Duffy was all too plausibly the stock family retainer.

But for whose benefit had they got themselves up to be so thoroughly convincing that, like even the best actors, they didn't quite convince? And who was it that had called them together and allotted them their parts in the shadow play?

Or was he imagining it all? There was always the danger, in his job, of seeing things that weren't there, of making a pattern where there wasn't one. The policeman insists that there be a plot. However, life itself is plotless.

Yet a man had been murdered, and someone had murdered him. That much had happened. And the person who had done the deed was hiding somewhere here, in plain sight.

Dominic spoke now, breaking in on the detective's thoughts. 'Can I ask you something?'

'Of course.'

'Why did you decide to become a detective?'

'Why?' Strafford looked away, suddenly self-conscious. This was the question he most disliked, and found most difficult to answer, even when he asked it of himself. 'I don't know that I can remember,' he said now, evasively, his eyes on the fire. 'I'm not sure that I did decide – I'm not sure anyone decides anything. It seems to me we drift, and that all our decisions are made in retrospect.' He paused. 'Why did you opt to study medicine?'

Now it was the young man's turn to look away. 'Like you, I don't know. I probably won't stay the course. I can't see myself in a white coat, dispensing placebos and peering up people's bums.'

'What would you prefer to do?'

'Oh, I don't know. Be a beachcomber, on an island some-where, anywhere, just so long as it's not here.' He looked about the lamplit room, with its shadowed corners. 'The house is haunted, did you know?'

'Yes, your sister told me. What sort of ghosts do you have?'

'The usual kind. It's all nonsense, needless to say. The dead don't come back – why would they? Anywhere would be bet-ter than this, surely.'

He reached down for his book on the floor. Strafford took the hint.

'Sorry,' he said, making to rise, 'I should leave you to your studies.'

'Ah, yes, my studies,' the young man said, with a sardonic laugh, sounding more like his sister than surely he would care to know.

Strafford was on his feet now, but still he lingered, with his hands in his pockets. The dog, half waking, raised up a little and looked at him, then let its head fall back on the carpet with a thud.

'A last question, Dominic, if you don't mind. May I call you Dominic?'

'Suit yourself. And go ahead, ask whatever you like.'

'Who was here, who was in the house, the night your mother died? Do you remember?'

The young man looked up at him quickly, with a puzzled frown. 'The night my *mother* died? Why do you want to know? It was years ago. I was a child.'

'Yes, I know.' Strafford assumed what he thought of as his most disarming smile. 'Can you remember, though, who was in the house?'

'No one in particular. Daddy, my sister – she was only, I don't know, seven or eight.'

'Mrs Duffy?'

'Yes, I suppose so. And we had two maids then, they had rooms in the attic. I can't remember their names.'

'And that was it? No one else?'

There was silence, and then from outside in the darkness there came a faint, soft, slipping sound. A section of snow, Strafford thought, must have slid off of the roof. Was a thaw setting in? Then there would be slush, first foe of the sleuth in search of clues.

'I believe *she* was here,' Dominic said.

'"She"?'

'Miss Harbison, as she was then. My stepmother-to-be.'

'Your stepmother?' Strafford said, startled. He had the sense of another soft slippage, but not outside this time. 'She was here when your mother—? I don't understand.'

From the hall came the hushed, reverberant note of a struck bronze gong.

'Yes,' Dominic said with a shrug. 'She was a friend of my parents. Didn't you know that? Well, a friend of my mother's, anyway, supposedly. That was the dinner gong, by the way. Will you be eating with us? I wouldn't advise it, frankly – are you familiar yet with Mrs Duffy's cooking?'

Strafford said nothing, only smiled. He was thinking of the steak-and-kidney pudding.

13

And no, he would not be staying. Colonel Osborne had invited him to dine, but he had excused himself, saying he must get over to the Sheaf of Barley, since it was late already, and the roads would be increasingly treacherous as the night went on.

Coming down the front steps, he stopped to look out over the gleaming fields. The sky had cleared, and stars sparkled in the depthless velvet dark. Far off, in the woods, a fox barked. The icy air made his face sting. He was tired, so tired. The day already seemed to have lasted longer than was natural, and it probably wasn't done with him yet.

His car, an elderly black Morris Minor, was encased in a glittering shell of hoar frost. He scraped the ice from the windscreen as best he could. The engine wouldn't start by the ignition key, and he had to get it going with the crank handle. Half a dozen shoulder-jarring turns were required before the thing would catch. He worried the handle would spin backwards and smash his wrist.

As he manoeuvred his way down the drive, he could hear the ice on the road crackling under the tyres. He turned to the left, slotting the front wheels into the two parallel black ruts in the snow. Frost-laden trees, ghost-white and stark, reared up at him in the headlights, their boughs thrown upwards as if in fright.

A jigsaw puzzle, Dominic had said, and he was right. The pieces were scattered, and there was no illustration on the lid of the box to guide him. There wasn't even a box.

By the time he reached the Sheaf of Barley his eyes ached from the glare of the snow-lined road. He had been negotiating a particularly sharp and treacherous bend when into the light of his headlamps a white-faced form had come gliding down at him out of the darkness on wide-spread wings. It was a barn owl. He had flinched from it instinctively, this great savage creature, and almost ran the car into the ditch.

The Sheaf of Barley was no more than a long, low, white-washed cottage with a thatched roof and tiny windows, all of them brightly lit tonight. He parked the car well in off the road and heaved his overnight bag from the back seat. He had brought only a toothbrush and razor, pyjamas, a couple of shirts and some changes of underwear. He approached the door of the pub – or an inn, was it? – with deep misgivings. He had put up at places like it in the past. His sole wish was for a hot meal and a warm bed. Gloom settled on his heart.

The door was on the latch, and when he opened it and stepped inside he was met by the reek of porter and an eye-watering fug of turf smoke. The bar was cramped and low-ceilinged, with a high counter and high wooden stools. Newspaper cuttings, unframed, were pasted on the walls. They were yellowed from age and curling at the edges. The stories in them told mostly of sporting victories of the far past. On the sill of one of the little windows there was a pair of miniature hurleys mounted on a varnished wooden plaque, the sticks proudly wound round with a ribbon dyed in the county colours.

Joe, Strafford understood, was Mrs Reck's name for her husband. This wasn't surprising. 'Jeremiah' had an altogether too resoundingly biblical ring to it.

He told her about the barn owl that had flown into the headlights on the road and how it had startled him, yet how marvellous a sight it was. She said they were 'fierce savage things, them owls'.

She gave the counter another swipe with her cloth.

'Terrible business, up at the House,' she remarked, studiedly casual, and not meeting his eye.

The 'House', as Strafford guessed, was how local people in general referred to the Osborne residence.

'Yes, terrible,' he said, looking into his glass.

'Poor Father Tom – I hear he fell down the stairs and broke his neck?'

It was clear from the manner in which she said it that what she had heard was not what she believed to have been the case.

'Yes,' Strafford said without emphasis, 'the poor man did indeed suffer injuries to the neck.'

She gave him a level look. 'So they're saying.'

And there they let the matter rest.

He took his dinner at a small table in a corner of a room adjoining the bar. This room was, by day, a combined grocery and butcher's shop. The meat counter was hidden delicately from view under a sheet of grey canvas, with rusty smears of tell-tale blood on the edges of it. Ranged on shelves along the opposite wall were jars of sweets and glass-lidded tin boxes of biscuits and cream crackers and lumps of broken fruit cake.

He was served by a girl with red hair and a broad face sprinkled all over with freckles. When she smiled she displayed an overlap in her front teeth.

'Are you the detective?' she asked. No beating about the bush here, he noted. When he said yes, she laid a hand on her hip and scrutinised him with friendly scepticism. 'You don't look like one.'

'So people tell me.'

She set before him a plate of sliced corned beef, which, as he found when he tested a forkful of it, was juicy and soft but with a satisfyingly crunchy texture. On the side there were four large boiled potatoes bursting out of their jackets, and cabbage that was green and actually looked like cabbage, unlike the stewed grey mush that places such as this usually served up. He found he was hungrier than he had thought.

How pleasant it was, he reflected, and how easy, to let oneself subside into the old simplicities. It was like leaning one's back against the sun-warmed side of a haystack.

Customers had begun to straggle into the bar next door. He could hear their voices, and the scrape of the legs of wooden stools on the tiled floor. Opening hours were flexible in the countryside, and tonight was no exception, even with an officer of the law on the premises. By now there would be no one in the townland, and beyond, who wouldn't know who and what he was. A peeler was a peeler, even in a three-piece suit.

Mrs Reck, having shown him to his table, had returned to the bar to serve the newcomers. Now she ducked back in and asked if he was ready for another drink. He shook his head – he had taken no more than a few sips of the first one. Mrs Reck cocked an eyebrow.

'How about a glass of sarsaparilla?' she asked, with a straight face.

He wished he had some prop behind which to hide, even if it was only a book. He felt exposed, and was sure he must cut a doleful figure, sitting there dully chewing his food and staring vacantly before him. Why was it so hard to eat one's dinner alone? Presently he sensed, not for the first time today, that he was being observed. He glanced behind him covertly, under the pretence of studying a faded copy of the 1916 Proclamation of Independence framed high on the wall behind the counter. An elderly fellow in a stained and threadbare suit had put his head around the bar-room door and was having a squint at him. When he saw that Strafford had spotted him he stepped back, withdrawing his head on its tortoise neck from the doorway.

The girl came and offered him seconds. 'You can have anything you like,' she said, and gave him a calculated look from under a fringe of her red-gold hair, biting her lip.

He thanked her, and said he could not eat any more than he already had. She lingered, standing over him and very slightly swaying her hips.

'Don't mind Matty,' she said, nodding towards the door. 'He's as nosy as an old woman.'

'Ah,' he said. 'So that's Matty.'

'Don't say you've heard of him?'

'I have.'

'Well, that's impressive. And what's your name, do you mind me asking?'

'Not at all. Strafford – with an *r*.'

'Is that your Christian name?'

'No.' He smiled up at her.

'I'm Peggy,' she said.

He nodded. His own first name could wait for a later time.

'I wonder, Peggy,' he said, 'if I might ask you for a glass of water?'

She took the tumbler and filled it and brought it back to the table. 'There you are,' she said, 'and mind you don't let it go to your head.'

And she winked.

It was late, but he was not ready to go up to his room just yet. The whiskey had set up a buzzing in his temples. He rose, pushed open the door and went back into the bar.

The old fellow who had spied on him was sitting on a high stool, with a bottle of Guinness's porter poured out into a glass that stood at his elbow. He was long and skinny, all sharp elbows and bony knees. All of the lower half of his face was collapsed around a mouth devoid of teeth. He nodded to Strafford as if he had never seen him before. Strafford pointed to the emptied Guinness bottle, the sides of which were streaked with yellow foam.

'Will you have another one of those?'

'I won't,' Matty said. 'But I'll have a small one.'

Strafford signalled to Mrs Reck and ordered the half glass of whiskey. She poured the measure and set it on the bar. 'There you are, Matty Moran. Aren't you in luck tonight?' She turned to Strafford. 'Mind out for this fellow. He'd drink all night if someone else is paying.'

'*Sláinte*,' Matty said, tipping his glass towards Strafford. 'Are you not having anything yourself?'

'Perhaps, in a while,' Strafford said.

At a table under one of the small square windows two more customers sat, big, red-faced men with colourless eyelashes and hands like hams. They too had nodded a guarded greeting to the newcomer, then gone back to their drinks.

Jeremiah Reck appeared, and took his wife's place behind the bar.

'Ah, so you managed to find us,' he said to Strafford. 'Can I offer you a welcoming glass? I'm told you're a whiskey and lemonade man.'

'No, thanks,' Strafford said. 'I've just had dinner.' He looked about. 'Did someone bring my bag up to the room?'

'Someone did, indeed. You've seen it, the room, I hope?'

'Not yet,' Strafford said. 'I'm sure it will be fine.' Again he glanced around the bar, feeling at a loss – how much less awkward it would be if only he were a drinker.

Matty was watching him from the corner of his eye. He took a drink of his whiskey and munched on it appreciatively, his collapsed mouth slackly working. Strafford was reminded of Colonel Osborne, and that way he had of jerking his jaw sideways, seeming to chew on something elastically resistant.

Reck, behind the bar, was drying a pint glass and reciting to himself, in the tone of the psalmist, '*O Lord, thou hast pleaded the causes of my soul, thou hast redeemed my life!*'

'I hear they brought poor Father Tom off up to Dublin,' Matty said, addressing no one in particular.

Reck glanced at Strafford and winked.

'There's nothing Matty doesn't know,' he said. 'Isn't that so, Matty? We should appoint you the town crier.'

Matty ignored this sally.

'Aye,' he said, 'took him up in an ambulance.' He sniffed. 'Down here wasn't good enough for him, it seems.'

Mrs Reck came ducking back through the archway, wiping her hands on her apron.

'Matty Moran,' she said, 'will you put your teeth in, for the love of God! I can't bear the sight of you. Do you know what you look like without them? A hen's hole.'

Strafford heard himself ordering another whiskey. He knew he would regret it in the morning, but he didn't care. He even eschewed the lemonade, this time.

Matty brought out a set of pink and yellowed dentures from his pocket and fitted them into his mouth. They didn't make much of an alteration to his appearance.

Jeremiah Reck was pouring Strafford's drink when the door opened and a swirl of snow came in, followed by a short spry man in a sheepskin coat, shiny black gloves, and a trilby hat cocked low over one eye. All turned to stare at him, but he ignored them. He removed his gloves finger by finger, and shook the snowflakes from his hat brim.

'There's a night!' he said.

He stopped at the bar and unbuttoned his coat. Beneath it he wore a double-breasted suit that was just a shade too well-cut, Strafford thought, and a regimental tie stuck with a pearl pin. He was in his early forties but clearly imagined himself to look much younger. He might have been a soldier, or a returned colonial, or both. To Strafford's sceptical eye, yet another actor had stepped on to the stage. And not a convincing one, either.

'Bloody weather!' he exclaimed, and grinned, showing off a set of small white teeth the sparkle of which added to the overall impression of mild and gamesome fraudulence. ''Evening, Reck.'

'Good evening, Mr Harbison. What'll it be?'

Reck's wife took one look at the newcomer and ducked back out through the archway.

'Hot whiskey, I think,' Harbison said, rubbing his hands vigorously. 'Bushmills, with just a dash of lemon, and plenty of cloves.' Now he noticed Strafford, off at the other end of the counter, fingering his glass of whiskey, and nodded to him in friendly fashion.

This would be, Strafford thought, Mrs Osborne's brother, the Freddie Harbison whom Doctor Hafner had mistaken him for that morning – the same one who, if the doctor were to be believed, was barred from Ballyglass House. It was true, he looked every inch the black sheep.

He peered more keenly at Strafford now, quickly registering the tribal markings – the good but shabby suit, the gold watch chain, the narrowly knotted tie. How easily one was spotted, Strafford gloomily reflected. For all their dissimilarities, they were, the two of them, of a class apart.

Reck set the hot toddy on the counter, and Harbison drank off a good half of it in one go.

'Ah, that's the ticket,' he said, giving himself a doggy shake inside his big sheepskin coat.

He drank the rest of the drink in three quick sips and set the glass down with a bang. 'Same again, landlord!' he said, with another rub of the hands. 'It's a night for the antifreeze.'

He glanced again at Strafford, and moved along the counter, passing by Matty Moran as if he were not there.

'Mind if I join you?' he said to Strafford. 'I know who you must be.' He pointed to Strafford's glass. 'Stand you another?'

'No, thanks,' Strafford said, rolling the tumbler on its base on the counter. 'This is my nightcap.'

The two farmers over by the window were whispering together and glancing in Harbison's direction. One of them snickered. Harbison took no more notice of them than he had of Matty Moran, or of anyone else in the bar, save Strafford.

Reck brought him his second drink, and he clinked his glass against the rim of Strafford's tumbler.

'You would be the detective, now, I'm guessing,' he said. 'I heard about the demise of the sky pilot. Great excitement, the county can talk of little else.' He took a swig from his glass. Glances were being exchanged all over the bar. 'Murdered, so I hear,' Harbison said, deliberately loud. 'Bound to happen, sooner or later. Damned fellow had it coming. Caught the killer yet, have you?'

14

Strafford regretted not having gone to bed when he had the chance. Harbison asked Reck to open the snug behind the bar, and invited the detective to join him there. The snug was a tiny brown room furnished with a couple of shabby armchairs and a small low table. There were framed prints on the walls, showing riders in hunting pink galloping full tilt over stylised greensward. The sole source of heat was a single-bar electric fire. Here Harbison, nursing his glass of grog and pulling his greatcoat close around him, settled down in happy anticipation of a night's talk. Strafford could think of no reasonable excuse to get away. Good manners were a part of his inheritance, like left-handedness or haemophilia.

He knew Harbison's kind, the minor blackguards in overly good suits tailored in London, speaking in the cut-glass accent of their caste and upbringing, masquerading as hard-riding gentlemen, scions of the few decent families that had stayed on in this benighted country after independence. Clubbable chaps who would do you a favour when they could, and then make sure you spent the rest of your life paying for it. Frequenters of the racecourse and the annual Royal Dublin Society Horse Show, fixed ornaments of the city's better hotel bars and Jammet's restaurant on Nassau Street. The gay blades who ran up bills with Mitchells the wine merchants and Smyths on the Green, grocers to the gentry, that gentry of which they considered themselves the last fine flowering.

'Sorry, haven't introduced myself,' the fellow said now. 'Freddie Harbison. I'm Sylvia Osborne's brother – I suppose you've met her. My place is up in Wicklow, in the mountains. The family seat, don't you know, ha ha. Bloody awful location, worse than here. And you're—?'

'Roslea. Bunclody way.'

'Ah. Right. Roslea.' He shut one eye. 'Don't think I've been there, have I?'

'I doubt it,' Strafford said. 'There's only my father, and he's not particularly sociable. I'm not sure we ever were, even when there were more of us.'

'Right, right,' Harbison said again, fingering his military moustache. He hadn't been listening. 'I didn't want to discuss it in front of the yokels out there in the bar, but what the hell is going on over at Ballyglass? – or Mount Glassyball, as I like to call it. What happened to the priest? The story is he fell down the stairs – you know that's how the first Mrs O. broke her neck, years ago? Dreadful business – and now it's happened again. Someone pushed him, yes? Don't say it was my mad sister.'

'Why would you think that?' Strafford enquired. 'And why do you think it wasn't an accident?'

'Well, it wasn't, was it?'

'There's to be an autopsy in the morning.'

'Oh, come now. You wouldn't be here if it was anything except murder. Someone gave him a shove, I'd take a bet on it.' He shook his head in gratified wonderment. 'Poor old Colonel! The Osbornes will shut him out for good, this time.

Maybe it was him who pushed the padre? There would be a thing – I've always suspected he did in the first wife, you know.'

He brought out a cigarette case and proffered it to Strafford.

'No, thanks.'

'Don't smoke, won't let a chap stand you a drink? You're not the usual run of detective, or have I been reading the wrong kind of mystery stories?'

The electric fire was drying out the air, and Strafford's eyes were stinging worse than ever. He was dizzy from the whiskey – he shouldn't have had one, never mind two – and his brain ached. This day seemed set never to end.

'Do you see your sister often?' he asked.

'Hardly ever,' Harbison answered. 'I'm sort of persona non grata out there, as you've no doubt heard by now. Not sure what I ever did to earn the displeasure of the master of the house, but he's made it clear on more than one sticky occasion that I'm not welcome under his roof.' He paused. 'You do know Sylvia is batty, don't you? I mean, really off her chump. She has periods when she's convinced she's other people. I don't know what Geoffrey was thinking of when he married her. She was young, of course – fellows like Geoffrey always go after the young ones. And then, she was on the spot and available, having been the first wife's best pal, or so she pretended, anyway. I always thought the first one was a bit' – he held a hand out flat before him and waggled it from side to side – 'you know. I suppose I shouldn't say it of my sister, but there was something distinctly iffy between those two, our crazy Sylvia and the first Mrs O. But here I am, talking too much, as per usual.'

He drank the last of his drink, and rose and tapped on the little square serving hatch beside the empty fireplace. When the hatch was opened, he passed his glass through it and asked for another – 'just whiskey straight this time, I've had enough of those cloves, my mouth tastes like a bag of Bull's Eyes.'

'Tell me,' Strafford said, 'did you come down here this evening all the way from the Wicklow mountains?'

'God, no. The roads up there are snowed up tight as a nun's what's-it. I was in Wexford yesterday afternoon, seeing a man about a horse.'

'So you were here for two nights?'

Harbison gave him a chary sideways glance.

'I often put up here, at the Sheaf,' he said defensively. 'The grub is decent, and you'll have seen Peggy the red-head, *she's* easy on the eye. But speaking of horses, listen—'

Reck appeared at the serving hatch with Harbison's glass of whiskey on a dented metal tray.

'Put that on the slate, will you, Jeremiah my friend?'

Reck said nothing, but catching Strafford's eye made a long-suffering face.

Harbison took a sip from his glass. 'Damn it, this is Jameson's – he knows bloody well Bushmills is my tipple. Do you think he's trying to make some sort of papish point?'

Bushmills was supposedly the whiskey favoured by Protestants, while Jameson's was the Catholics' choice. Strafford thought it absurd, another of the multitude of minor myths the country thrived on.

Harbison put down the glass and lit a cigarette. 'What was I saying?'

'Something about a man and a horse.'

'That's right, yes. Thing is, the priest had one, Mr Sugar, magnificent beast. Old Geoffrey puts him up at Ballyglass House, free, gratis and for nothing. There's a young fellow there, looks after the stables, Fonsey somebody. He's a halfwit, but my God does he know all there is to know about horse flesh.'

'I've met him.'

'Have you?' Harbison seemed amazed. 'Then you'll know what I'm talking about. I mean' – he tapped his forehead – 'as far as this goes, you can forget about it.' He took another sip of whiskey and made a face. 'Jameson! Tastes like maiden's pee. But anyway, the point is, that horse.'

'What about it?'

'I was going to make an offer for it, to what's-his-name, the padre.'

'Father Lawless.'

'That's it, Lawless. But you see my difficulty now.'

'You mean, now that he's dead?'

'Well, yes.'

Strafford fixed his gaze on the fire and its single glowing bar. It kept giving off little sparks, as drifting dust motes landed on the filament. To a microbe, he mused, each tiny burst of fire would seem a vast conflagration, like a storm on the face of the sun. He thought again of the snowy fields outside, smooth and glistening, and over them the sky of stars burning in icy brightness. Other worlds, impossibly distant. How strange a thing it was to be here, animate and conscious, on this ball of mud and brine as it whirled through the illimitable depths of space. A chill ran down his spine, as if the tip of something cold had touched him briefly at the very core.

In his mind he saw the priest lying dead on the floor in the library, his hands joined and his eyes open. No longer conscious, no longer animate.

'Mr Harbison—'

'Call me Freddie.' He sat forward in his chair. 'Now, about that horse—'

'Mr Harbison, a man has died, in questionable circumstances, in the home of your sister and her husband. I hardly think this is the time to—'

'All right, all right!' Harbison said, giving him an injured look. 'Life goes on, you know.' He rose and went to the hatch again – 'and Bushmills, this time, mind!'

He sat down, pulled off one of his shoes and held his stockinged foot close to the fire's rust-red element.

'It'll be a bloody disgrace if that horse is left with my brother-in-law,' he said with sudden violence. 'He doesn't know the back end of it from the front, for all that he imagines he's a natural in the saddle. Someone should take the beast off his hands, and I don't see why it shouldn't be me. The question is, who owns Mr Sugar now?' He rubbed his chin thoughtfully. 'Did the priest leave a will, I wonder? Probate could take forever, and meanwhile that magnificent animal's muscles will be turning to jelly for want of proper exercise.' He put a hand on Strafford's arm. 'Now that would be a shame, wouldn't it? You have to grant me that.'

The hatch in the wall opened, and a hand pushed through it the metal tray bearing the glass of whiskey. Reck's big face appeared in the opening. 'On the slate again, Mr Harbison?'

'Good man,' Harbison said, taking the glass. 'And listen, Reck – heard anything about the priest's horse? You know, the big gelding, Mr Sugar?'

Reck leaned down at the hatch, closer this time, and caught Strafford's eye again, then swivelled his attention back to Harbison. 'Are you after him, yourself?'

'Well, I'd be interested, if he was up for sale.'

'Father Tom had a sister,' Reck said, withdrawing from the hatch. 'Talk to her, why don't you.'

When the hatch was closed they heard Reck, from beyond it, intoning in his prophet's voice, '*She weepeth sore in the night, and her tears are on her cheeks.*'

Harbison sat down. This was his fourth or fifth drink – Strafford had lost count – and his eyes had taken on an excited glassiness.

'So the padre has a sister, eh?' he mused. 'I wonder how I'd go about getting in touch with her.' He was talking to himself, lost in eager speculation. Strafford rose from his chair. Harbison stared up at him. 'You're not going, are you?'

'Yes. I'm tired. I'll say goodnight.'

He went to the door.

'Listen,' Harbison said behind him, 'if you hear anything, you know, about the horse, you might—'

'Why don't you speak to your sister?'

'Sylvia?' He snorted. 'I told you, she lives in cloud cuckoo land.'

Strafford smiled vaguely, and opened the door. 'Anyway, goodnight.'

Mrs Reck came through the archway, yawning.

'Can you tell me how to get to my room?' Strafford said.

'Come on, I'll show you,' the woman said, and yawned again.

She led the way up a narrow, ill-lit staircase. Strafford wondered what had become of Peggy, she of the flame-red locks. She would probably be in bed by now. He recalled her overlapping tooth, and the saddle of freckles on the bridge of her nose.

'Will Mr Harbison be lodging here tonight?' he asked, of necessity addressing Mrs Reck's broad rump as it preceded him up the steps.

'He will,' she answered over her shoulder. 'I wouldn't send even him out in that black weather. He stops over when he's visiting the sister, above at the House.'

'He sees her, then, Mrs Osborne, does he? I had the impression—'

They came to the landing.

'Wait up a minute, till I catch my breath,' Mrs Reck said, putting a hand on his arm and pressing the other to her collarbone. She was panting. 'That stairs will be the death of me, one of these days.' She moved on. 'He's a caution, isn't he,' she said, 'the bold Freddie? You'd want to watch out for him, mind – he's a fierce rogue.'

'How often does he put up here?'

'Oh, not often. Now and then. It's handy for him. And of course' – she chuckled – 'he's after our Peggy.'

'Your daughter, is she?' Strafford asked.

She stopped and stared at him. 'God, no.' She laughed again, shaking her head. 'I wouldn't be wanting Peggy Devine for a daughter, grand girl though she is.'

There were three rooms on either side of the corridor. Mrs

Reck stopped outside the middle one on the right. From the pocket of her apron she took a set of keys on a big metal ring and sorted through them.

'What was he talking to you about, anyway?'

'Mr Harbison? A horse. Mr Sugar. It belongs – belonged – to Father Lawless.'

'Oh, aye, he was a great one for the horses, and the hunting, all that. Hard to believe he's gone. Not, mind you, that I was all that fond of him, God forgive me.'

'Oh, yes? Why not?'

He could see she regretted what she had said. She turned away, busying herself with the jumble of keys. She selected one, and crunched it into the lock.

'Bingo!' She pushed the door open. 'This is our deluxe suite.' She gave him a broad grin.

The room was small, with a narrow wooden bed, a chair and an oversized tallboy. An enamel jug and basin stood on a pine table under the window. The curtains were drawn. A pink satin eiderdown covered the bed, plump and smooth and shiny as a pie crust. Strafford's bag, which someone had set beside the bed, seemed to regard him smugly, as though, having got here first, it considered itself the rightful occupier.

'Very nice,' he said faintly. 'Thank you – very nice.'

'I hope you'll be comfortable. There's a hot-water bottle in the bed for you.' She turned to go, then paused. 'Mr Harbison's room is the one opposite, by the way. Mind out you don't bump into him in the morning, he'll be like a bear with a sore head, after all that drink he took tonight, and him after driving all them miles in the snow.'

'He's not a morning person, then,' Strafford said, laying his suitcase on the bed.

'Well, he certainly wasn't this morning – wouldn't eat the rashers and eggs I went to the trouble of making for him.'

'So Mr Harbison *was* here last night, yes?' Strafford asked, turning to her.

'Aye, he was. He left to go home but he got caught by the snow and came back and stopped over again.' She gave him a questioning look. 'Why do you ask?'

'Oh, no reason. Goodnight, Mrs Reck.'

He opened his bag and began to unpack. The woman was still standing in the doorway.

'Will you tell me, Inspector Stafford—' she began.

'Strafford.' He smiled apologetically, as he always did when he had to make this correction.

'Sorry – Mr Strafford.' She paused. 'Only I wondered, you see. Father Tom—' Her voice trailed off.

'Yes? What about him?'

'They're saying in the town—' Once more she hesitated, then went on in a rush. 'They're saying he didn't fall down the stairs at Ballyglass at all, or that if he did, the fall wasn't what he died of.'

'Oh, yes? And what else are they saying, in the town?'

'There's all kinds of rumours flying around – you know what it's like, when there's big news in a small place.'

He nodded. He knew all about small places.

'We're investigating the circumstances of Father Lawless's death,' he said. 'We've a long way to go before we'll know anything for certain.'

'There was a thing about it on the wireless tonight.'

'Was there?'

'On the ten o'clock news. Just that a priest had died in an accident in Ballyglass – they didn't even say it was Ballyglass House, so it might have been anywhere in the village. They didn't give his name, either.'

He thought for a moment.

'There will have been a press release from the Archbishop's palace, I imagine. Press releases never give much away, especially the ones the Archbishop issues.'

'His poor sister,' she said. 'What's she going to do, with him gone?'

'Were they very close?'

'They were. She'll be lost without him.'

'Does she live here, in Ballyglass?'

'No, over at Scallanstown, in the presbytery there.'

'They lived together, she and Father Lawless?'

'They did. She kept house for him for years, since she was a girl, I think.'

'I'll go and talk to her tomorrow,' he said, 'or' – he consulted his pocket watch – 'today, I should say.'

She didn't take the hint, but remained standing in the doorway. There were things she might say, he could see, but she would not say them. Big news, and bigger secrets, in a small place.

'I don't envy you making that visit,' she said.

'Yes. These things are never easy. Goodnight, Mrs Reck.'

He resumed unpacking, pointedly turning his back to her, but still she lingered. He was so tired. He thought of the hot-water bottle awaiting him in the bed.

'Yes, goodnight to you,' the woman murmured distractedly. She stepped into the corridor, but stopped yet again, and turned back to face him. 'Was he killed, Inspector?' she asked. 'Father Tom. Was he murdered?'

'As I say, we're investigating the circumstances in which he died.'

He laid out his pyjamas on the bed.

'Right.' She stood nodding to herself. 'I'll leave you in peace. Is there anything I can get you, before I turn in, myself?'

'No, thank you.'

'Right, so.' Pause. 'The lavatory is at the end of the corridor.'

'Thank you.'

When she had closed the door at last, he drew back the curtains and switched off the light in order to look out into the darkness. The glimmering landscape materialised slowly before him. Such stillness. He might have been the last man in the world.

15

He rose early, before the dawn, observing Mrs Reck's warning about the inadvisability of an encounter with Harbison and his hangover. He went downstairs, and took his breakfast at the corner table where he had sat the night before. The dog lay in front of the stove with its muzzle on its paws, watching Strafford with deep suspicion. He broke off a crust of bread, dipped it in the yolk of one of his fried eggs and offered it to the beast, but was rebuffed with a disdainful stare.

He was finishing his food when Sergeant Jenkins arrived. There was still only the faintest glimmer of daylight in the window. Jenkins had come down from Dublin. Like Harbison, he was not a morning person, it seemed. He had the look of one who had been held forcibly under a cold tap and scrubbed until his skin glowed red and raw.

'What time did you set out at?' Strafford asked. 'Did you sleep at all? What are the roads like?'

'Terrible. Black ice at every turn.'

'But it's not snowing?'

'Not yet. It snowed in the night, and will again, soon.'

'Sit down, sit down. Have some tea. There's toast left but I'm sure it's cold by now. What did the Chief have to say?'

Sergeant Jenkins eyed the table doubtfully. It was plain he was hungry, but wasn't sure of the propriety of sitting down to his breakfast with his superior officer, especially in an establishment such as the Sheaf of Barley. In the end, hunger overcame doubt. He took off his overcoat and hat, hung them up and pulled up a chair.

Jeremiah Reck appeared. He wore baggy corduroy trousers and a pair of carpet slippers – they looked like identical dead cats – and a jumper with moth holes in it.

'There's rashers and eggs,' he said gravely to Jenkins, 'or rashers and sausage and eggs, or rashers and sausage and black or white pudding and eggs. Or there's eggs.'

Jenkins regarded him warily, wondering if he were being made fun of. He had a keen ear for the faintest hint of mockery. He put a hand to his buffed-up hair, and said he would have an egg, just an egg, soft-boiled.

'You're a great disappointment to my missus, the two of you,' Reck said. 'She's out there in the kitchen, like Ruth amid the alien corn, with the rashers in one hand and the sausages in the other, only waiting for the word to set them sizzling. Anyway, an egg it is. The chickens will be happy, at any rate.'

He went off to the kitchen, murmuring to himself.

'A great joker, that fellow,' Jenkins said sourly.

Strafford nodded, saying nothing. He had long ago learned not to let his gaze stray higher than Jenkins's hairline. It really was a remarkable head.

'The Chief said to keep on as you're going,' Jenkins said.

'Did he, now. That's very helpful of him, very helpful. Any possibility of his coming down to have a look around for himself, do you think? It would be good to have someone to share the blame, when the newspapers get hold of the story and start baying at us and demanding why we haven't found the killer yet.'

Jenkins shrugged. He had no time for sarcasm.

'You know there's a story already in the paper?' he said. He fetched a rolled-up copy of the *Irish Press* from the pocket of his coat on the rack. 'Page four,' he said.

'Page four? Hardly hot news, then. I suppose we should be thankful.'

Strafford opened the paper.

WEXFORD
PRIEST DIES
IN MISHAP
By Peter McGonagle

A Wexford priest, Father Thomas J. Lawless, PP, died at an address in the village of Ballyglass, Co. Wexford, in the early hours of yesterday morning. The circumstances of his death have not yet been disclosed by the Gardaí, but it is understood he fell down a flight of stairs and sustained fatal injuries.

Father Lawless, known to all as 'Father Tom', was popular throughout the county. He was a keen horseman, and rode regularly with the Keelmore Hunt, the Master of which is Colonel Geoffrey Osborne, DSO, of Ballyglass House, Ballyglass.

Father Lawless was also involved in many youth organisations, especially the Boy Scouts, and was a strong supporter of the Wexford Junior Hurling Team. He was chaplain of the Ballyglass branch of the Legion of Mary. When he was still a seminarian he travelled to Rome, where he was honoured by an audience with the Holy Father.

Tributes were paid to the late Father Lawless by the Bishop of Ferns, Most Rev Tony Battley, by his colleagues in the Church, by the business community, by sporting organisations and by parishioners.

Father Lawless is survived by his sister, Rosemary, and by numerous cousins in America, Canada and Australia. Funeral arrangements will be announced later.

'That's good,' Strafford said. 'Either they don't know the actual circumstances of his death, or they have orders from on high to hold off. Either way, it means they won't be crawling all over us, for a while at least. I hear it was on the wireless last night – probably from the same press release. The Archbishop's people don't waste time, do they.'

'We should have put out a statement ourselves,' Jenkins muttered. Jenkins disapproved of Chief Inspector Hackett and what he considered his lackadaisical methods. 'Will you go and see the sister?' he asked.

Reck came with Jenkins's boiled egg, and slices of toast wrapped in a checked napkin. Strafford asked him to bring a fresh pot of tea.

'By the way,' he said, looking up from the newspaper, 'where's Peggy this morning?'

'She only does nights,' Reck said, reaching over and taking up the toast rack with its three shrivelled slices of cold toast. 'By day she runs the local Ballyglass branch of the Bank of Ireland.' Jenkins stared at him. 'That was a joke. She does the odd shift in the Boolavogue Arms, our esteemed rival down the road. She's there now.'

He went off, doing that buzzing whistle through his teeth.

'This country has more than its fair share of comedians,' Jenkins said darkly.

Strafford only smiled. He had a high tolerance for eccentrics, having grown up among so many of them.

'Yes,' he said, 'I'll talk to the sister. Though I won't be expecting much enlightenment.'

'How did you get on yesterday?'

'I didn't get on, and I didn't get anywhere. At least, I don't think I did.' He folded the newspaper and laid it on the table beside his teacup. 'It's the way it always is, at this stage. I'm convinced the answer is staring me in the face, plain as day, but I can't see it. What do you think?'

Jenkins considered the tablecloth, biting abstractedly into a slice of toast. After a moment he shook his head. 'I don't know what to think.'

Strafford nodded, sighing.

'Who would have wanted the priest dead?' he mused. 'That's the question.'

'That's always the question,' Jenkins observed drily.

'Yes.' Strafford pushed a limp lock of hair up from his forehead. 'He seems to have been about a lot at Ballyglass House. The daughter described him as "oogey" – have you come across that word?' Jenkins shook his head. 'Well, that's what she said, that he was oogey, and that he was always hanging about the place. In fact, the son, Dominic, said the same thing, that he was around a great deal. Hardly a motive for murder, though, would you say? Hanging about the place and being oogey couldn't be considered a capital offence.'

Reck returned with the pot of fresh tea and set it with ceremonial care on its cork mat.

'Your pot of plenty, gentlemen, straight from the Golden Orient.'

He went away again, whistling as before. Strafford, tolerant or not, was becoming a little tired of the fat man's ponderous wit.

He poured the tea. The fragrance of it, on this wintry morning, wafted straight up out of childhood.

'So what now?' Jenkins asked.

'Eh?'

'What do you want me to do?' He could see Strafford wasn't listening. 'Will I drive you up to see the sister?'

Strafford sipped his tea. As usual, he took it black, without sugar. He had noticed Jenkins noticing, and not being pleased. Jenkins had a keen sense of the class divide, the signs of which were of the tiniest moment, tea with or without milk, the buttoning of a waistcoat, the pronunciation of a name.

'You know, it's funny,' Strafford said, 'but either no one at Ballyglass House had a motive for killing the priest, or everyone had.'

Jenkins looked askance at the room where they sat. He was impatient of Strafford's dreamy metaphysics. The art of detection was a matter of fact.

'Maybe it was somebody from outside,' Jenkins said, defiantly spooning sugar into his milky tea. 'Somebody could have had a key to the front door, or maybe there's another way into the house. Those old places have all sorts of coal-holes and trapdoors and God knows what, that get overgrown and people forget about.'

Strafford, his gaze fixed on the floor beside the table now, was lost in his own thoughts.

'And no one had an alibi,' he said, 'not one of them, even the housekeeper. All asleep in their beds, even the insomniac Mrs Osborne. It doesn't make sense, or it makes too much.'

'Maybe they all did it,' Jenkins said, with a snicker. 'Like in the book by what's-her-name.'

No, Strafford thought, there was no sense to it. The thing was entirely implausible, and yet there it was, the deed was done, the man was dead. He felt as if he were stumbling through a snowstorm, the snow dense and blindingly white. There were others around him, also moving, dim grey ghosts, and when he reached out to touch them he grasped only an icy emptiness.

Abruptly he stood up.

'Yes, I'll go and talk to the sister,' he said. 'She lives in Scallanstown, in the presbytery – any idea where Scallanstown is?'

'It's up the road, about ten miles – I passed through it on the way here. You must have, too. There's not much to it, but you can't miss the church – ugly big barn of a thing.'

Strafford stood thinking.

'I wonder if I should telephone her,' Strafford murmured. 'I should let her know I'm coming. Somebody told me her name – Rose, is it?'

'Rosemary,' Jenkins said. He took up the newspaper, showed it. 'There, look. "Survived by his sister, Rosemary".'

'Right,' Strafford said, nodding. 'Rosemary.' He heaved a sigh. 'Oh, God.'

'I'll go with you. I'll drive you up and we can both talk to her.'

'What? No, no. You go over to the house, have a look round again. Talk to anyone who's there.'

'Talk to them about what, in particular?'

'Just – talk. Be polite, be friendly, even. Don't press, just listen. The more you let them talk, the more likely they'll give something away. They can't all be innocent.' He turned to go, then turned back. 'By the way, was the whiskey glass found, the one the priest had in his room?'

'No. Nor the light bulb. Someone knows where they are.'

'Yes, and isn't saying.'

He sat down again at the table and rolled a crumb of bread into a ball. 'I thought this was going to be an easy one,' he said. He sat for some moments, frowning, then stood up a second time, and a second time stopped. 'I knew there was something I meant to say. Mrs Osborne's brother is staying here. Harbison, Freddie Harbison. He was here last night, and also the night before, though for some reason he didn't tell me that. Have a word with him, before you go over to the house.'

'Did he know the priest?'

'He knows his horse,' Strafford said.

He went into the bar. It was empty, the stove was cold. He put on his trench coat, his hat, his scarf. Everything felt unreal. Priests didn't get murdered, it simply didn't happen. And yet it had.

There was a pair of galoshes under the hat stand, probably Harbison's, Strafford guessed. He considered borrowing them, but thought better of it. He would not put his feet where that man's feet had been. He stood in the glare of snow-light coming in at the low windows, each one with its four small square panes. He looked about. He had the sense of something important left undone, though he couldn't think what. Later, he would think it had been a premonition. He should have taken up Jenkins's offer to come with him to Scallanstown.

He went out into the cold, moist morning. He thought of the Christmas hymn, 'Good King Wenceslas'. When he was young, he always misheard it as

Good King Wences last looked out
On the fist of Stephen,
When the snow lay round about
Deep on Crispin's even

and didn't care that it made no sense. Most things made no sense, when he was young. Yes, he would think later, yes, he should have kept Jenkins with him. He should have kept him safe.

> *'Sire, the night is darker now*
> *And the wind blows stronger;*
> *Fails my heart, I know not how,*
> *I can go no longer.'*

That bit he had got right.

16

The sky was loaded with a swag of mauve-tinted clouds, and the air was the colour of tarnished pewter. It wasn't snowing, but there had been the fresh fall in the night that Jenkins had mentioned. The land all round was smooth and plump as a pillow. The gnarled bare boughs looked as if they had been blackened in fire. Strafford watched his breath smoke in the air. Summer was unimaginable.

There was a thick layer of opaque ice on the windscreen of his car, etched with rune-like scratches and squiggles. He had to go back inside and fetch a kettle of warm water from Mrs Reck to melt it with. It took six groan-inducing turns of the crank handle to get the engine shuddering to life. A ragged jet of black smoke billowed from its exhaust pipe at the back end. When he released the clutch the tyres skidded, sending up showers of slush and frozen mud.

He had gone a good mile along the road before it came to him that he had forgotten to telephone ahead to Scallanstown to let the priest's sister know he was on his way.

The short journey took far longer than expected, for he had to drive most of the way in low gear. A few vehicles had been out before him, leaving ruts in the road that gleamed like black glass.

Scallanstown squatted in a hollow between two low hills. Driving along the main street, he counted five pubs, three grocery shops, two hardware stores. There were also a pork butcher's – Hafner's: surely a relative of Ballyglass's doctor – a barber's, a newsagent's and post office combined, and Bernie's Beauty Parlour. The streets were empty. The only vehicle to be seen was a milkman's cart, abandoned by the milkman. A mongrel dog was worrying at a soiled scrap of greaseproof paper in the gutter outside Hafner's.

The church stood on a rise overlooking the town from its northern end. It was an imposing granite edifice of a peculiarly unpleasant shade of reddish-brown. There were black railings, a broad, arched doorway, and a short stump of spire absurdly out of proportion with the massive structure it was attached to. On the right there was a graveyard, each headstone sporting a neat topping of snow, incongruously reminiscent of slabs of ice cream. On the other side, and standing at a slightly lower level, was the presbytery, a substantial, many-chimneyed house built of the same plum-coloured stone as the church.

A mourning wreath of black crape was attached to the front door knocker. It reminded Strafford of a gentleman gunslinger's elaborate neckwear in some movie he had seen long ago.

Rosemary Lawless was a tall, lean woman, handsome in a somewhat forbidding way. She had a thin pale mouth and prominent, dull-grey eyes. She wore a black skirt and a black jumper and a black woollen cardigan. She was in her early thirties. He had expected her to be older, he didn't know why. She had a taut, parched look that Strafford recognised, the look of a person caught in the furnace-glare of grief.

He introduced himself. They didn't shake hands – it would

have seemed in some way inappropriate. Death makes everything difficult.

'Forgive me for bothering you, at such a time,' he said, picturing the words in print, as in the pages of an etiquette book.

Rosemary Lawless moved aside in the doorway and gestured to him to enter. The black-and-white tiled hallway was chilly. The house, beyond, was a zone of silence. On a bog-oak table, shiny as hewn coal, stood a vase of dried chrysanthemums that must have been crimson once but were faded now to palest pink. Everything here had a faded look.

'I thought it would be Sergeant Radford who would come,' the woman said, unable to suppress a note of peevishness.

'He's unwell,' Strafford said. 'The 'flu, apparently.'

'The 'flu. I see. So that's what they're calling it now. You know he's a drunkard.'

'I'm told he lost a son.'

Something closed in her expression, like a door shutting.

'I haven't lit the fire in the parlour yet,' she said. 'But the stove is going in the kitchen. I'll make tea.'

She went ahead of him along the hall, then through a narrower corridor where the tiles gave way to linoleum. The air in the kitchen was stiflingly hot; Strafford felt an immediate constriction in his chest. There was a dresser with cups and plates, a table of scrubbed deal, four stiff-backed chairs and, beside the iron stove, a rocker, across the back of which was draped a tartan rug.

Rosemary Lawless pulled a chair out from the table for Strafford, and a second one for herself. For a moment, in the silence, there was a sense of helpless teetering. Strafford could think of nothing to say.

The rocking chair, facing the stove, was a presence of its own in the room.

Rosemary Lawless had fixed her gaze on Strafford in poised expectancy.

'I'm sorry for your loss,' he said, and winced again, at another hackneyed phrase.

'Thank you,' the woman responded, and looked at her hands, folded lifelessly before her on the table. 'I hope you've come to tell me the truth about what happened to my brother.'

Strafford glanced at the rocking chair.

'May I ask, how did you hear of his death?'

'Someone telephoned, I can't remember who. Someone from the Guards' barracks in the town, I think. Not Sergeant Radford.'

'Probably the Guard on desk duty. What did he—?'

'Just that there had been an accident at Ballyglass, and that my brother was dead. Then there was a story in the paper this morning' – she put a hand to her forehead – 'it said he had fallen downstairs and died. They said it happened in Ballyglass. I suppose that means he was at the House.'

'Yes. He stayed the night there.'

'Oh, of course he did,' she exclaimed, her tight lips tightening further and turning a shade whiter. 'He couldn't keep away from them, his grand friends.'

'So he was there quite a lot?'

'Too much, as far as I'm concerned.'

'Why is that? Do you dislike the Osbornes? Did you disapprove of the family?'

She shrugged dismissively.

'It's not for me to disapprove of them or not. They aren't our kind, and we're not theirs. Tom wouldn't listen to me, oh, no. He wanted to be like them, with his horse riding and fox hunting and all the rest of it.' She stopped, and frowned. 'I'm sorry. I offered you tea, then I forgot.'

'Don't worry,' he said. 'I don't need anything.'

'I can't get myself organised. My brain is spinning, round and round. I feel nothing will ever be right again. I suppose that will pass. They say it does.' She gave a low, bitter laugh. 'Time is a great healer, that's what they say, don't they? They're all so wise.'

She tugged at a loose thread in the sleeve of her cardigan. To Strafford it seemed as if she were made of fine spun glass, tinted grey and black, that might shatter at any moment under its own internal pressure.

'I can't believe he's gone,' she said, and she too turned her eyes to the rocking chair. 'I can't believe it.' She paused, and again she laughed. 'Of course, that's what everyone says too, isn't it.'

Strafford looked away. Other people's pain embarrassed him. He wished, as so often, that he was a smoker, for at least then he'd have something to do with his hands. Maybe he should take up the pipe. He wouldn't even have to light it, he could just fiddle with it, as pipe smokers do. Anything can make a mask.

'Will you tell me about him, about your brother?' he asked. 'Or tell me about your family, at least – have you other siblings?'

She shook her head. 'There was only the two of us. Thomas was the eldest.'

'Did you always keep house for him? – I mean, after he became a priest?'

'Yes. Except when he was over in the west for a couple of years, as chaplain at a place there for orphans.'

'Oh, yes? Where was that?'

'Carricklea, it's called. It's an industrial school.'

Carricklea. He knew about Carricklea. And he had heard it mentioned recently – by whom?

'What did you do, then,' he asked, 'when he was away, in the west?'

She stared at him, baffled. 'What did I do? I did nothing. I took care of my father. He was dying.'

'He must have been young, your father, when he died?'

'Yes, he was only in his fifties.'

He nodded. It was the old story, the son sent off in glory to the priesthood, while the daughter stayed at home to tend the parents until they were gone and she was left alone, young still but old already, untrained for anything other than spinsterhood.

He thought of his own father. What would happen when he became too old to look after himself – who would care for him then?

'I wanted to be a teacher,' Rosemary Lawless said, 'but it was unheard of in the family, a daughter going to the university. Tom, our Tommy, got everything.' There was no rancour in her words. That was the natural order, that the son would be the favoured one. That was how it always had been, and how it was.

'Are you acquainted with the Osbornes?' he asked. 'Do you know them?'

She stared at him. 'Do you think they'd have anything to do with *me*? I can't even ride a horse.' She drew herself back on the chair and cast about the room with a look of desperation. 'It's so stuffy in here,' she said, with a sort of gasp. 'Do you mind if we go out? I usually go for a walk at this time of the morning. I know the weather is terrible.'

'Of course,' he said. 'It's not snowing now.'

She looked down past the table at his shoes. 'Would you wear a pair of his boots? They'd probably fit you.'

'Of course,' he said again, too hastily, as he realised too late. Try as he might, he did not have it in him to care enough for her distress. Yet what of it? No one cared enough, not really, for all the kind words and the mournful smiles they lavished upon the bereaved. The living live, the dead are dead. He almost heard his father's soft, heartless chuckle.

In the silence he studied the woman before him, as she sat with downcast eyes, her hands folded on the table. So much anger, so much resentment, so much loss. What if she had come by a key to Ballyglass House, and had gone there last night, by some means or other – he had seen no sign here of a car – and had let herself in by the front door and gone upstairs and unscrewed the bulb from the passageway and hidden herself in the darkness to await her moment?

Our Tom got everything.

But no, he told himself, no. She might have killed him, in a fever of fury – it was possible, he knew it – but she would not have mutilated him in that way. For such violence, another level of rage would have been called for, another extreme of vengefulness. But all the same—? He looked about him. What things might have gone on in this house, between a brother and a sister?

The woman stood up from the table.

'Well then,' she said, 'will we go?'

In the hall she produced a pair of high-sided walking boots – 'Tom brought them back from a holiday in Italy' – and he tried them on.

'Are they too big?'

'They are a little on the roomy side, yes.'

She went upstairs, and presently came back, bringing with her two pairs of men's thick socks. He put on both pairs. As he did so, an image flashed into his mind of the priest lying on the floor at Ballyglass House, his hands folded on his chest and his eyes open, and he felt a momentary flutter of revulsion. He would be wearing not only a dead man's boots, but a dead man's socks as well. No end to life's grotesqueries.

They walked together along a path traversing the hillside where the house stood. She said it was a pity about the mist – the landscape looked like a smudged pencil drawing. 'When it's clear there's a nice view along the Slaney Valley towards Enniscorthy.'

The snow was patchy here on the lee side of the hill, and scraps of sheep's wool were snagged in the bare heather.

Rosemary Lawless wore a heavy black overcoat and a wool hat with a bobble. Strafford tightened the knot of his scarf at his throat. He thought wistfully of last night's hot-water bottle. He thought of Peggy the barmaid, too, of her red hair and her freckles, and of her eyes as green as – as whatever is greenest green, eyes that had, in their moment, quite eclipsed the memory of Sylvia Osborne's grey and melancholy gaze.

Look at you, he told himself, daydreaming about a girl in a country pub. Was he not the son of a stern and dutiful people? What would his Strafford forebears, who had fought and slaughtered for Cromwell at Drogheda and Wexford, what would they think of him, mooning like this after a girl? Sometimes it came to him that he was lonelier than he knew.

'Will you tell me about your brother?' he prompted for the second time.

'What do you want me to tell you?' she snapped impatiently.

'Well, from all accounts he was a very popular cleric, not only in the parish, but in the county, and beyond.'

She looked off into the mist. 'He should never have gone to be a priest,' she said bitterly. 'He was wasted on it. He could have been anything, he could have done anything.' She gave a sour little laugh. '"It was God calling him," they'll tell you. If so, why didn't he call *me*? I could have been a nun, it would have suited me, better than it suited Tom to be a priest.' They came to a stop at a rocky ledge. 'You know who we are, don't you,' the woman asked, turning to him, 'the Lawlesses? My father was John Joe Lawless – JJ, as everyone called him.'

'Ah. No, I didn't know that.'

JJ Lawless had been a notorious figure in the Civil War, one of the IRA leader Michael Collins's most unwavering supporters and a ruthless director of the Big Fellow's death squads. JJ had been sentenced to be hanged, but was reprieved on the direct intervention of the British prime minister, who had seen his potential in the Treaty negotiations that were about to take place. Later, when the Civil War ended, Mr John Joseph Lawless became a barrister and set up his own firm, specialising in the defence of unreconciled IRA men who had been marked for the scaffold by order of the Free State government. When peace came, or what was called peace, JJ Lawless & Son was the leading law firm in the province of Leinster, until JJ's premature death ten years before. So, Strafford thought, *those* Lawlesses.

'That would have been a weighty inheritance, for a son,' he said, minding his words. 'For a daughter too, of course.'

This last she ignored.

'It was why Tom went for the priesthood,' she said, with an odd vehemence, 'I've no doubt of that. It was his only way out. There was no competing with Daddy. Tom had to make his own way, and his own name. Daddy never forgave him when he announced to the family that he had a vocation – oh, the fights they had! – but Tom held out and made his escape.'

'And you went with him?'

That caught her by surprise.

'I suppose you might say that.'

'Your father didn't relent, where your brother was concerned?'

'They didn't speak for years, the two of them. Anyone else would have been proud to have a son in the priesthood. Not Daddy.' She gazed off into the mist. 'I believe he lost his religion after all that cruel fighting in the wars – he was in the 1916 Rising, in the War of Independence and then the Civil War. He must have seen terrible things. "I'll pray for you to be at peace," those were Tom's last words to him, before he went off to the seminary.'

She stepped away from Strafford, to the brink of the stony ledge.

'It took a long time for Daddy to reconcile himself to the fact that someone had stood up to him and got away with it.' Her nose was red from the cold and her eyes were watering – or were those tears on her cheeks? She didn't seem the weeping kind. 'I suppose all this is foreign to you – the fight for freedom, all that? I'm assuming you're not a Catholic.'

'Protestants fought in all those wars you mentioned,' he said, 'and not a few of them on the nationalist side.'

'Yes, and your people suffered too, and weren't thanked for it. I'm well aware of that. We all suffered. I sometimes wonder if it was worth it – if independence, so-called, was worth even one life.' Suddenly, to his surprise, she smiled, for the first time since his coming here. 'I must say,' she said, '*you* were a surprise, when you turned up out of the blue. Do you mind me asking why you became a policeman? Most of the men recruited for the Guards, when the Force was set up, were former gunmen, after all – the people who killed your people.'

Far off, the clouds parted for a moment, and a shaft of sunlight struck through the mist like a searchlight, but was soon doused. More snow was on the way, he could feel it.

'Perhaps, like your brother, I felt I had to take a stand, make a break for freedom.'

He heard himself say it and knew it wasn't true. But why then had he 'joined up'? He didn't know. He must have known, once, but if so he had forgotten. Sometimes he thought he should give up policing and try something else – but what? He had never wanted to be anything in particular, until somehow he hit on the idea of 'going for the Guards', which was how he learned to put it. His father had been at first amused, then baffled, then angry, though of course he would not say so.

'Freedom?' Rosemary Lawless said now, seizing on the word. 'Tom wasn't free. Oh, he played at being the new kind of priest, going all over the place and seeing people, staying at their houses – Ballyglass was his favourite, of course – riding to hounds, all that kind of thing. But that wasn't him. That was only how he wanted people to think he was, while all the time he was someone else.'

'I see.'

She pounced again. 'Do you?' she almost snarled. 'Do you see? I very much doubt you do.'

'No,' he conceded, 'I'm sure you're right. I'm not very good on people and why they do the things they do. Which is not very good, in a detective.'

He smiled, but she took no notice. They had turned and were walking back the way they had come. The path was so narrow that in places they had to go in single file. A cattle truck went past on the road below them, the same one, by the look of it, Strafford thought, that had driven up behind him yesterday and honked at him derisively.

'He had secrets,' Rosemary Lawless said. 'I could see it in his face, the way it would change sometimes. When I looked at him I saw two people, the priest that everyone knew, Father Tom, the life and soul of the party, and then the other one, hiding in there, behind his eyes.'

'Do you think he was unhappy?'

'I think he was in torment.' She was impassive, her dull grey gaze fixed straight before her. 'I said it already,' she went on, 'he should never have gone for the priesthood. But once he was in, that was it. I don't believe he fully realised, before he went, that he was letting himself in for a life sentence. All he could think of was getting away from Daddy, by whatever means.'

She stumbled on a loose piece of rock and he put a hand under her elbow to support her. She righted herself, and drew away immediately from his touch.

'Did you try to persuade him away from the priesthood?' he asked.

'Me?' she scoffed. 'Who ever listens to me? Anyway, I was young, I had no voice in the house. Daddy had this smile he would put on whenever I spoke up about something, a little sort of twitch at the side of his mouth, that's all it was, but, oh my, it said so much about what he thought of me.'

They were almost at the house now, descending the last of the slope, and the ground underfoot was a treacherous mixture of mud and ice and slippery gravel. Strafford watched the figure in black making her way ahead of him. She was trapped, just like her brother, but his had been a roomier cage.

She was fumbling for the keys in the pockets of the outsized overcoat she was wearing. 'This was Tom's coat,' she said, 'his Sunday best. Someone might as well get some use out of it, and it might as well be me. It still smells of the Churchman's cigarettes he used to smoke. He joked that maybe he could get them to pay him to do an advertisement for them: "A Churchman's for a churchman."' They were on the doorstep, and now she turned to him, with a sudden, intense light in her eyes. 'Are you going to tell me what happened to him?' she said. 'Are you going to show me that much respect?'

17

He spared her the worst of it, more out of cowardice than consideration. He couldn't bring himself to tell her what had been done to her brother as he lay dying. What would be the point of her knowing that detail? With luck, she would never hear of it – no newspaper in the country would dare print such shocking facts.

What he did tell her was bad enough. As he spoke, he stood by the coke stove in the kitchen, batting his hat against his thigh, while she sat on the straight chair with her ankles crossed and her hands clamped on her knees. She wept without tears, her shoulders heaving, now and then letting fall a harsh, dry sob.

'But who would kill him like that, sticking a knife in him?' she wailed softly, looking up at him in a kind of desperate wonderment. 'He never did any harm to anybody.' She closed her eyes, and he saw the traceries of tiny blue veins in the stretched, paper-thin lids.

'I told him,' she said bitterly, 'I warned him not to be going to that house, not to be mixing with those people and trying to pretend he was one of them. They only laughed at him behind his back. Colonel Osborne was forever telling people how he allowed Tom to keep his horse in the stables there, letting them think he wasn't charging him, while in fact Tom was paying him through the nose for the privilege. They're great at that kind of thing, the Protestants, lording it over us and pretending everything they do for us is a favour, and then pocketing our money without a word of acknowledgement.' She stopped, and her brow coloured a little. 'I'm sorry,' she said, 'but it's true.'

He said nothing. He felt no resentment. Both sides in this troubled country had their cause for bitterness.

A robin redbreast flew on to the windowsill and stood with head aslant, as if to eavesdrop. He had seen a robin yesterday, too, somewhere. It was the time of year for them. Christmas. Yule logs. Holly wreaths. Loneliness.

I, said the Sparrow, with my bow and arrow, I killed Cock Robin.

'You felt your brother had secrets,' Strafford said, in a mild and purposely distracted tone, for Rosemary Lawless was just as liable to take fright as the bird outside on the sill. 'Do you know what they might have been?'

She shook her head, tight-lipped.

'He didn't talk to me,' she said. 'He used to, when he was young. He was afraid of Daddy – we both were – and sometimes he'd say something about that.'

'What would he say? – what kind of thing?'

'Just – oh, just that he couldn't sleep, thinking about him.'

'Did your father beat him?'

'No!' she exclaimed. 'He never laid a finger on him. Or on me. He was never violent like that. Only—'

'Only?' he prompted.

'He didn't need to hit us. All he had to do was look at us, that was all.' She shifted on the chair, and when she spoke again it was as much to herself as to him. 'They were very close, you see, the two of them. It was funny. Tommy was afraid of Daddy, and yet he was – yet he was *attached* to him. There was a bond between them that excluded other people, me especially. They were like – I don't know. Like a magician and his assistant.'

The robin flew away. Random flakes of snow drifted past the window, swaying as they fell.

Snow falls absent-mindedly, Strafford thought, absent-mindedly.

'Was that what you meant when you said he was in torment?' he asked.

She looked up, frowning. 'What? What do you mean, torment?'

'You said it earlier, that your brother was in torment. That was the word you used.'

'Was it?' She looked at her hands gripping her knees. The knuckles were white. 'Isn't everybody in torment, more or less, in this world? My father, too, he must have been tormented, otherwise he wouldn't have—' She stopped, still staring at her hands.

Strafford waited, then said, 'Wouldn't have what, Miss Lawless? What wouldn't he have done?'

'He would have let poor Tom sleep at night, instead of making him worry and fret.' Her voice sounded faraway and dreamy.

They were silent for a moment, as if at the passing of some dark thing in the air.

'You haven't mentioned your mother.'

'Haven't I?' She had begun to rock herself back and forth on the chair. It was a tiny movement, almost imperceptible, in time perhaps with her heart's metronome.

'Mammy didn't get a look-in, not where Tom and my father were concerned. *I'm only a piece of furniture*, she said to me one day, I remember it. She was standing there, just there where you're standing now. She was looking out of that window. It wasn't like today, it was summer, the sun was shining. I was sitting at this table, doing my homework. History. I was always good at history. She was so quiet I'd forgotten she was standing there, behind me, and then suddenly she said it, with no more feeling than if she was commenting on the weather: *I'm only a piece of furniture.*'

Strafford looked down at her. He had the feeling something had occurred that he had missed. It was something to do with the priest and his father. Something she knew without knowing she knew it. Something she had suppressed.

'And she's still alive, yes?' he asked. 'She's still living, your mother?'

'Yes,' Rosemary Lawless answered dully.

She said nothing more for a long time, then a sort of shiver ran through her, from her shoulders all the way to her crossed ankles.

'What am I going to do?' she said, with a new, quick urgency. 'What am I going to do, now? They'll put me out – there'll be a new parish priest and I'll have to vacate the house. Where will I go?'

'Well,' he said, 'perhaps you might live with your mother? You know what they say about home, that no matter what happens or what you do, when you go there they have to take you in.'

Suddenly the woman laughed, shrilly, flaring her nostrils and letting her teeth show.

'Oh, yes,' she cried, 'oh yes, where Mammy is, they'd take me in there, all right. She's in the madhouse, up in Enniscorthy. All are welcome, there.'

18

He drove as fast as he dared through the town and out on to the Ballyglass road. His pulse was racing, and his palms were moist on the steering wheel. There was a nightmare he had, it recurred with awful frequency, of being trapped in the dark in what seemed to be a sort of fish tank, filled not with water but some heavy, viscous liquid. To escape from the tank he had to clamber up the side, his fingers and toes squeaking on the glass, and heave himself over the rim and squirm off into the darkness over a smooth, slimed floor.

The snow was falling heavily, coming down in big flabby flakes the size of Communion wafers and lodging in icy clumps around the edges of the windscreen and making the wipers groan against the glass. The frozen mist was thicker now, so that he had to press his face close to the windscreen, squinting and blinking, until his chin was almost resting on the top of the steering wheel.

When he looked at the dashboard clock, he was surprised to see that it was only a little after eleven. Since his arrival the previous day in Ballyglass, time had become a different medium, moving not in a seamless flow, but jerkily, now speeding up, now slowing to an underwater pace. It was as if he had strayed on to another plane, on to another planet, where the familiar, earthbound rules had all been suspended.

He thought of telephoning Hackett and asking to be taken off the case, this case in which he was floundering, and in the slime of which he might drown.

The priest's death had seemed at first just another crime, much like any other, except more violent than most. It had not been long before he realised how mistaken that first impression had been. Everything was upended, everything swayed and wallowed. He was in the tank again, up to his neck, and each time he managed to get himself out and flop on to the floor he was scooped up by invisible hands and tossed back in.

He arrived at last at the Sheaf of Barley. He went into the bar. The place was empty, and had the mysteriously dishevelled air that bars always have at that time of day. He should phone Hackett and ask his advice. Hackett would help him, would bring him to his senses, those senses he felt he was in danger of losing.

The encounter with Rosemary Lawless had shaken him, in a way he didn't quite understand. He had felt, in that cold stone house, and then out on the cold hillside, the touch of something that was new to him, something impalpable that yet was vividly there, like a freezing fog. Was it evil he had encountered, at last? He had never believed in evil as a force in itself – there was no evil, he always insisted, there were only evil deeds. But was he mistaken?

He went up to his room and lay down on the unmade bed, still in his overcoat. Going down that morning for breakfast he had left the window open a crack, to air the room, and now it was so cold he could see his breath, rising above him like billows of thin, quickly moving smoke.

He had slipped into a restless doze when he heard the door opening, and he jerked upright as if he had been pulled by a string. For a second he didn't know where he was – why was there all this white light around him? – but then he turned and saw Peggy in the doorway, looking at him in surprise and seeming about to laugh. She had a stack of folded linen over her arm, and was carrying a bucket and a mop.

'Oh, pardon *me*,' she said in a tone of mock accusation. 'I thought you were gone out.'

He rubbed a hand roughly over his face, grimacing. Then he rolled off the mattress – the bed was uncommonly high – and set his feet unsteadily on the floor. He felt distanced from himself. This, he imagined, must be what it would be like to be drunk.

'I'm sorry,' he said, his voice slurring. 'I did go out, but now I'm back.'

Peggy snorted. 'Well, I can see that for myself!'

She dumped the linen on the bed and put down the mop and the pail. He felt shy and slightly ridiculous in her presence. She had a way of tucking in her chin and looking at him with a teasingly humorous light in her eyes.

'Do you sleep here?' he asked, and went on quickly, 'I mean, have you a room here, that you stay in?'

She pointed a finger towards the ceiling. 'Up there. And I'd hardly call it a room – more a cupboard with a cot in it.' She gave a throaty chuckle. 'You should come up and see it some time. I only stay there when I'm working late. I live over at Otterbridge, with my Ma and Da.'

'So you slept here the night before last?'

'I did.'

'I wonder if you heard anyone going out, late? It would have been long after midnight.'

She shrugged her plump shoulders. 'I never hear anyone or anything – I sleep like the dead. Anyway, who would have been going out in the middle of the night, in this weather?'

'I thought Mr Harbison might have had somewhere he needed to go to.'

Peggy snorted again. 'Him? Most nights he's so far gone in drink he can hardly get up the stairs, and certainly not back down them again. And I'd say we won't be seeing much of him today, either. He's a terrible man for the booze.' She sat down on the bed, with her hands on her knees. 'Were you comfortable last night?'

'What?'

'Is it all right for you, here? Is the bed all right? There's two more rooms that are empty, if you want to look at them.'

'No, no, thank you.' He had retreated to the window, from where he watched her out of the corner of his eye. 'Mrs Reck put a hot-water bottle in the bed for me.'

'No she didn't – I did.'

'Oh, it was you, was it? Well, thank you.'

'Don't mention it.'

Strafford looked out of the window. The snow had stopped again, and an icy miasma hung over the fields. There was no wind. There hadn't been any wind for days, he realised. It was as if the world had come to a gelid standstill.

'I wish I could talk like you,' Peggy said.

He looked at her over his shoulder in surprise. 'How do you mean?'

'I've always wanted to have a nice accent, like yours. I sound like a tinker half the time.'

'But you don't!' he protested. 'You don't at all!'

'Yes I do. You're only being nice.'

'No, I mean it.'

'Oh, go on! You're such a fibber.'

She smiled at him. She had spread her palms on the mattress, and was leaning back a little, with her elbows straight and her shoulders lifted, swinging one foot. He folded his arms and set a shoulder against the window frame.

'What about Mr Harbison,' he asked teasingly, 'do you like his accent? I'm sure he speaks much the way I do, no?'

'I don't know,' she said dismissively, 'I never listen to him. I keep away from him. He's always after me – anything in a skirt.' She paused. 'What happened to the priest – I mean, what *really* happened to him?'

He drew back his head, startled by the sudden change of subject.

'Don't you know?' he asked.

'It said in the paper he fell down the stairs. Did he?'

'I'm not sure that he fell.'

Her eyes widened. 'Did someone push him?'

'We're trying to find out what happened, exactly.'

She nodded, still swinging her foot. 'You don't give much away, do you?'

To this he only smiled.

'What age are you, Peggy?' he asked.

'Twenty-one.'

'You must have lots of boyfriends.'

She made a sour face. 'Oh, sure! They're queueing up.

Anyway, there are no fellas worth a second glance in this hopeless bloody place.' She looked him up and down with her lips pursed. 'Where do you live in Dublin?'

'I have a flat.'

'Yes, but where?'

'Baggot Street. It's over a shop. Very small, just a living room, bedroom, bathroom. It's a bit like a prison cell, I always think.'

She threw back her head and laughed. 'Oh, that's a good one! The detective who lives in jail!' She grew wistful. 'God, I'd love to have a flat in the city. I suppose you're always out in restaurants and pubs, and going to dances, and concerts, and – oh, I don't know – all sorts of things.'

'I'm afraid I'm not much of a dancer, and I've a tin ear when it comes to music.'

'You must have a girlfriend, though.'

'No. I had one.'

'But you haven't now?'

'No. She broke up with me.'

'She must have been mad.'

Her directness made him smile. She said whatever came into her head. He envied her.

'We still see each other, now and then.' He hadn't thought about Marguerite in a long time. He didn't like her name. The moment he admitted it to himself was the moment when he knew there would be no future for him with her. They had gone out together for three years, and had slept together twice. Then one night she arrived unannounced at the flat, pale and trembling, to present him with an ultimatum. Either he would marry her, or it was over. There was a fight. Or at least she had fought, while he perched on the edge of a sofa, twisted around himself like a corkscrew. In the end she threw a wine glass at him and walked out. He hadn't seen her since that night. Why had he lied? Now he heard himself lie again. 'Her name is Sylvia,' he said.

'Oh? Same as Mrs Osborne.'

'Yes, yes it is. Coincidence. I hadn't realised.'

But he had.

They were silent, then she exclaimed, 'Look at me, sitting on a guest's bed! At least it's in the middle of the day. Mind you, if Mrs Reck saw me I'd get my marching orders on the spot.'

Yet she made no attempt to rise, only sat there, looking at him. Her nether lip glistened.

'You have another job here in the town, Mr Reck tells me?' Strafford said.

The atmosphere in the room had thickened noticeably.

'At the Boolavogue Arms. I'm going to give it up. The men that stay there, commercial travellers mostly, they're worse than here, always pawing at me and making smutty remarks.'

She was pretty, he thought, with those red-gold curls, and those freckles, and that generous mouth. If he were to walk over to her now and put his hands on her shoulders and kiss her, she wouldn't resist – quite the opposite, to judge by the look she was giving him. But ah, it would be a mistake, he knew that. He thought of the wine stain on the wall in his flat, beside the fireplace, where Marguerite's glass had struck. He had tried to wash it off, but wine was stubborn stuff, he discovered, and a discernible trace of it remained, shaped like the faded map of a lost continent.

'I'll leave you to your work,' he said, clearing his throat and moving away from the window.

'Where are you off to now?' she asked. 'You've only just come back – I heard your old jalopy of a car.'

'I'm going over to Ballyglass House.'

'That's right,' she said. 'To see Sylvia.'

His eyes skittered away from hers. He was blushing. How did women know so many things?

He brushed past her with a muttered word and hurried from the room. In the corridor he stopped, and through the open doorway he heard the girl sigh, and a moment later there was an ill-tempered clatter as she took up her mop and pail.

Down the stairs he plunged, taking them two at a time. Oh yes, he thought, run away, yet again. Peggy should have thrown the bucket at him, much better than a wine glass.

He was opening the door of the Morris Minor – his jalopy, Peggy was right – when Matty Moran appeared at his shoulder, seemingly out of nowhere.

'Are you going over to the House?' he asked. At least, that was what Strafford thought he had said, for Matty hadn't got his dentures in, and when he spoke his lips made a noise like that of a loose tent flap blowing in a high wind. Now he said something else, of which the only word Strafford could be sure of was 'lift'.

'You need a lift, do you?' Strafford sighed. 'Yes, well, all right, get in.'

Despite the weather, Matty wore no overcoat, and had on only his threadbare pinstriped suit and a collarless shirt. He didn't seem to notice the cold, although his nose was a shade of purplish-red, and there was a blue sheen on the back of his hands.

In the confines of the car, he smelled to Strafford, mysteriously, of soot, the solid kind that gathers on the inside of a chimney.

Matty spoke again. He was talking about the weather, it seemed, for Strafford was sure he had caught the word 'snow'.

'Matty,' he said, 'would you mind putting in your teeth?'

'Righ', righ',' Matty mumbled, and brought out his dentures. He picked off some pieces of fluff that had stuck to them, and fitted them into his mouth, gagging and slurping as he did so.

They went on a mile or two in silence. Matty, it was clear, wasn't accustomed to travelling by motor car. He sat with his back very straight and his palms clamped on his splayed knees, craning forward with his eyes fixed unblinkingly on the road ahead. At every bend he drew his shoulders up and made a sucking sound with his lips, convinced a catastrophe awaited them and it was only a matter of time before it occurred.

Suddenly, he spoke.

'I seen you talking last night to your man Harbison.'

'Yes,' Strafford answered. 'He was looking for someone to get drunk with him, but he chose the wrong man.'

'Why's that?'

'I don't drink. Well, not the way he does.'

'Umm,' Matty said, making a muffled clacking sound with his dentures. 'He had a skinful himself, all right. He'd drink whiskey off a sore leg, that fellow would.'

'Do you see him, ever, at Ballyglass House?'

'Oho, no.' Matty was greatly amused by this. 'The boss barred him from the place, years ago.'

'Colonel Osborne?'

Matty didn't deem this worthy of reply. After all, how many bosses could there be in Ballyglass?

They went another mile, Matty keeping his eyes unwaveringly on the road.

'A right whoremaster, too, that man,' he said.

'Colonel Osborne?' Strafford said, startled.

'No!' Matty returned scornfully. 'Harbison. He was at it again, last night – no, the night before last.'

Strafford had for an instant a clear image of Peggy, sitting on the side of his bed. But she had said she kept away from Harbison, when she could. Had she been lying?

'The roads were very bad, that night, weren't they?'

'They were,' Matty said. 'But when I was on my way home, Harbison passed me by at the crossroads, down along here at Ballysaggart, in that big car of his, going hell for leather.'

'I see,' Strafford said slowly. 'And what time would that have been?'

'I don't know – I've no watch, ever since the one I had broke last year. I was on the bike, when he comes roaring up behind me, flashing his lights and skidding in the snow. Bloody madman, and him full of drink.'

Strafford was frowning at the windscreen. 'About what time would you say that was, approximately? Two o'clock? Three?'

'Around three, I'd imagine. It was awful cold, but it wasn't snowing, and the stars were out.'

'Which direction was he going in?'

'He was headed for the town, by the look of it. He have a lady friend there that he goes to see.'

'Has he?'

'Aye – Maisie Busher. She works in Pierce's, the hardware. She leaves the key at the front door, on a string inside the letter box. Harbison is not the only lad who comes calling on Maisie of a night.'

'And you think that's where he was going, when you saw him?'

'It's where he usually goes when he's in the vicinity, and has a few on him.'

'You don't think he could have been on his way to Bally-glass House?'

Matty turned his head and looked at him. It was the first time he had taken his eyes off the road.

'Didn't I tell you he's barred out there?' he said, in a tone of exasperation. Plainly he believed he was dealing with an idiot.

'All the same—' Strafford let his voice trail away.

They were approaching a crossroads. 'This'll do,' Matty said, 'let me off here.'

Strafford, bringing the car cautiously to a halt on the icy verge, peered up at a snow-clad signpost. 'Is this where he overtook you?'

'That's right. This is Ballysaggart.'

'Did he turn off, to left or right, or did he drive straight on?'

Matty was uncoiling himself, sloth-like, from his seat. 'Straight on, he went, looking neither right nor left. He'll wrap that car of his around a tree one of these nights, so he will.'

He slammed the door behind him and was gone. Strafford

sat motionless for some moments, thinking. The road led not only to the town, but also, beyond it, to Ballyglass House.

When Strafford arrived at the house, Mrs Duffy let him in at the front door. She pointed to a note on the hall table, addressed to him.

'There was a telephone call for you,' she said. 'Colonel Osborne took down the name.'

He picked up the note. *Detective Chief Superintendent Haggard telephoned. He asked if you would call him back. Osborne.*

The telephone, an ancient one, with an earpiece and a horn to speak into, was kept on a little table in an alcove off the hall, behind a curtain of moth-eaten black velvet, as if it were a thing of dubious taste and must be kept discreetly out of sight. Strafford squeezed into the alcove, took up the receiver and wound the metal handle, which made the bell inside the machine tinkle faintly. The operator came on. Strafford hesitated, then said he was sorry, that he had made a mistake. He hung up.

He didn't feel up to dealing with Hackett, just now.

Instead, he went in search of Jenkins.

19

Jenkins, however, was not to be found. He had spoken to Mrs Duffy, so she told Strafford, and had quizzed her about her having cleaned up the blood in the library and on the stairs. Then he had wandered about the house for a while, examining again the room where Father Tom had slept and the spot in the corridor where he had been set upon and stabbed. The housekeeper had followed in his footsteps as he poked about, to keep an eye on him, suspecting, Strafford supposed, that even though he was a policeman, or precisely because of it, he would be inclined towards pilfering. After that he had put on his coat and hat and had left the house, at which point Mrs Duffy had judged her duty done, and had gone down to her room in the basement to get out her sewing box and turn the collar of one of Colonel Osborne's shirts.

Maybe, she ventured, Sergeant Jenkins had brought Sam out for a walk. Sam was the black Labrador. It had taken a shine to the sergeant, she said. Strafford tried to picture Jenkins and the dog tramping through the snow, the dog nosing after rabbits and Jenkins discovering in himself the nature lover he had never known himself to be, until now.

Strafford walked away, laughing to himself.

The house was deserted. Dominic had gone off to an afternoon Christmas party at the home of friends of his in New Ross, Mrs Osborne was resting, and probably comatose –

Doctor Hafner had called while Strafford was at Scallanstown – and Lettie had been dispatched to Sherwood's pharmacy in Enniscorthy to renew a prescription for her stepmother. Colonel Osborne was out at the stables with the local vet. Despite the impression Strafford had got, from the Colonel's airy references to them, that 'the horses' must consist of a couple of dozen thoroughbreds at least, in fact there were only four – two mares and an elderly stallion, along with Father Lawless's gelding.

Father Lawless's gelding, Strafford thought, and made a pained face, recalling the bloodied front of the priest's trousers.

Now he too walked about the house, meeting no one. He heard a stove being riddled, the scullery maid singing, an ancient lavatory flushing. It was an ordinary afternoon in a country house in the south-east of Ireland. This was the life, and these its circumstances, that Strafford was thoroughly familiar with, and yet he felt estranged, an interloper in a foreign world of violence and malefactors, of stab wounds and blood.

He had told Rosemary Lawless he had become a policeman as a way of breaking free from what his upbringing would have made of him. Yet what he had become was an outsider, an observer. Was that freedom? At Ballyglass House, he seemed to himself the ghost of what he might have been. He was out of place, out of time, the very model of a man cut adrift.

He went to the alcove behind the curtain and again wound the handle of the telephone, and again was spoken to by the operator, a weary-sounding woman suffering from a heavy head cold. He gave her the number of Pearse Street Garda

Station, and after a long wait was put through to Detective Chief Superintendent Hackett. Who was not in the best of humour.

'It's about time,' Hackett grumbled. 'I called two hours ago – where were you?'

'I went to see the priest's sister.'

'And? What did she have to say?'

'Not much. Did you know her father was JJ Lawless?'

'Are you telling me *you* didn't know?'

'Who was there to tell me? Getting information out of these people is like – I don't know what it's like, but it's very difficult.'

'I thought you'd know your way around down there. It's why I put you on the case.'

To this, Strafford said nothing. He was slowly learning to negotiate the treacherous waters of his boss's moods. Hackett was a decent man doing a difficult job, and Strafford respect-ed him, was fond of him, even, in a muted sort of way. It wasn't long since Hackett had been promoted to Detective Chief Superintendent – the inflated title embarrassed him – and the last thing he needed, in the early days of his new posi-tion, was to have to deal with a murder, especially the murder of a priest. Now he asked, 'Is that all she had to tell you, the sister, that her father was JJ Lawless?'

'Yes. She was in distress, as you can imagine. It was clear that relations between her brother and his father were less than warm.'

'Is that so? Well now, isn't that a surprise. Do you know anything at all about the bold JJ Lawless? Lawless – the name suited him, even if he did make a fortune out of the law. In the Civil War he used to shoot people in the face. It was his trademark.'

'I didn't know that,' Strafford said.

'And drove his wife into the asylum. Oh, a hard man, the same JJ.'

'The sister said he was tormented.'

'Who, JJ, or the priest?'

'She meant her brother.'

'It would be remarkable if he wasn't tormented, given what he came from. Anyway, the clergy are all half-cracked – only don't say I said so. Speaking of which, that's what I was calling earlier to say to you. You've been summoned to an audience with His Grace the Archbishop.'

'The Archbishop?'

'Doctor McQuaid himself – who else? He has a place down there, outside Gorey, on the coast. It's his summer retreat, as they say. His' – a chuckle – 'Castel Gandolfo. He's there now, though God knows it must be a chilly spot, in this weather. Maybe he's on retreat, pondering the state of his soul. Anyway, you're to go over and see him.'

'Why?'

'How do I know?'

Strafford sighed. He felt as if he had been summoned to an interview with the Grand Inquisitor Torquemada.

'I saw the story in the *Irish Press*,' he said.

'So did I. What about it?'

'I suppose the press release came from the palace?'

'We issued one too, but it was ignored. Church business is none of our business.'

'Even when it's a murder?'

192

Hackett was silent.

'The paper had it that he fell down the stairs,' Strafford said.

'And?'

'And he didn't fall down any stairs.'

'That's a technicality.'

'No, it's not.'

'Reporters get things wrong,' Hackett said wearily. 'Anyway, what does it matter how he got down the stairs? They could have said he flew down and it would be all the same.'

'The man was murdered.'

'Don't shout at me, Inspector.'

'I'm not shouting!'

Strafford shifted uncomfortably in the cramped space of the alcove. The receiver was hot in his hand, and seemed to breathe, like a mouth, into his ear. He was unnerved by telephones, by the humid sense of intimacy they offered. Even the most bland and guileless remark sounded like an insinuation over the phone.

'Have the results of the post-mortem come in yet?' he asked.

'There's nothing in them we didn't know already,' Hackett replied. 'The man died from shock and loss of blood – there's science for you, Harry Hall and his henchmen at their most subtle. It was "a frenzied attack", as the newshounds would say.'

'Yes, if they knew about it,' Strafford said. Hackett chose to pretend not to have heard.

'By the way,' the Chief said, clearing his throat, 'there was another stain on the priest's trousers, apart from blood.'

'Oh? What was it?'

'Semen.'

Strafford tapped his nails against his teeth.

'Just semen?' he asked. 'Nothing else? No traces of female fluids?'

'No.'

They were silent for some moments, then Hackett spoke again.

'Go and see McQuaid,' he said. 'It'll be the usual guff: discretion vital – preserve the good name of the Church – save the reputation of the son of one of Mother Ireland's finest heroes. Tell him what he wants to hear. Have you encountered him before?'

'No.'

'Then watch out. He's smooth, and he's not stupid – far from it, whatever you might think. Oh, and listen, I wouldn't tell him about, you know, the stain on the priest's trousers.'

'Tell me, Chief, am I supposed to solve this case, or am I not?'

Hackett cleared his throat, making an angry rumbling that in the receiver sounded like muffled thunder. 'What do you think I sent you there for?'

'It strikes me everyone would be happier if the thing was left alone. Is that what the Archbishop is going to tell me, in his smooth, unstupid way?'

'Just go and talk to him, will you, Detective Inspector? Will you do that? I'd be grateful, really, I would.'

Hackett wasn't good at sarcasm.

'Right, sir,' Strafford said, sarcastic in his turn. 'I'll get up there tomorrow.'

'Today, lad. Today.'

'All right. I'll leave now.'

He hung up. His ear throbbed from the pressure of the receiver against it, and the background hubbub on the line had left a buzzing sensation in his head. He pushed the curtain aside – the odour of dusty velvet was another echo out of his childhood – and stepped into the hall. For a moment he felt dizzy. The house around him seemed suddenly a maze from which, whatever way he turned, he would find no way out.

Yes, he should have been a lawyer. He wasn't cut out to be a policeman. Too late now to change. He felt at once ridiculously young, a sort of monstrous child, and at the same time hopelessly old.

The Dublin road, when he reached it, was almost clear of snow, and the going was easier than on the side roads he had been travelling since he had arrived in Ballyglass. He turned the heater to its highest. When he tried to make the wireless work, he got only a jumble of static, worse than the noise on the telephone line.

There was very little traffic. Solitary crows, blacker than black, flapped across fields of unblemished snow. A herd of piebald cows stood in a muddy corner under the scant shelter of bare trees.

A car had skidded on the bridge at Enniscorthy and was slewed across both lanes of the road, and he had to wait while it was being moved. He left the engine running. There must have been a crack in the exhaust pipe, for the car soon filled with fumes, and eventually he was forced to switch off the ignition. In the ticking silence he watched the river flowing under the low arches of the bridge in a roiling, dark-silver surge. He tried to identify repeating patterns in the way it flowed, but couldn't. Further on, where the river had room to widen, the water slowed down, and whirlpools formed on the brimming surface, formed, and then swallowed themselves. The snow, where it stopped at the edges of the banks on both sides, was folded under like a thick woollen blanket.

He thought back over the exchanges with Hackett on the phone. Did the Chief really want this case to be solved? Or had he been sent to Ballyglass merely to go through the motions of investigating the priest's murder, reach no conclusion, and return to Dublin after a few fruitless days, write up his report and file it safely away on a high shelf, where it would rest undisturbed and be forgotten, the pages yellowing and the cardboard folder curling at its corners? Reality wasn't as it was in the movies, he reminded himself, and the majority of murderers were never caught. Maybe he should just wrap the thing up and go home. Rosemary Lawless was the only one truly affected by the priest's death. Even her sense of grievance would dissipate in time.

But no – there was such a thing as duty, even if carrying it out was futile. He had been assigned to a case, and he was bound to prosecute it until he reached a resolution, or failed. Harry Hall and his henchmen, as Hackett had called them, might not care a fig who the killer was, and Hackett might fear the consequences of the mystery being solved. But he wasn't Hackett, and certainly he wasn't Harry Hall. Forces were ranged against him. The Archbishop would wag a finger at him before pressing it to his lips to counsel discretion, but Strafford was impatient of being discreet. A man had been attacked, brutally – it was only in the politer detective novels that the victim ended up on the library floor without first having passed, albeit briefly, through a living hell of agony and anguish – and had died. He deserved more than a few mendacious paragraphs in a newspaper.

The stalled car had been towed away from the bridge, and the lorries in front of him began to move, trumpeting like elephants and snorting blue-grey clouds of exhaust smoke. He started the engine and jiggled the gearstick, engaged the clutch, and drove on. The windscreen was misted on the inside, and he had to keep rubbing at it with the side of his hand.

He had no illusions about the task facing him. Hackett had sent the wrong man, perhaps deliberately. Strafford wasn't good at solving puzzles, everyone knew that. His mind wasn't made that way. He was what the Chief called a trudger. Probably he shouldn't have been promoted, but left as a Garda on the beat. His people weren't imaginative, and neither was he. The priest's death might be an inconvenience to everyone, to the Osbornes, to Hackett, no doubt to the Archbishop, too. Was he the only one who took it as an affront? He couldn't grieve for the dead man, as Rosemary Lawless was grieving, but it wasn't grief that was required of him. He had lost faith long ago in the notion of justice, but might he not make kind of a reckoning? That wasn't too much to ask, surely.

A mile outside Ballycanew he ran into a patch of ice and felt the tyres lose hold, and for a second or two the car seemed to leave the road and take to the air as it glided gracefully to the left and mounted the grass verge, and the engine coughed and died. Strafford let his hands fall from the wheel and swore. He would have to flag down a passing motorist, go back to the town he had just come through and call for assistance. He swore again, more violently this time. He didn't often swear. It was a matter of upbringing. He had never heard his father utter an oath or use a four-letter word. There were other, subtler ways of cursing the world and one's fate in it.

He had expected to have to get out and use the dreaded starter handle. However, the car was a sturdy and resourceful little beast – he had nicknamed it Warthog – and he had only to turn the ignition key once for the engine to cough itself back to life, with a shake and a shudder. He drove on.

The Archbishop's house stood at the end of a zigzag of ever narrower laneways that culminated in a muddy track with a grassy ridge along the middle of it. Strafford got lost repeatedly, and had to stop a number of times to ask for directions, once at a pub and twice at a farmhouse – the same farmhouse on both occasions, as it turned out, to the rich amusement of the farmer and the farmer's wife. The house, when at last he got there, presented to him a forbidding frontage. It stood on a bleak promontory, facing the sea. It was a low-built pebble-dashed bungalow with blank windows and a narrow front door that made Strafford think of a coffin. He had to get out to open a black iron gate that gave on to a short gravelled drive. To his left, a flock of sheep was scattered across a snowy slope. On the other side, down a flight of rough stone steps, a beach curved away northwards, soon dissolving into a ghostly sea mist.

In a shed beside the house was parked an enormous black Citroën – this time, Strafford thought of a hearse. The car's windows had fringed cloth blinds that could be pulled down to ensure archiepiscopal privacy. The windscreen glass was so thick Strafford wondered if it might be bulletproof. Perhaps the thought was not so far-fetched, Strafford reflected, given the recent, sacrilegious slaughter of Father Tom Lawless.

The door was opened by a small elderly man of vaguely ecclesiastical aspect, with watery eyes and a cluster of broken veins high up on each cheekbone. He wore a long black tubular apron, the string of it wound twice around and tied in a double knot at the front. Strafford gave his name, and the man nodded and said nothing, only took his coat and hat and gestured for him to enter. He led the way down a dim passageway, at the end of which he opened another door on to a nondescript room in which a coal fire was burning. Two identical, buttoned leather armchairs stood one on each side of the fireplace, and between them was set a small square table with carved and curlicued legs. Above the mantelpiece there hung a framed reproduction of a painting, in fleshy pinks and creamy whites, of an impossibly comely, soft-bearded Jesus, tilting his head languidly and pointing two stiff fingers at his bared and profusely bleeding, flame-fringed heart. The Saviour's expression was both mournful and accusatory, as if to say, *See what you did to me?* His father called this portrait, prints of which were on display in every other parlour in Catholic Ireland, The Bearded Lady.

'His Grace will be with you shortly,' the little man said, and went out, shutting the door behind him noiselessly.

Strafford looked out at the tin-coloured sea and a sky of clouds like trodden-on chalk dust. Gulls wheeled and swooped out there, vague chevron shapes, like wisps of cloud come loose.

The door opened behind him and the Archbishop came in. He was chafing his hands, and for a moment Strafford was reminded, incongruously, of his first sight of Sylvia Osborne, when she entered the kitchen at Ballyglass House, doing the same thing with her hands.

'Good day to you, Inspector. It was good of you to come, in such inclement weather.'

'Good afternoon, Your Grace.'

The Archbishop was a spare, trim person with concave cheeks and ears that stuck out. He had thin lips and a fat, fleshy nose too big for his face. His eyes were small and keenly alert, the lids somewhat swollen and pulpy. He wore a full-length cassock, with a broad silk sash wrapped around his midriff, and, on the crown of his long narrow head, a crimson silk skullcap. Another player steps on stage, Strafford thought grimly, though this one would know his part to the last aside. The man extended his archbishop's ring for Strafford to kiss, but seeing Strafford had no intention of doing so he altered the angle of his hand and used it to point to one of the armchairs, as if that was what he had meant in the first place. Smooth, that had been Hackett's word for him. Oh, very smooth, and smoothly sinister.

'Sit down, Inspector, please. May I offer you a glass of sherry?' He touched the bell push beside the fireplace. 'Such harsh weather! I came down only for a little break, and I'm sorry now that I did. This is a summer residence, and there's no keeping out the draughts and the freezing gales that come in off the sea.' They seated themselves, facing each other. Strafford noted the toes of the Archbishop's crimson velvet slippers, peeping out from under the hem of his cassock.

'Yes,' Strafford said, 'it's certainly cold.'

The Archbishop regarded him with a wintry smile. 'Ah well, we mustn't complain. The weather is another of the trials it pleases God to impose upon us, for the good of our souls.'

Strafford was uncomfortably aware of those sharp little eyes scanning him intently.

'I'm sorry it took me so long to get here,' he said. 'A car was stuck on the bridge at Enniscorthy, and then I skidded off the road at Ballycanew.'

'Oh, goodness me! Are you all right? You weren't hurt? Was your car damaged?'

'No. I got it going again easily enough.'

'I'm glad to hear it.'

There was a tap at the door and the little man in the apron appeared again. The Archbishop addressed him as Luke, and asked him to bring sherry – 'the Oloroso, please.' The little man nodded, and withdrew. 'I don't know what I'd do without poor Luke,' the prelate said. 'He had a bad time in the war – the first war, that is. Shell shock. He has been with me for longer than either he or I can recall.'

There followed a silence. The Archbishop turned his head aside and looked into the heart of the fire, where a lump of burning coal was making a sharp whistling sound. From outside could be heard faintly the mewling of the gulls, and, fainter still, the soft plashing and hissing of waves on the shoreline.

'Such a terrible business, down at Ballyglass.' The Archbishop put his hands together, with his thumbs linked. His hands were as bloodless as his face.

'Yes, terrible,' Strafford said.

Luke the servant came back with the sherry bottle and two tiny, ornate glasses on a wooden tray covered with a lace doily. There was also a plate of Marietta biscuits.

'Will you be wanting anything else, Your Grace?'

'No, not for now, Luke, thank you.'

'Then I'll go into Gorey. We're in need of eggs.'

'Of course, Luke, of course' – again that cold, dry smile, for Strafford's benefit – 'we can't afford to be without eggs!'

Luke nodded, and again withdrew, again closing the door behind him carefully and without a sound. He might have been shutting the door of a vault.

The Archbishop poured from the bottle and passed a glass to Strafford. They drank. The sherry was dark and dry, though somewhat treacly in texture. Strafford thought it must be good, though he was no expert.

'These little glasses,' the prelate said, holding his up at eye level, 'were a gift from Cardinal Mindszenty, all the way from Budapest. They came by diplomatic bag – you know, of course, that the Cardinal is living at the American embassy in Budapest, where he was granted asylum after the Soviet suppression of the Hungarian uprising. He's likely to be there for some time to come, if the newspaper reports of the state of things over there are to be believed, and I have it on good authority that they are. The poor man – another of the Church's persecuted warriors for peace.'

Strafford knew about the warlike Mindszenty and his opposition to the Communists, about his imprisonment and torture. He also knew of the accusations against him as a Nazi enthusiast and an implacable anti-Semite. He supposed the mention of his name was intended as a test of some sort, but if it was,

Strafford declined to meet it, and said nothing. He took another sip of his sherry.

He heard from outside the growl of the Citroën's engine starting up.

'Your Grace, may I ask why you sent for me?'

The Archbishop held up both hands in feigned shock.

'Oh, but I didn't "send for you"! I mentioned to the Garda Commissioner – Commissioner Phelan, do you know him? A good man, a sound man – I mentioned to him that it might be well for you and I to have a chat.' He turned his eyes to the fire again. 'Poor Father Lawless.'

'Are you aware of the details of how Father Lawless died?'

'Indeed I am. Commissioner Phelan telephoned me today, after he had the results of the post-mortem. A dreadful sin has been committed. Dreadful. Father Tom, God rest his soul, was one of the most popular priests in the diocese, and in the whole county – indeed, it's not too much to say that he was known throughout the length and breadth of the country. His death is a great tragedy. Will you have another drop of sherry? The fire is not too hot for you? We could push our chairs back a little, perhaps. I feel the cold increasingly, these days.'

'Your Grace, there was a story in the *Irish Press* today—'

'And the *Independent*, too. Though not, I notice' – he pursed his lips – 'in the *Irish Times*. I imagine the *Times* would be your paper? I understand you're one of our separated brethren.'

'My people are Protestant, yes, if that's what you mean,' Strafford said. 'I only saw the *Irish Press*.'

'The report in the *Independent* was much the same.'

'No doubt, and no doubt equally – shall we say incomplete, as you'll know, from your talk with Commissioner Phelan.'

The Archbishop set down his glass.

'I imagine,' he said, 'that would be due to the fact that the post-mortem results only came out this morning, while the papers would have been printed last night.' He leaned back in his chair, set his elbows on the arms of it again and joined his fingers together at their tips. 'People so often forget,' he said, gazing up at the ceiling, 'that what's in the papers is always yesterday's news. The wireless, of course, is supposed to be much more up to the minute, but I notice often the broadcast news is little different to what appears in the papers. Indeed' – he leaned forward with a conspiratorial smile – 'I suspect the people in Radio Éireann themselves depend on the daily papers for their news more often than they'd care to admit. Or am I being bad-minded? What do you think?'

Strafford too put down his glass, with half the sherry undrunk. He could feel the stuff sticking to his teeth.

'Doctor McQuaid,' he said, 'I'll be submitting my report on Father Lawless's death in the next day or two. I've already conveyed my preliminary findings, by way of a colleague, to my superior in Dublin. You say the post-mortem results came out this morning. They didn't.'

'No?' the Archbishop murmured. 'But I thought—'

'That's to say,' Strafford went on stolidly, 'a highly selective version of them was released to the public. Father Lawless didn't die from a fall. You know how he did die, if Commissioner Phelan gave you a full account of the pathologist's findings. When the papers get hold of the real facts of the case—'

'"When"?' the Archbishop said softly. He was gazing at his steepled fingers, with a deliberately preoccupied expression. 'I like to think there's only one thing I have in common with the gentlemen of the press, and that's curiosity. There's a "story" here, as they'd say, a tragic story but also a sensational one, and they will go after it, you can be assured of that. They wouldn't be doing their job if they didn't. But will they find it, Inspector, their sensational story? Will they find it, do you think?'

There was almost a merry light in the prelate's eye. It was the eye of a cat toying with a still living mouse.

'What I think,' Strafford said, 'is that some things are too big to be suppressed.'

The Archbishop leaned forward, picked up the metal tongs and lifted two nuggets of coal from the scuttle, and set them amid the flames of the fire.

'"Suppressed"?' he said. 'Now, that is a word that troubles me, I have to say.'

'Then may I ask for a better one, Your Grace?'

'"Withheld", I think, might be more accurate, and certainly more advisable, in this context. Would you not agree?'

Strafford made to speak again, but the Archbishop, smiling, held up a hand to silence him and, still smiling, rose from his chair and paced to the window, where he stood, with his hands clasped at his back, looking out at the bleak cold prospect of metal-grey sea and greyer sky.

'Ours is a young nation, Inspector Stafford—'

'Strafford.'

'Forgive me – Strafford. A young nation, as I say, with much of our original innocence intact – I do believe there is original innocence, as well as original sin. There was a time before the apple of knowledge was eaten.' He glanced back at Strafford over his shoulder and caught his deprecating look.

'Oh, I know, I know, you feel the people have been deliberately kept in ignorance. We might have grown to maturity, had we been allowed. But centuries of English oppression kept us back, kept us down – kept us, as I say, innocent. I hope I don't offend you by speaking of these things? Your people—'

'"My" people? With respect, Your Grace, I'm as Irish as you are.'

'Of course, of course.' The Archbishop turned from the window to face his guest. 'But I remember that fine Anglo-Irish novelist, Elizabeth Bowen, saying to me once – it was at a party given by the British ambassador, one summer afternoon in the back garden of the embassy in Merrion Square – I remember her saying to me that she felt her true place was a point smack in the middle of the Irish Sea, halfway between England and Ireland. I thought it a very candid and telling admission. It must be strange, to be stranded like that. Although of course' – a faint chuckle – 'one couldn't, strictly speaking, be situated in the middle of the sea.' He made a diving gesture with his left hand. 'One would sink, Inspector. One would sink.'

He paced back slowly to the hearth, with his head down, looking at the tips of his slippers where they appeared alternately, like crimson tongue-tips, from under the hem of his cassock. He stopped before the fire and held out his hands, which were as pale as cuttlefish bones, to the muttering flames.

'I have the greatest respect for your Church and your creed, which has produced so many fine minds – and fine sensibilities, if I may put it that way. But then' – here he gave a little sigh – 'Protestantism is not so much a religion as a reaction against a religion, isn't that so?' He smiled at Strafford's stony stare. 'Again, please, do not be offended. I'm merely stating a fact. What was the Reformation, after all, but a protest against the traditions of the Church of Rome? – a protest not unjustified, I regret to say, in the days of Luther and his followers. It's not for nothing that the word itself, *protest*, is still enshrined in the very name of your faith.'

'I was brought up as a member of the Church of Ireland,' Strafford said.

'Ah, yes. But then, as myriad-minded Shakespeare says, what's in a name?'

The Archbishop, still standing in front of the fire, leaned a hand on the mantelpiece and bowed his head towards the flames, which gave a lurid tinge to his thin, pallid face.

Strafford made to rise from his chair, ostentatiously consulting his watch. 'Your Grace, much as I find this conversation stimulating, I really can't spare the time to engage in a theological discussion—'

'Yes yes yes, forgive me! I know how busy you must be. But Father Lawless's death is a great shock to us all, and it will be a particularly heavy blow to his parishioners, and to Catholics in general.'

'To *people* in general, Catholic or Protestant, wouldn't you say?'

'Of course, yes, that's what I meant – to all of us.'

The two men were on their feet now, facing each other. Strafford looked to the window and saw that it had begun to snow again. He thought of the state of the roads. He wouldn't care to be trapped here, in this cold place, with this cold man. He made a show again of looking at his watch.

'Yes, you must be on your way, I understand,' the Archbishop said, lifting a placating hand. 'But before you go, a last few words, while I have the opportunity.' He looked down. 'As I've said, we retain, as a nation, a remarkable – some would say a *deplorable* – degree of innocence. In many ways we are like children, with a child's simplicity and charm, as well as, I confess, the child's capacity for wickedness. It will take us a long time to achieve full maturity – growing up, after all, is a slow and often painful process, and one that shouldn't be hurried. The duty falls to some of us to calculate what is best for the congregation – forgive me, for the *population*, at large. As Mr Eliot says – I'm sure you're acquainted with his work? – "humankind cannot bear very much reality". The social contract is a fragile document. Do you take my point, at all?'

Strafford shrugged. 'Yes, I suppose I do. But all the same, the truth—'

'Ah, the truth' – the Archbishop lifted both his hands before him, the palms turned outwards, as if to ward something off – 'such a difficult concept. There's not much to be said in favour of Pontius Pilate, yet one feels a flicker of empathy for him when he asked, in his helplessness, What is the truth?'

'In this case, Doctor McQuaid,' Strafford said, 'the question is easily answered. Father Lawless didn't fall downstairs and break his neck. He was stabbed in the neck, and after that—'

The Archbishop shook his head, letting his eyelids close lightly for a second. 'Enough, enough,' he breathed. 'I know, from Commissioner Phelan, what came next.' He paused a moment, then moved a step closer to Strafford. 'Do you think, Inspector, do you really think, that any good, any good at all, would result from the public disclosure of such lurid, such terrible, facts?'

'Your Grace, as Shakespeare said, murder will out, and so will the truth, however terrible.'

The Archbishop smiled. 'Ah, yes. Life, though, is not a play, but all too real. And some aspects of reality are better – what was the word I used earlier? – are better withheld. I see you don't agree. Well, you must do as you think best. You have your duties' – here, a hard glint came into his eyes – 'as I have mine.'

Strafford was preparing to depart. He wondered where his coat and hat were to be found – Luke the Indispensable hadn't returned from his shopping trip. The Archbishop put a hand lightly on his shoulder, and they moved together to the door.

'Thank you for coming so far, Inspector, in such inclement conditions. I wanted to meet you in person. Your Commissioner speaks very highly of you. He believes you have a bright future before you, in your work as a detective.'

'I'm glad to hear it,' Strafford said drily. 'He's not a man given to lavish praise.'

'Yes,' the Archbishop said abstractedly, 'yes indeed. I often think how hard it must be for a young man to make his way in the world of today. So many frightful things have happened in our time, so many wars and revolutions, so much death and destruction.' They stepped into the hall. 'Once again, thank you for coming.' At the front door, the prelate smiled, thinly, palely, his little dark eyes glittering. 'Be assured, Inspector,' he said softly, with his sharp, cold little smile, 'I shall be watching your progress with the keenest interest.' Strafford's coat and hat were hanging on hooks by the front door. 'And here are your things. Such a light coat, for such a cold day!'

When the door was opened a gust of icy air swept in from outside, bringing with it a flurry of snowflakes, one of which settled, a brief, icy benediction, on Strafford's forehead.

He was halfway to the car when the Archbishop called out his name – 'Inspector Strafford, a moment' – and he turned and trudged back along the path, treading in his own reversed footsteps.

'Chaucer,' the prelate said.

Strafford was baffled. 'I beg your—?'

'"Murder will out." It's Chaucer, not Shakespeare. It appears in the Priest's Tale, in fact. "Murder will out, that see we day by day."'

'Ah. Right. Thank you, I'll remember – Chaucer, not Shakespeare.'

The Archbishop smiled again, and sketched a quick little blessing with two upraised fingers. Strafford was reminded of the portrait of Christ showing off his Sacred Heart.

He drove off, and at the gate glanced back to see the Archbishop standing in the doorway still, a hand lifted in farewell. There was snow on the front of his cassock. He didn't seem to notice.

20

The drive back to Ballyglass was not as hair-raising as he had feared it would be. After he had gone a mile or two the snow suddenly cleared, and he was able to switch off the windscreen wipers. At Enniscorthy he manoeuvred the car over the bridge with care. On the other side he met the big Citroën, with Luke perched elf-like behind the wheel.

He arrived at Ballyglass House and was left standing outside the front door for a full five minutes, banging the knocker repeatedly and getting chilled to the bone, before Mrs Duffy arrived at last to let him in. She said she was sorry not to have come sooner, but she had been downstairs, washing up after lunch. At the mention of lunch, he remembered that he hadn't eaten since breakfast time. Mrs Duffy said she could 'throw on' an omelette for him.

He asked if Jenkins had returned, and was told he hadn't. He turned back and looked at the snowy landscape all round. Then he went and squeezed himself once more into the alcove behind the velvet curtain, his elbows pressed to his ribs, and called Pearse Street, and asked again for Chief Superintendent Hackett.

'So, how did you get on, yourself and His Eminence?' Hackett asked with a chuckle.

Strafford could hear him lighting a cigarette, in that way he did when he was on the phone, putting the matchbox on the desk, trapping it under his elbow and manoeuvring a match out of it and scraping it slowly and carefully along the strip of sandpaper. It was one of his little displays of flamboyance.

'He gave me a lecture on religion, and saw me off with a warning,' Strafford said.

'Oh, aye? What sort of a warning?'

'He said he'd be keeping an eye on me. He made a point of letting me know it.'

'He's a sore man, is Doctor McQuaid. There's no love in that fellow.'

'He wants the thing hushed up, of course.'

'And what did you say?'

'As little as possible.'

There was a pause.

'He's a dangerous man, Strafford, and not to be crossed. You don't need me to tell you that.'

'Do you think he can keep the lid on something as big as this?'

'He's done it before.'

'Oh, yes? Care to elaborate?'

'No. But I'm telling you, watch out. Comrade Stalin's right-hand man Mr Beria will never be dead while His Grace is alive.'

Strafford scowled. He itched to know when and how McQuaid had 'done it before', in another case – or cases? – as large and potentially scandalous as this one. He would have to ask Quirke about it, when Quirke came back from his honeymoon. Quirke knew where many a body was buried, legitimately and otherwise. He was the State Pathologist, after all.

'Jenkins has gone missing,' he said. 'Have you heard from him?'

'What do you mean, gone missing?'

'I sent him over here, to Ballyglass House, to question the family again. He arrived, talked to the housekeeper, then went out, according to her, and hasn't been seen since.'

'Where would he have gone to? Is it now snowing down there, like it is here?'

'Yes, Chief. Snow is general all over Ireland.'

'Is it?'

'It's a quotation – never mind.'

Strafford heard his superior breathing down the line. Hackett valued Strafford, but also considered him too clever by far.

'So how long has he been gone?'

'Three or four hours,' Strafford replied.

'Is that all? For Christ's sake, he's probably having a quiet pint and a ham sandwich somewhere. Three or four hours, indeed.'

'It's not like him, Chief, to go off like that and not leave word for me.'

Hackett was becoming exasperated. He was exasperated much of the time, nowadays. Promotion, it was clear, didn't suit him. He had liked being a working detective. Now he spent most of his time stuck at his desk, dealing with paperwork.

'I'll wait a while longer,' Strafford went on, 'and then I'll call the local fellow, Radford, and see if he can help.'

'Radford? Who's he?'

'A sergeant at the barracks here, in the town. Haven't seen him yet. He's supposed to be down with a dose of 'flu. I believe he's a drinker.'

'Well, isn't this a fine situation?' Hackett said. 'Your man is gone missing, and the local bobby is down with the DTs. Good luck.' And he hung up.

Mrs Duffy had said she would let him know when his omelette was ready. While he waited, he wandered into the drawing room and stood at the window, where yesterday – could it have been only yesterday? – he had stood with Lettie and watched the snow falling on the lawn and the fields beyond. The hill in the distance was barely visible today, a ghostly, floating form, like Mount Fuji in the background of a Japanese print.

A robin landed on a twig outside the window and perched there, fluffing up its feathers. Strafford was at once convinced that it was the same one he had seen – when? When had he seen it before? Yesterday? Today? Time was playing tricks on him again. Could it be the same bird, following him?

The thought of his mother came back to him, his mother on her makeshift deathbed, watching the birds on the lawn, as the light faded, the light of day and her light, too. Why was she so much on his mind? He had hardly given her a thought in recent years, but now, whenever he saw a bird in the snow, her ghost was there. Who was it had said this house was haunted? Certainly it seemed to be, for him.

He thought back over his interview with the Archbishop. He had been delivered a warning, no doubt of that – there had been no mistaking the undertone of menace in the prelate's calculated politeness, his subtle insinuations. They liked to show off their power, these unctuous churchmen. He thought of the Reverend Moffatt, the vicar at Roslea when he was a boy. Poor Moffatt, with his silver hair and pink scalp, his pale incompetent hands, his bubblingly apologetic manner. John Charles McQuaid would gobble up the likes of the Reverend Moffatt as a snack before compline.

Strafford had never met the Commissioner, Jack Phelan. Had Phelan really spoken highly of him, as the Archbishop had claimed? He suspected Phelan had never heard of him, before now. Anyway, whatever Phelan thought of him, it would take only a quiet word from His Grace John Charles to have him banished to some town in the windy west of Ireland, where he would punch in his days seizing illicit poitín stills, and his evenings stopping schoolboys with no lights on their bikes.

He had been hearing the sound since he had entered the room, but only now paid attention to it, and realised what it was. Someone, a woman, he thought, outside the room but nearby, was weeping, quietly, steadily. The sound was coming from behind a door in the corner of the room. At his knock, it stopped abruptly, and there was silence. He tapped on the door again, but still there was no response. He turned the doorknob.

In her chocolate-box parlour, Sylvia Osborne was reclining on the yellow sofa, with her legs drawn up and covered by a blanket. Her pink-rimmed eyes made the rest of her face appear even paler than it was. Her cheeks were smeared with tears and her mouth was swollen in a way that made her look ugly. She was clutching a sodden handkerchief, which now she quickly hid behind her back. She wore a white blouse and a pale-blue cardigan.

'It's you,' she said, and seemed relieved despite her sorrow. 'I thought you were Geoffrey.'

Strafford stepped into the little room. It seemed less gaudy today than it had yesterday. A weeping woman always lends an air of the serious, he supposed.

'Mrs Osborne, what's the matter?' he said, moving towards her. 'What's happened?'

She said nothing at first, but then her face crumpled and she began to cry again. 'It's all my fault!' she wailed, in a choking voice. 'It's all, all my fault!'

He sat down at the far end of the sofa. 'I don't understand,' he said. 'What do you mean, it's all your fault? Are you talking about Father Lawless's death?'

She hid her face in the crook of her elbow, where the sleeve of her cardigan muffled her sobs. She said something that he couldn't make out. He touched her on the wrist, but she wrenched herself away.

'Tell me what's wrong,' he said softly, as to a child. He pictured himself taking her in his arms, and her resting her head on his shoulder and sighing, her breath warm against his cheek. Briefly he marvelled at himself. Such mad imaginings!

'I'm sorry,' Mrs Osborne mumbled. She had stopped crying.

From the hallway came the sound of Mrs Duffy's voice, calling Strafford's name. His omelette was ready. He had forgotten about it.

'It was because of me he came here,' Sylvia Osborne said, between soft hiccups. 'It was because of me he kept coming. I should have put a stop to it. I should have told him to stay away.'

'Father Lawless, you mean? Father Tom?'

He tried not to seem surprised. Good God, had they been

having an affair, she and the priest? Such a possibility had not occurred to him – how would it? Priests did not have love affairs with ladies from the Protestant landed gentry. It was unthinkable. And yet here he was, thinking it.

'You mean,' he said – 'you mean he was fond of you? That you and he were—?'

She shook her head quickly, frowning, as if at something absurd. Yet what else could she have meant, by saying she should have made him stay away?

'Did he say anything to you?' he asked. 'Did he give you the impression that he was—?'

'He talked to me one day. I think he'd been drinking already, and I gave him some sherry, which I shouldn't have, and he drank that, glass after glass of it, I don't think he was even aware. He was sitting there, just where you are now. His eyes were so strange, as if he was seeing something – I don't know. Something awful.'

'And what did he say?'

'He talked about how difficult it was, being a priest. He said I wouldn't be able to understand, of course, but that priests had feelings like anybody else. He said he didn't know what to do. He looked – he looked so strange, so agitated. He frightened me. I couldn't think what to do, what to say.'

She brought out the wadded handkerchief and blew her nose into it. Her nostrils were a delicate, almost translucent pink along their edges.

'Had he ever talked like this to you before?'

'No, never.'

'And had you any idea how he felt about you? I mean, had you known before that day?'

'Of course not,' she said, wearily dismissive. 'It was a complete surprise to me – and a shock. I thought priests were supposed to be – well, celibate. You know how the RCs go on about – well, sex, and all that. And I was afraid Geoffrey would barge in, the way he does, and what would I have said?'

They were silent, busy with their thoughts. Strafford felt in some manner delicately captured and held fast, as if a net had been thrown over him, a net of steel yet so fine as to be invisible.

'When did this happen?' he asked. 'I mean, when did he come here and say these things?'

'I don't know – not long ago. Weeks. He finished the sherry – he'd drunk a whole bottle, nearly – and went off. He drove back to Scallanstown. I was surprised he didn't have an accident. I thought – I thought he might kill himself, that he might drive deliberately into a tree or something, he seemed so desperate. Then the next time he came it was as if nothing had happened. He was his usual self, joking with Mrs Duffy – by the way, wasn't that her calling you, just now? – and talking to Geoffrey about horses, which is all they ever seemed to talk about, horses, and hunting, and those bloody, *bloody* hounds. I didn't know what to think. I should have said something. I should have taken him aside and told him not to come to the house again, after the way he'd behaved, babbling on at me and drinking all that sherry. But I didn't say anything. And now he's dead.'

She began to cry again, quietly this time, almost absent-mindedly, then stopped, dabbing the handkerchief to her nose and delicately sniffing. The rims of her nostrils were rawly inflamed by now. Strafford thought of a pet rabbit he had kept when a boy. One night the fox got it. In the morning all that was left were patches of dried blood, rather a lot of it, and a single tuft of fur.

'And you think,' he said, 'you think his coming here, and talking to you the way he did that day – you think it had something to do with his death?'

She stared at him. 'What do you mean?'

'You said it, a moment ago, that it was all your fault.'

'Did I?'

'Yes, just now, when I came in, you said—'

'Did I really? Sorry, my memory is terrible these days, I can't remember a thing—' She stopped suddenly, and stared at him again, wide-eyed. 'You don't think I'm suggesting my husband killed him, do you?' She gave a choked little shriek of laughter, pressing the balled-up handkerchief to her mouth. 'You poor man – what you must think of us all! We must seem like the characters in one of those novels about mad people in country houses.' She laughed again, less shrilly this time. 'Lettie says *I'm* mad, you know. Has she told you that?'

'No, of course not.'

'Yes she has – I can see it in your face. I don't care. She hates me. I'm the wicked stepmother, according to her. Have you got a cigarette, by the way?'

'I'm sorry, no. I don't smoke.'

'It doesn't matter.' She looked about vexedly. 'There's never anything here when you want it,' she muttered.

They heard Mrs Duffy calling Strafford's name again, in a tone of mounting grievance. He thought of the omelette waiting for him. He was really quite hungry, as a matter of fact.

A lock of hair had fallen across his forehead, and he pushed it away.

'You were a friend of Colonel Osborne's wife, weren't you? – the first Mrs Osborne?'

The woman's tears seemed suddenly forgotten. She took a powder compact out of her purse and opened it and peered into the little mirror in the lid. 'Oh, God,' she said, 'look at me!' She dabbed powder around her eyes and at the glowing pink sides of her nose. 'The first Mrs Osborne – it sounds like something by one of the Brontës, doesn't it? I wasn't her friend – my mother was. She used to bring me here, on visits, when I was a child. Then she died – my mother, I mean – and I started coming on my own, and Millicent sort of adopted me.'

'Millicent? That's Mrs Osborne?'

'Yes. Mrs Osborne – funny, you know, to think of her as that, now, when I'm also Mrs Osborne.' She gave a little laugh. '*The Second Mrs Osborne*, starring Vivien Leigh. You can almost see it, can't you? The fog swirling around the dark old house, the peacocks shrieking on the lawn—'

Strafford touched a finger to her arm, giving it almost a poke.

'You were here the night she died, weren't you?' he said.

'Yes, of course!' she snapped. 'I was always here.' She applied the powder puff to her throat this time, then shut the lid of the compact. 'God, I'd kill for a cigarette.'

'Shall I go and see if I can find some for you?' he asked.

'No, please, don't bother.' She frowned. 'That was Mrs Duffy calling you again, wasn't it? Why does she want you so urgently?'

'She was cooking something for me. An omelette.'

'Why don't you go and have it?' A far-off note of agitation had come into her voice. 'You should. She'll be cross at me, for keeping you. Go and eat it now. It'll probably be cold, mind you, but cold omelettes are quite nice, I find.' She glanced about. 'Doctor Hafner was here,' she said. 'He's probably gone by now. He sent Lettie to get my prescription. I suppose she stayed in town, with those awful friends of hers. She goes about with all sorts, you know. The sooner she's back at school the better.' She blinked. 'I've such a headache. Are you sure you haven't any cigarettes? Oh, but I forgot, you don't smoke. Pity.'

He had moved to the fireplace, to get a safe distance from her, but he came back now and sat beside her again.

'Can you tell me something about that night, the night that Mrs Osborne died?'

She looked at him distantly for a moment, as if she had forgotten who he was, her head wobbling a little, so that it seemed in danger of toppling off of the pinion of her long, pale neck. The skin between her eyebrows was knotted in an effort of concentration.

'Well, there'd been a fight, as usual,' she said, 'and, as usual, she was drunk.'

'Millicent?'

'What? Yes, Millicent, of course. Who else?'

'So she was an alcoholic?'

She considered, twisting up her mouth at one corner.

'I don't know about that, but she was drunk every night, practically. Is that what it means to be an alcoholic?'

'And who had she fought with?'

'Geoffrey, of course. They were always at it, hammer and tongs. Or she was. He would just sit there, looking miserable and staring at his plate, while she went on and on at him. He was a bit afraid of her. Well, more than a bit – everyone was. She was a big woman, you know, enormous shoulders and a great square jaw, like a man's. She always dressed in the most ridiculous girlish things, like a flapper, or something, out of the twenties. Her people were very grand, or thought they were – the Ashworths, of Ashworth Castle. It's in the west, on Lough Corrib. I was there, once. Ugly great place, fake Tudor, with battlements and round towers and things. And the food! It amazed me that anybody ate it. I certainly didn't. For all the time I was there I survived on chocolate bars and biscuits that I got from the shop in the post office in the village. I was dreadfully sick afterwards.'

Strafford nodded. He knew the Ashworths, or had known them – he had stayed at the castle on the lake himself, once. They were what his father, in that straight-faced ironical way of his, which many dim people mistook for pomposity, would describe as 'a notable family'.

'You must have been very upset, when she died.'

She fixed him again with her wobbly stare. She had a way of extending her already long neck and lifting her chin high that gave her something of the look of a haughty and petulant swan. She was the very model of those willowy young women with diaphanous complexions and vague stares, the daughters of county families, whom he used to fall for when he was young, but never had the nerve even to address.

'I wouldn't say I was upset, exactly,' Mrs Osborne said thoughtfully. 'I was shocked, of course. Even if she was drunk, it must have been awful to go tumbling down the stairs like that, head over heels, with your suspenders showing and everything. Mind you, it was bound to happen, or something like it, sooner or later.'

She drew back the blanket under which she was sitting and scratched her ankle. She was barefoot, and wore no stockings. There was a chilblain on her little toe, delicately pink and shiny, like her nostrils. Her skin had two shades, milk, and strawberries crushed in milk.

'By that stage I hated her, of course. She kept me as a sort of unpaid lady's companion, making me run her bath and iron her things and run errands for her. Every Saturday I had to take the bus into Walker's in Wexford to fetch her weekly supply of gin. I had to clear up after her, too. She used to throw her things down any old where. Honestly, she was a dreadful cow. One morning I came in to wake her and she had' – she grimaced – 'she had dirtied herself, in the night, in bed, from being so drunk.'

She shivered, and said she was cold, and thrust her hands into the pockets of her cardigan. Then suddenly she brightened. 'Look!' She took her right hand out of her pocket and held up in triumph a single, crumpled cigarette. 'I found one! Be a sweetheart and fetch me a match, will you? There's some over there on the mantelpiece.'

He found the box of Swan Vestas and came back to the sofa.

'Damn,' she said, showing him the cigarette, 'it's broken in the middle. Why do fags have to be so breakable? I'll have to smoke it in two goes.' She tore the two halves carefully apart and put one of them between her lips. He struck a match, and she leaned down to the flame, lifting her eyes to his as she did so.

Jenkins! He had forgotten about Jenkins. He wondered if he had returned yet, from wherever it was he had taken himself off to. Maybe Hackett was right, maybe he had gone into a pub somewhere – the Sheaf of Barley itself, even – to escape the weather and warm himself up. But he didn't really think that was the case. No, he didn't think so at all. He felt the first touch of real alarm, cold as the snowflake that had settled on his forehead outside the Archbishop's house.

'It's funny she died the way she did,' Sylvia Osborne said pensively. 'I used to have a fantasy about pushing her down the stairs, you know – really, I did. I could see myself running up behind her, on tiptoe, without a sound, and putting my hands against her shoulder blades and just *pushing*, like that, not hard, but firmly.' She mimed it for him, dropping cigarette ash down the front of her cardigan. 'I'd imagine how it would feel, watching her fall. Though I didn't think of her as falling, but rather of launching out, slowly, gracefully, the way high divers do, with her head down and her hands joined in front of her, swooping out in an arc and then smashing on to the tiles in the hall below, like a bird against a windowpane.' She stopped, and blinked, and looked at him, lengthening her neck. 'Isn't that terrible?'

He thought of taking her hand, the one that wasn't holding the cigarette, but didn't.

'She must have been very unhappy,' he said. 'Was she?'

She was still gazing at him, her head trembling faintly on that slender stalk of neck.

'I don't know,' she said, 'I never thought about it. I suppose she must have been. Some people make it their life's work, being unhappy. And making everyone around them unhappy too, of course. It probably begins as a kind of game, in order not to be bored, or something, and then it just sort of hardens into a way of life, and you don't notice any more that you're doing it to yourself.' She paused, gazing blankly before her. 'There isn't very much to do, when you live in the country.'

'Yes,' he said, 'I know.'

She lit the second half of the cigarette from the glowing end of the first, which she crushed into the ashtray. She dug her hands into the pockets of her cardigan again, and smiled at him crookedly. He noticed that her left eye was set lower than the right. It was what gave her face that slightly lopsided look. He recalled that the Greeks deplored symmetry, and considered beautiful only things that were a degree or two out of kilter. Mrs Osborne wasn't beautiful, exactly, and yet—

'I think you want to kiss me,' she said suddenly, breaking in on his thoughts. 'Do you?'

'Mrs Osborne, I—'

She took the cigarette out of her mouth, crawled along the short length of the sofa on hands and knees and put her mouth to his. Her lips were cold. He felt the brief touch of the sharp little tip of her tongue. She drew back, but remained for a moment on all fours, peering closely at him and frowning, like an anaesthetist, he thought, waiting for the anaesthetic to take effect. Then she moved away and sat down again and drew the blanket over her knees.

'Try to get the fire going, will you?' she said. 'I'm absolutely perished.'

He squatted in front of the hearth and fiddled with the

embers. They were grey and powdery on the outside but still red within. He found some bits of kindling and pushed them deep into the glowing ash. He sat back on his heels.

'It will light,' he said, 'I think.'

He should have held her in his arms and kissed her properly – wasn't that what she had wanted him to do? Women don't kiss you without expecting you to kiss them back. He was a hopeless case, clumsy and inept. He had an image for a second of his father's eye fixed on him disparagingly.

Sylvia Osborne held the stub of the half cigarette between the tips of a finger and thumb and sucked from it the last of the smoke. 'You know,' she said, 'I think we're quite alike, you and me. Neither of us has a clue who we are. Don't you think? I try on versions of myself the way I'd try on dresses in a shop.'

'Yes, I've noticed,' he said.

'Have you? – Ow!' The cigarette had burned her fingers, and she dropped the last of it into the ashtray and watched as it sent up a tall straight plume of grey-blue smoke. 'And what about you?' she asked. 'Aren't you the same?'

'Me? Well, I suppose I've hit on the version of myself that I prefer, or that I think will do, for the present. I mean' – he smiled – 'until something more plausible comes along.'

She made a sour face. 'Lucky you.' She lifted her arm and peered closely – was she short-sighted? – at the little silver watch strapped to her wrist. 'Where *is* that blasted Lettie, with my prescription?' She looked at Strafford, where he stood by the fire. The kindling suddenly caught, and a pale flame leaped up. 'Come and kiss me again, will you?' she said. 'The first one didn't quite take.'

It was only afterwards, when he had left her, that he re-membered all the further questions he had meant to ask her, in particular about her brother, the black sheep Freddie Har-bison. Did he come to the house the night the priest died? If so, it would have been she who let him in. He felt he should go back and confront her, but he couldn't face returning to that humid chocolate box of a room.

He ate his omelette cold. Mrs Duffy, in a sulk because he hadn't come when she called him, rattled pots and pans loudly in the sink, then took up a straw broom and began to sweep the floor while he was still eating, stirring up dust and making him lift his feet so that she could get the broom under them. Kathleen, the skivvy, poked her head out of the scullery to have a look at him – it was the first time she had seen him – and withdrew hurriedly when the housekeeper glared at her.

Jenkins hadn't come back. Strafford wasn't really worried yet, not really – Jenkins was tougher than he looked, and would be able to look after himself – but all the same, it wasn't like him to be gone for so long, without leaving word of where he had gone to.

Colonel Osborne came in from the stables, bringing with him a whiff of hay and horse dung, and sat down at the table opposite the detective and drank a mug of tea. Strafford felt his brow grow hot. Here was her husband facing him, and all he could think of was the touch of Sylvia Osborne's lips on his, the fragile, underwater paleness of her skin, the taste of her smoky breath, the fragrance of the excitingly cloying, musky perfume that she wore, and that had enveloped him and made him feel dizzy when they kissed a second time. Madness, madness.

'Your chap still missing?' the Colonel enquired. 'Hope he

has boots and a warm overcoat – there's going to be more snow, the wireless says. A blizzard is in store, it seems.' He paused. 'How are they treating you, at the Sheaf of Barley? Reck is quite a fellow, isn't he? You don't meet many butchers who have read all of Shakespeare and can quote you reams of stuff from the Bible.'

Strafford gave an account of his meeting with Rosemary Lawless.

'Ah, yes,' the Colonel said, frowning. 'That can't have been easy.'

'She told me about her father. Did you know who he was?'

'JJ Lawless? Oh yes, I knew.'

'Did Father Lawless ever speak of him?'

The Colonel's frown deepened.

'No, he didn't, and I thought it best to do the same. That man was a ruthless killer, a murderer in a Sam Browne belt, and he didn't change, for all that he presented himself as a champion of law and order when the fighting was done with. You know he accused a man of being an informer and had him shot, all in order to get hold of his house? A thorough bad lot, no doubt about it. Round here, of course, he's a hero, you can't say a word against him. I had great respect for Father Tom for defying him the way he did. To be honest, though, I think the man was wasted as a priest.'

'His sister would agree with you.'

'Oh, yes? Well, she's right, and she would know. Still, he made the best of it. Everybody spoke well of him – he was great friends with the vicar at St Mary's, you know.' He shook his head, frowning at the steaming mug on the table. 'I still can't believe he's dead.' He looked up. 'Made any progress on tracking down the killer? I hear there's a gang of tinkers camping over at Murrintown – maybe you should haul in a few of them for questioning.'

'I'm afraid that would be a waste of time,' Strafford said. 'It wasn't tinkers who killed Father Lawless.'

'Well, somebody did!'

Strafford said nothing. He couldn't but admire Osborne's tenacity in insisting, against all indications to the contrary, that the murderer was someone from outside who had broken into the house without forcing a lock or smashing a pane of glass.

Strafford had finished the omelette – it had left a layer of fatty scum on the roof of his mouth – and now he wiped his fingers on a napkin and stood up. He thanked Mrs Duffy, who pretended not to hear. She was still cross with him. He wondered if she had guessed where he had been when she called him, and what he had been doing? Servants knew everything that went on in a house, upstairs and down, as he was well aware. Mrs Duffy, he had no doubt, would be a dedicated listener at keyholes.

'You off?' the Colonel said to him.

'Yes. I'm going to the Garda station in Ballyglass. They may have heard from Sergeant Jenkins, or had reports of his whereabouts. He has to be somewhere.'

'If he gets back while you're gone, I'll have him phone the barracks to let you know,' the Colonel said. He walked with Strafford to the front door, and pressed him to borrow an overcoat – 'That thing of yours is no good in this weather' – and a pair of gloves and a cap with ear flaps. He put a hand on his shoulder, just as Archbishop McQuaid had done. 'Don't worry,' he said cheerily, 'your fellow will turn up.'

Strafford nodded. He wasn't sure which he found harder to take, Osborne the ramrod-straight, no-nonsense officer and decorated veteran of Dunkirk, or this other version of himself that he was putting on now, the decent sort, bluff and avuncular, the kind of chap you could depend on in a tight corner.

He accepted the coat and the gloves, but declined the cap with the ear flaps. There were limits, and a deerstalker hat was well beyond them.

It wasn't snowing yet, but soon it would be. Strafford drove past Enniscorthy again, and came out on the Wexford road at Camolin. Cattle stood about the snowy fields, looking baffled and lost. He supposed they didn't know what to make of their green world turned suddenly white. Or did they even notice? Hadn't he read somewhere that cows are colour-blind?

The barracks in Ballyglass had once been a town house, granite-built, four-square and dourly imposing. A merchant would have lived here, or a successful solicitor. Strafford could see him, a fat fellow in gaiters and a frock coat and a stock, his wife a cheerful frump, his son a rake, his daughters chafing at the narrowness of small-town life yet fearful of the wider world. Gone, that world, all gone. Even Roslea House had electric light, his father having at last relented when his sight began to fail and he could no longer read the *Irish Times* by candlelight.

He parked in the yard at the side of the barracks and went in by the open front door. There was the familiar yet mysterious smell of house dust and pencil shavings and scorched paper. It was the smell, he suspected, of every police station in the country – perhaps even in the world.

The Guard at the duty desk was a tall, skinny pinhead with bulging fish eyes and no chin. He looked about eighteen but must have been older. He gave Strafford a wary stare, recognising authority and resenting it. Strafford identified himself, showing his badge.

'Sergeant Radford, is he about?' he asked.

'He's at home with the 'flu,' the Guard replied curtly. It was clear he wasn't going to kowtow to some hotshot down from Dublin, with his cashmere coat – borrowed from Colonel Osborne, in fact – and his fancy accent.

Strafford looked at him for a moment in silence.

'You don't use titles down here, at all?'

'He has the 'flu, *Detective Inspector*.'

'So I hear. Very bad, is he? In the bed, hot-water bottle and hot lemonade, wife at his bedside mopping his burning brow?'

'All I know is, he's sick. His missus phoned in this morning to say he won't be in.'

'How long has he been sick?'

The Guard shrugged. 'A week. Ten days.'

'Which is it, Guard, ten days, or a week?'

'Friday week was the last time he was in.'

'Was he at work that day, or did he just happen to drop by to say hello and collect his wages?'

'He was at work.'

'Good. And you are—?'

'Stenson.'

'Heard anything of my colleague, Sergeant Jenkins?'

'Who?'

'Jenkins, Sergeant Jenkins. We're out at Ballyglass, where, as you may know, there was a killing yesterday.'

'Why would I hear from him?'

'He hasn't been seen since this morning. I thought he might have called in.'

But if he had come here, how had he travelled? Strafford wondered. He might have hitched a lift. Somehow he couldn't see Jenkins compromising his dignity by standing at the side of the road with his thumb stuck out. Jenkins too had his inviolable limits.

The Guard stood and gazed at him without expression. A clock high on the wall behind him ticked. Strafford wondered what Chief Superintendent Hackett would do in the face of such a blatant display of dumb insolence.

He sighed, and looked about. Assorted notices were thumbtacked to a green baize board. A stencilled poster advertised a Christmas raffle – BUMPER PRIZES! BUY A BOOK OF TICKETS NOW! – and there were ragwort alerts, and something to do with rabies. Always the same notices, always the same green baize board. His was a narrow world. He pictured himself once more in wig and gown and celluloid stock, with a bundle of briefs under his arm and a lady solicitor trotting at his heels. Was everyone haunted by a self that had never been? He knew in his heart he wouldn't be any more content as a barrister than he was as a detective, so why did he keep toying with the thought of being that impossible other, the one his father had wanted him to be? Do all sons, he wondered, defy all fathers? He was thinking of the priest and JJ Lawless, the man who shot people in the face.

'Get Sergeant Radford on the phone for me, will you?'

'Why?'

Strafford took a deep breath.

'How would you like a transfer, Garda Stenson?' he enquired pleasantly. 'North Donegal, say, or the Beara Peninsula? It could be arranged, I'd only have to give the Commissioner a tinkle.'

The Guard, his mouth tightening into a knot at one corner, picked up the receiver and pressed a green button on the side of the phone. Strafford heard a click at the other end of the line, and then, indistinctly, a woman's voice.

The Guard said, 'Hello, Mrs Radford. Will you tell the boss there's a detective here from Dublin wants to talk to him.' Again the woman's voice, and the Guard put his hand over the mouthpiece. 'She says to tell you he's in the bed, with the 'flu.' He grinned.

'Tell her I'll be round there shortly.'

'He says to say he'll be round there shortly.'

There was a pause, then a man's voice, hoarse and rasping, came on the line. Garda Stenson listened to him for a moment. 'Right, Sarge,' he said, and hung up the receiver. 'He says to wait.'

Strafford waited, sitting on a wooden bench under the green baize noticeboard. Garda Stenson went back to his ledger, glancing up now and then with studied indifference. Time passed. An elderly woman in a headscarf came in to complain that her neighbour's greyhound had been worrying her hens again. Garda Stenson opened another ledger and wrote in it. The woman looked at Strafford and smiled timidly.

'Right, missus,' Stenson said perfunctorily, 'I've noted that.' He shut the ledger. The woman left. 'That's the third time this month,' Stenson said to Strafford. 'There's no greyhound.'

'A widow, is she?' Strafford asked.

Stenson eyed him suspiciously. 'How did you know?'

'They get lonely.'

After ten minutes, a car pulled into the yard. A door opened and was slammed shut. Plodding footsteps approached.

Sergeant Radford was a heavy-set, slack-jowled man in his middle forties. He had three or four days' growth of beard. The bristles were rust-coloured, and glistened at the tips. His uniform looked too small for him, and the tunic bulged where it was buttoned, showing the edge of a blue-and-white striped pyjama jacket. He had a congested look. His forehead was flushed and his cheeks were sunken, and there were livid pouches under his eyes. Maybe he did have the 'flu, Strafford thought. After all, even drunks fall ill sometimes. Strafford caught a whiff of his breath. It smelled of Polo Mints and, more faintly, of whiskey.

'Sorry, what was the name again?' he asked, and coughed heavily. He glanced here and there at nothing in particular. The Guard at the desk he ignored. Strafford guessed there was no love lost between the two men.

'I'm Strafford. Detective Inspector.'

'Didn't they tell you I was sick?'

'I have a man missing.'

'What do you mean, missing?'

'I sent him to Ballyglass House this morning to take statements from the Osborne family. You do know about the killing there?'

Radford ignored the sarcasm.

'What's his name, your fellow?'

'Jenkins. Detective Sergeant Jenkins.'

'What happened?'

'He arrived there, spoke to the cook, then at some point he left the house, and we haven't seen or heard from him since.'

There were beads of sweat on Radford's forehead, and his eyes looked as if they ached. He needed a drink.

'What do you want me to do about it?' he asked.

'You could organise a search.'

'A search?' Radford stared at him. 'In this murk?'

Strafford calmly returned his stare.

'I've told you, the man is missing,' he said. He looked up at the windows and the louring sky beyond the wire-meshed panes. 'I'm concerned about him, in this weather. He's not the type to go off without letting me know. I want him found. How many men have you got here?'

Radford looked at Garda Stenson, who said, 'Five, including me.'

'That's not much good.' Strafford sighed. 'What about the Fire Brigade? The St John Ambulance Brigade – can you call them out?'

'You think he's outside? That makes no sense.'

'He hasn't got a car.'

Now it was Radford's turn to look up doubtfully at the windows and the leaden sky. 'Surely he'd have taken shelter somewhere.'

'Maybe so. But I'm worried he may have injured himself – taken a fall, or something. He'd have got to a phone before now, to let me know his whereabouts.'

'Come up to the office,' Radford said, and he pushed past him, lifted the counter flap and set off with weary tread up the narrow wooden staircase.

Strafford turned to Stenson.

'Get the men in,' he said, 'as many of them as you can find. Tell them they'll be outside, so they'll need weather gear.'

'Am I taking orders from you now?'

'Yes. I don't see anyone more senior around, do you?'

Radford had stopped at the top of the stairs to listen to this exchange. Now, without a word, he tramped on upwards. The desk man's face was flushed with anger.

'And get on to the Fire Brigade and the St John Ambulance people,' Strafford said, 'and anyone else you can think of.'

'What about the Boy Scouts?' This with a sour smirk.

'Good idea,' Strafford said, and turned away.

He followed Radford up the stairs.

'And why not the Girl Guides?' growled Garda Stenson, below.

In Radford's office there was a film of ice on the inside of the window.

'Bloody heating's gone again,' he said. 'Everything is going to hell. First the priest gets himself killed, and now you've lost this Strafford fellow.'

'Jenkins,' Strafford said, 'Detective Sergeant Jenkins. I'm Strafford – Strafford with an *r*. Do you know my boss, Chief Superintendent Hackett?'

'In Pearse Street? I've heard of him. What was that murder case he didn't solve? – somebody called Costigan, found in the Phoenix Park with his neck broken, right?'

Strafford pulled up a chair and sat down in front of the desk. 'There's something about this entire business I really don't understand – maybe you can enlighten me.'

'What is it?'

'A parish priest gets stabbed in the neck, and castrated too, for good measure, yet no one seems all that concerned about it. There can't be that many murders round these parts, can there? I mean, you'd think the place would be agog.'

Radford's attention had strayed, and his eyes were vacant. He took a packet of Player's from the breast pocket of his tunic and lit one. On the first lungful of smoke he began to cough so violently that he had to double over, jerking up a knee and squeezing his eyes shut and clinging on to the desk with one hand. 'Jesus!' he gasped at last, throwing himself back on the chair and giving himself a shake. 'These things will be the death of me.' He sucked air into his lungs and shook himself again. 'Sorry, what were you asking me?'

'Doesn't matter. I hear he was very popular, your Father Lawless.'

Radford took another drag at his cigarette, bracing himself, but this time no cough came.

'He was popular, all right, in certain quarters,' he said.

'But not in others?'

Radford vaguely eyed the muddle of papers on his desk.

'Let me put it this way,' he said. 'He was never going to die among his own, that fella.'

'What do you mean?'

'Just what I say. Too fond of his fancy friends. He'd have done better to look after his parishioners, instead of hobnobbing with the Prods. Anyway.' He waved a hand, dismissing the topic of Father Lawless's popularity, or lack of it. 'Give me a description of your man – what's his name again?'

'Jenkins,' Strafford said patiently, suppressing his growing sense of irritation. 'Detective Sergeant Ambrose Jenkins.'

'Ambrose?'

'Known as Ambie. Twenty-five, twenty-six. Average height, brown hair, blue eyes, or grey, maybe, I'm not sure.' He wondered if he should mention the distinctive shape of Jenkins's head. It was a distinguishing feature, after all. 'Brown overcoat, black shoes—'

He stopped, and looked up yet again at the high window, blank with sky. It had come to him, with a certainty for which there was no accounting, that Ambie Jenkins was dead.

22

The search party assembled on the lawn in front of Bally-glass House. They were an ill-assorted bunch, as Strafford saw with a sinking heart. There were three Guards, in capes and wearing balaclava helmets under their peaked caps, and along with them half a dozen members of the Fire Brigade, in oilskins and helmets, three or four pimply youths from the St John Ambulance Brigade, a Scoutmaster from Wexford going by the unfortunate name of Higginbottom, and a solitary Boy Scout, a hulking fellow with a bronchial cough, who was immediately sent home for fear he would get pneumonia. A dozen or so civilian volunteers had turned up, ghoulishly cheerful types. They were farmers and farmhands, a retired bus driver, a grocer's assistant and a Corporation labourer. And somebody's mother, very fat, in wellingtons and a man's cloth cap.

There was a festive air to the occasion. The men stood clustered in groups, smoking cigarettes and cracking jokes. Colonel Osborne had contributed three bottles of Algerian wine, which Mrs Duffy had made into a punch, with cloves and strips of orange peel and slices of apple, and which she carried out in a metal tea urn and set down on an upturned wooden crate at the foot of the front steps. Kathleen the scullery maid distributed an assortment of glasses, mugs, teacups and even a couple of jam jars. Colonel Osborne, in an army greatcoat and leather leggings, stood with Strafford on the top step outside the front door and surveyed the scene with some bemusement.

'It's like the morning of a hunt,' Osborne said. 'They could be drinking stirrup cups.'

The sky was clouded but the air was clear, although now and then a solitary flake of snow fluttered down uncertainly, like a drunken butterfly. On the drive were parked two Garda cars, an ambulance, a tractor, an earth mover and a jeep.

Lettie came back from Wexford with her stepmother's prescription. She offered to join the search, but her father forbade it – 'For goodness' sake, you could catch your death of cold, a slip of a thing like you!' – and she stamped off into the house, swearing under her breath.

The last of the punch had been drunk and the search was about to start when Sergeant Radford turned up, in his own car, a rattly old Wolseley with a fender missing. He wore a sheepskin coat and a woollen hat pulled down over his ears. His cheeks and nose were blotchy and bright-veined, his eyes watery in a nest of wrinkles. He was a sick man, lost in grief. His son was not three months dead. He greeted Strafford with a nod, and pointedly ignored the Colonel.

'Are you sure you should be out?' Strafford said. 'You don't look well.'

Radford shrugged.

'What was that everyone was drinking?' he asked peevishly. 'Punch? And I suppose it's all gone.'

He took charge, splitting up the search party into pairs and assigning them directions. The Colonel went off to the stables, saying he had to tend to the horses, and that he would join the search later. He didn't fancy plodding the fields with a crowd of locals. He had a position to maintain, after all.

Doctor Hafner arrived as the party was moving off. He rolled down the window of his car and called out to Strafford to know what was going on. Strafford told him.

'That's awkward,' Hafner said, 'losing a man. Should I borrow a pair of boots and join in? Not that I'm much good in open country. Anyway, I'm here to see her ladyship.'

Strafford wondered if he came every day. Such assiduous attentiveness to a single patient was surely beyond the call of duty. He looked at the fellow's bristling eyebrows, his sharply knowing eyes, his burly hands clutching the steering wheel. Would Sylvia receive him, too, in her parlour, reclining on the yellow sofa, with a blanket over her bare knees? Would she show him, as she had shown Strafford, the chilblain on her little toe?

Strafford and Sergeant Radford set off down the drive together. Radford was smoking a cigarette, which of course made him cough.

'I don't like this,' he panted, when the coughing fit had passed. He wiped his mouth with the back of a gloved hand.

'You don't like—?'

'Searching, like this.'

'You needn't have come.'

Radford was looking about and scowling.

'It's a couple of months since we lost our lad,' he said, with seeming inconsequence. He began to cough again, and threw the cigarette away half-smoked.

'How did he die?' Strafford asked.

'He rode his bicycle over to Curracloe strand one evening and walked into the sea. We searched for him all night.'

'What age?'

'Nineteen. He was going to be an engineer, had a scholarship to the university.'

They were passing by the line of parked vehicles. The fire engine smelled of oil and cooling metal.

'Do you know why he did it?' Strafford asked, and wondered if it had sounded callous.

Radford didn't answer, only shook his head.

They came to the gate at the end of the drive. Strafford looked to right and left. The flakes of snow were more numerous now, blowing this way and that on the blued air. Some of them were managing to fall upwards. The wind was light. A brumous glow lay on the fields. Strafford saw the figure of a young man walking into waves, striding forward effortfully and swinging his arms.

'Which way do you want to go?' Radford asked.

'I don't know. What do you think?'

'It doesn't make much difference. We're not going to find him, you know that as well as I do.'

'You found your son.'

Radford shook his head again. He was gazing off in the direction of Mount Leinster, a squat white cone on the horizon. He turned left, and Strafford turned with him.

'As a matter of fact, we didn't find him,' Radford said. 'Someone reported seeing him in Curracloe earlier that night, so we searched the shoreline, the dunes, the road up to the village. Three days we kept at it. I knew there was no hope. A week later he was washed up on the shore out at the Raven

Point. I had to identify him.' He glanced sideways at Strafford. 'Ever seen a body that's been in the water that long? No? Count yourself lucky.'

Reck's van approached behind them, its springs and mudguards rattling. Strafford glimpsed through the misted side window a big pallid face and a shock of red hair. It was Fonsey. He kept his eyes on the road as he drove past, and didn't slow down.

Radford tramped along, stoop-shouldered. His coat was so bulky he had to hold his arms out at an angle from his sides. He looked like a retired boxer, punch-drunk and exhausted.

'Laurence was his name,' he said.

'Your son?'

'Wouldn't let us call him Larry. His mother used to tease him. Gentleman Jim was her name for him. Told him he thought he was too good for us. They were close, the boy and his mother.' He pointed a thumb back over his shoulder. 'He used to go up there, to the House. Played tennis in the summer – there's a court out at the back – parties at Christmas. The Osborne girl used to invite him. She was sweet on him – what's her name?'

'Lettie?'

'I couldn't see anything there for him. A Garda sergeant's son and His Lord High Majesty Osborne's daughter? Ah, no.'

'Could that have been the reason why he—?' Strafford began, but stopped.

'Why he did away with himself? No. She was sweet on him, but I don't think' – he hesitated a second – 'I don't think it worked the other way.'

They came to the bend in the road where the barn owl had flown into Strafford's headlights. It was snowing steadily now. They stood together in the shelter of a thorn tree. Mount Leinster had disappeared in the falling whiteness.

'This is a waste of time,' Radford said.

'Yes, I know. I imagine the others will have given up by now, anyway.'

They turned and set off back the way they had come.

'I'm sorry about your son,' Strafford said.

'Aye. He was a good lad. I don't think his mother will ever get over it.'

Neither spoke again until they had come to the gate and were walking up the drive. The firemen had returned, and were gathered around the engine, peeling off their oilskins and cursing the snow, preparing to depart.

Strafford spoke to the driver. They had combed through Ballyglass Wood, the man said, and had found nothing. They would come out tomorrow again, if the snow cleared. Strafford thanked him, and waved farewell to the other men.

Radford had got behind the wheel of his Wolseley. 'Sorry about your man,' he said. 'We'd never have found him in this weather, and anyway the daylight will be gone soon. Probably he took shelter somewhere.'

Strafford shook his head.

'I don't think so,' he said.

'You think he's gone?'

'Yes. I shouldn't have called out all these men. It was a waste.' The snow was getting under the collar of his coat. 'Thanks,' he said.

Still Radford made no move to shut the car door. He had

started the engine and was giving the accelerator little jabs with his foot, making the engine whine.

'What will you do?' he asked.

Strafford looked away, frowning. 'I don't know.'

'Will we try again tomorrow?'

'I doubt it would be worthwhile.'

Radford, facing the windscreen, nodded. He was thinking of something else – his son again, probably.

'You know you said about the priest being popular?' he said.

'Yes.'

'He was – and a lot of people were popular with him.' He revved the engine again, sharply this time, and it gave a shriek of protest. The wipers were having a hard time dealing with the snow. He turned them off, and Strafford leaned over the bonnet and used his glove to make a clear patch in the glass. 'My son, my boy, *he* was popular with him,' he said, still looking straight ahead. 'Very popular, with the reverend father, he was. That I know for a fact.'

He put the car into gear then, slammed shut the door, and drove off down the potholed drive, the car rocking on its springs.

23

Strafford arrived in the hall just as Doctor Hafner was getting ready to leave. His black bag was at his feet, and he was knotting a tartan scarf at his throat.

'What's it like out there?' he asked. 'Bad as it looks?' Strafford said it was. The doctor was eyeing the big black coat that he wore. 'I thought you were the Colonel, when you came in the door.'

'Oh, yes, the coat,' Strafford said. 'He lent it to me.'

Hafner was adjusting the brim of his hat. He had already put on his galoshes. 'No luck with the search, I take it?'

'No.'

'Sorry to hear it.' He moved towards the door, then turned back. 'By the way, why didn't you tell me yesterday what happened to Father Tom?'

'What do you mean?'

'Why didn't you tell me he was stabbed, and thrown down the stairs?'

'He wasn't.'

'What?'

'He wasn't thrown down the stairs.'

'What I meant,' Hafner said coldly, 'was that you didn't say he was murdered.' He stepped closer, and lowered his voice. 'Is it true they cut his balls off?'

'"They"?'

'I assume it was burglars. That's what the Colonel says. Is he wrong?'

'Yes, he is wrong. It wasn't burglars.'

'Then—?'

'How is Mrs Osborne? How is she feeling?'

'This business hasn't done her nerves any good.'

'When you say "her nerves", what do you mean, exactly?'

Hafner chuckled. 'Now *you* expect *me* to give *you* information? Aside from the fact that it's none of your business, there is such a thing as the Hippocratic Oath.'

Strafford nodded. 'I just wondered what kind of treatment you were giving her. Which kind of drugs, for instance.'

Hafner's already florid brow had turned to a shade of brick red. 'I don't like your tone, Inspector. What's it to you, anyway, what I'm prescribing?'

'I noticed the pupils of Mrs Osborne's eyes.'

'Did you, now? You got close enough to have a good look?'

'They were contracted.'

Somewhere in the house someone was playing music on a gramophone.

'Do a bit of doctoring on the side, do you?' Hafner enquired nastily.

Strafford was imagining him as a student, flushed and sweating in crowded bars, always with a different girl on his arm, shouting at Saturday afternoon rugby matches, cheating in his exams.

The distant music stopped abruptly, as the needle was lifted from the groove.

Hafner said, 'Listen, Inspector – what's your name again?'

'Strafford.'

'Strafford, right – I'll remember it next time. A word of advice: stick to finding out whoever it was that murdered the priest, and keep your nose out of other people's affairs.'

He put on his hat and went to the door. Opening it, he stopped and turned, with a hand on the knob, gave Strafford a last bold stare, and was gone.

There was stillness all around. Strafford could hear Mrs Duffy and Kathleen the maid talking together far off in the kitchen. He stood motionless, listening. The music started up again, upstairs. He went into the drawing room. It was deserted, and the fire was out. Snow billowed against the tall windows. He thought of Jenkins. They weren't close. Hadn't been.

Ambrose Jenkins. He saw the name in his mind, the letters of it carved as if on a tombstone.

He tapped on the door of Sylvia Osborne's little parlour, and got no response. He put his head into the room. The only sign of her was the blanket, left in a heap on the sofa. Since Hafner had been here he supposed she would be upstairs, in her room, sleeping. He wondered what kind of drug it was that Hafner was giving her. Whatever it was, everyone would turn a blind eye, the family, the servants, the chemist, Sergeant Radford. Nowhere as discreetly forbearing as a small town.

He should phone Hackett and tell him about Jenkins, that he hadn't turned up, that most likely he was dead.

The music stopped again.

He went up by the back stairs, and into the corridor along which the priest had walked to his death. He knew by now, more or less, which bedroom was which. Dominic's was next to the window, and Lettie's was on the other side, two doors along. The little room where the priest had slept was on that side too.

That left three vacant bedrooms. He tried the doors. Two of them were locked, the third one, opposite Lettie's room, was not. He stepped inside.

The shutters were fastened, and in the gloom he made out the shapes of a bed, a wardrobe, a chest of drawers, a chair. The air was dank. He searched his pockets and found the box of Swan Vestas he had forgotten to put back on the mantelpiece in Mrs Osborne's parlour. He struck one, and crouched down and scanned the threshold. On the inner side of it there was a deposit of dust, smooth and undisturbed. No one had been in this room for a long time.

He walked back down the corridor, stepped through the narrow passageway – the missing bulb hadn't been replaced – and stopped again, looking back along the corridor. He tried to imagine the priest coming out of his room, fastening the button at the back of his clerical collar. Why had he put it on? Three paces would have brought him from the door to the entrance to the passageway. There would have been a light on in the corridor, but not in the passage – would he have noticed the missing bulb?

Maybe he hadn't been coming from his room. Maybe he'd been returning there, from somewhere else. He might have been downstairs. He might have been meeting someone. Sylvia Osborne had been awake, wandering the house, in a drugged stupor, but sleepless. He was thinking of the semen stain Harry Hall had found on the priest's trousers. Who could know all that goes on in an old house late at night?

The sound of the gramophone started up yet again, close by. It was coming from Lettie's room. He knocked on the door.

Lettie was wearing a pink and blue kimono. She flung open the door and stood in the doorway, a lock of hair fallen over one eye. 'This is my Dietrich look,' she said, in a sultry voice. 'What do you think?'

He tried to see past her, into the room. There was a narrow wooden bed with a crimson eiderdown, a desk by one wall, a table by another, with a cheap gramophone on it, the turntable spinning. The song was 'Falling in Love Again'.

'I didn't mean to disturb you,' he said.

'Yes you did.' She smiled, cocking an eyebrow. Her breath smelled of cigarette smoke. 'But you're not disturbing me, as a matter of fact. Or if you are, I don't mind.' She put her head out and glanced right and left along the corridor. 'What are you doing? I heard you poking about, thought it must be the Ballyglass ghost.'

'I wanted to check again – are you sure you heard nothing yesterday morning, when Father Lawless was attacked? There must have been a scuffle, a cry – something.'

She groaned, assuming a look of agonising boredom.

'I told you, I was asleep. Someone could have fired off a shotgun out here and I wouldn't have woken up. Do you not believe me?'

'I do, I do believe you. But people often hear things without realising it. Concentrate, and try to remember?'

'Concentrate how? Concentrate on what? I've told you. *I – was – asleep.*'

He nodded.

'If you're going to remain standing here, why don't you come in? What if Ma Duffy spotted you, loitering at the bedroom door of the daughter of the house? A girl has to look out for her reputation, you know.'

The song had ended; the needle clicked and clicked in the turning groove.

'I'm sorry,' Strafford said, and turned aside.

She stepped out into the corridor to watch him walk away. He could see her faintly reflected in the glass of the French window at the end of the corridor. She put out her tongue at him and flung open her kimono. Underneath, she was naked.

He went downstairs. Colonel Osborne met him in the hall.

'Any luck with your colleague?' The Colonel was wearing his shooting jacket, and still had on his leather leggings.

'No,' Strafford answered. 'We abandoned the search – the snow was coming on too heavily.'

'Yes, it's a fair old blizzard, all right. If it keeps up like this there'll be a foot of it by morning.'

It seemed to Strafford the snow was falling not only on the world but in his head, too. It might go on falling for ever, steadily, silently, muffling all sound, all movement. He shut his eyes and pressed a fingertip hard against the bridge of his nose. Explorers at the poles often imagined there was an extra person walking beside them.

'Look,' the Colonel said, being the bluff uncle now, 'seeing the night that's in it, why don't you stay and have a bite to eat with us? We're dining early, since the children are going to some party or other – though I'm blessed if I know how they'll get there, with the state of the roads.'

'Thank you,' Strafford said, caught off guard and without a ready excuse. So often a polite upbringing proved a disadvantage.

There was rabbit stew for dinner.

In the modestly sized dining room an enormous chandelier, converted to electricity, dangled oppressively over a mahogany table. The table was so vast it hardly allowed space enough for Mrs Duffy, going around with pot and ladle, to get past the backs of the diners' chairs. The Algerian rotgut made its second appearance of the day, in two cut-glass decanters, one at either end of the table. The wine gave off an evil rubious glitter. Everything on the table was old, the plates, the knobbly silver cutlery, the frayed linen napkins, the dented salt cellar. Strafford sighed. The old home, again.

The Colonel presided at the head of the table. He had changed into a dinner jacket. On the left breast was pinned an array of army decorations. Sylvia Osborne languished at the other end of the table. She wore an evening gown of dark-green silk, which gave her a shimmering, sylph-like aspect, or would have, if it hadn't been for the Colonel's tweed hunting jacket draped over her shoulders, inside which she huddled for warmth. Dominic looked handsome in a black silk jacket and an open-necked white shirt. Lettie was in her kimono still, under a heavy black overcoat, buttoned at the throat. She also had on woollen fingerless gloves, knitted in shades of purple and orange. The room was very cold.

Conversation proved desultory. Mrs Osborne, sunk in deep distraction, picked about in her food, as if she were

255

searching in it for something she had lost.

The Colonel turned to Strafford. 'Why don't you tell us something about yourself, Inspector,' he said, showing off his dentures in a desperate imitation of a grin. 'Married, are you? – kiddies?'

'No,' Strafford replied. 'I'm single.'

He winced. He had bitten on a pellet of buckshot, embedded in a piece of rabbit meat, and thought he might have cracked a molar.

Lettie smiled at him brightly.

'So you're a queer, then?'

'Lettie!' her father fairly bellowed. 'Apologise to Mr Strafford at once!'

The girl put a finger to her lower lip and simpered. 'Oh, I'm tho thowwy, Inspecto' Sthwaffod.'

Sylvia Osborne lifted her head and looked about vaguely, as if she had heard her name spoken.

Lettie winked at Strafford.

On his side of the table, Dominic Osborne was eating steadily, his face lowered over his plate. Lettie threw a crust of bread at him.

'And why don't you tell us about yourself, Dom-Dom,' she said. 'Got any matrimonial plans? A nice little wife and a few kiddies would be just the thing to smarten you up. Eh, brother dear?'

'Shut up,' Dominic said. He turned to his father. 'Has she been drinking again?'

The Colonel's eyebrows shot up. 'She doesn't drink, does she?' He turned to his daughter in alarm. 'Do you?'

'Of co'se not, Daddy,' she said, doing her baby voice again.

She laughed. 'Unless you count the odd gin and tonic before lunch, a spot of champers around the middle of the afternoon, and a couple of brandies last thing before bed. Strict teetotal, otherwise.'

The Colonel turned to his son again, pleadingly. 'She's joking, isn't she?'

Dominic, concentrating doggedly on his food, said nothing.

Mrs Duffy came to clear away the dinner plates. There was tapioca for dessert, she announced.

'I'm going up to change,' Lettie said.

She tossed aside her napkin, pushed back her chair and stood up, drawing the black overcoat tightly around her like a cape. Again she winked at Strafford. Her father began to say something to her, but she ignored him and stalked out, throatily doing her Dietrich voice.

Falling in love again,
Never wanted to—

Sylvia Osborne looked up again. 'What?' she murmured, frowning.

The Colonel too threw down his napkin.

'You'll have to forgive my daughter's rudeness,' he said crossly to Strafford.

'Oh, I don't mind,' Strafford said.

Dominic looked up suddenly and fixed him with a venomous glare.

'You're such a good sport, aren't you,' he said, with acid sarcasm. 'What are you doing here, anyway, when you should be busy hunting down the murderer? And what about that other detective, what's-his-name, I hear he's gone missing – why aren't you out searching for him?'

'Dominic, Dominic,' his father said quietly. 'The Inspector is our guest.'

The young man scrambled to his feet, almost knocking his chair over backwards, and strode out of the room, slamming the door behind him. There were tears in the young man's eyes, though he had tried to hide them. Strafford wondered what kind of tears they were.

Colonel Osborne sat silent, looking down at the table, his bow tie askew. 'I don't understand the young,' he said. He looked up at Strafford. 'Do you? Of course, you're hardly old, yourself.'

Strafford too stood up now. 'I must get back, while the roads are still passable.'

'Oh, but hang on!' the Colonel exclaimed. 'The children will be leaving shortly, for their party. They can give you a lift, and drop you off along the way. I've told them they can take the Land Rover. That brute of a motor will drive through anything. And so it should,' – he laughed grimly – 'it costs me enough to run.'

'Oh, but I wouldn't want to delay them—'

'Nonsense! They'll be happy to drop you at the Sheaf of Barley.' He stood up. 'I'll tell them to wait for you.'

He rose from his chair and strode out of the room, calling after his departed children. Strafford lingered uneasily, a hand braced on the back of his chair. Sylvia Osborne sat hunched around herself at the end of the table, gazing at the floor. He suddenly felt a rush of pity for her. She seemed so small and frail there, under the great chandelier hanging over her like a suspended shower of icicles.

Mrs Duffy appeared with five white bowls on a large wooden tray. She looked around in annoyed surprise. 'Where have they all gone?' she demanded, looking accusingly at Strafford. She set the tray down in the centre of the table with such a bang that the bowls on it rattled. She glared at Strafford again. 'And I don't suppose you want any? Well, it won't be my fault if it gets cold,' she said, and swept out of the room, muttering under her breath. She had not so much as glanced in Sylvia Osborne's direction.

Strafford crouched down beside Sylvia's chair. 'Are you all right?'

'I did see him, you know,' she said, looking up at him suddenly. The pupils of her eyes were two dark dots.

'Who – who did you see?'

She turned her face away from him now, remembering.

'There was someone, coming out of the library—'

'Yes?' He held his breath. 'Who was it?'

'I don't know. It was dark in the hall, I just saw a shadow. I thought it might be—'

Her voice trailed off. Strafford caught her smell, at once sweet and bitter. She drew the tweed jacket more closely about her. The skin in the crook of her elbow was silver-grey, the colour of a polished knife blade.

'Did you think it was your brother?' he asked urgently. 'Did you think it was Freddie?'

She looked up at him again, frowning, as if in a daze. How thin and pale her lips were, like two faint pencil lines.

'Freddie?' she said, sounding baffled. 'No, of course not. He never comes here – Geoffrey won't let him.'

'Then where do you see him?'

'Who?'

'Your brother.'

'Oh' – she shrugged – 'he comes round to the gate at the end of the Long Meadow, or if the weather is bad I meet him in town, in Grogan's tea shop.'

'Do you give him money?'

She bit her lip. 'Sometimes. He's always broke. He's a dreadful person, really.' She smiled fondly. 'Poor Freddie.'

Strafford drew up a chair.

'So you saw someone coming out of the library, but you don't know who it was?'

'No. I told you. It was dark. There was only the bulb on the landing.' She was frowning again, trying to concentrate. Morphine, he thought. It must be morphine, or one of the barbiturates, anyway. He was no expert on drugs, but he knew their effects when he saw them.

'And then you went into the library,' he said, 'didn't you?'

'Yes, I went in. I didn't turn on the light. Or did I?' She put a hand to her forehead. 'I saw what they had done to him. I saw the blood—'

'And then? – what did you do then?'

'I screamed, I think, and ran out into the hall. Geoffrey came down. He looked so silly, in his nightshirt – he always wears a nightshirt, never pyjamas.' She giggled, and covered her mouth with the tips of her fingers. 'All that was missing was a nightcap and a candlestick.'

'You recognised who it was in the library – you knew it was Father Lawless?'

'I suppose so. He was lying on his back. So much blood. I'd never seen so much blood before. I knew it was him, of course I did – the black suit, the collar—' She sighed, and sat up a little straighter. When she spoke, she was suddenly matter-of-fact, almost brisk. 'I never much cared for him, you know. And I didn't want him in the house. Geoffrey, however—' She gave a shivery little laugh. 'Poor Geoffrey, he thinks he's so much better than Freddie, but they're just the same, really, except that Geoffrey doesn't gamble and keep losing all his money all the time, the way Freddie does.' She paused again. 'Anyway, the priest is dead now, and I can't say I'm very sorry. Is that awful? I suppose it is. You won't be too hard on them, will you?'

'"Them"? Who is "them"?'

She waved a hand limply before her, as if shooing away something annoying. 'Oh, all of them. Dominic. Poor Lettie. And the other one. They're just children, really.'

'The other one?' he said sharply. 'Who is the other one?'

'What?' She looked at him, bleary-eyed, blinking like a tortoise.

He drew forward, until their knees were almost touching. 'Dominic, Lettie, and who else?' he urged. 'Who, Mrs Osborne?'

'What?' she said again. She was still gazing at him, still slowly blinking. 'I don't know what you mean. I don't understand.'

Colonel Osborne appeared in the doorway.

'Step lively!' he said to Strafford. 'Those two are waiting for you in the Rover. The snow has stopped, but it looks like it's going to freeze.' He looked at his wife. 'You all right, my dear? Time for bed, I think.' He rubbed his hands. 'Christmas Eve!' he said, and added with a roguish twinkle, 'I wonder what Santa Claus will bring us?'

Christmas Eve. So it was. Strafford had forgotten.

INTERLUDE

SUMMER, 1947

I was their shepherd, and they were my flock. That was how I thought of it, and I believe they did, too, in their way. I did my duty by them, more than my duty. I'm only human, with all a human being's frailties. Nevertheless, I believe I did my best, whatever anyone might say against me.

They were a wild bunch, but when you got past all the smart talk and the tough-guy posturing, you realised they were just boys, after all. Just children, really, most of them. Of course, there were real ruffians among them, dyed-in-the-wool bad lads, and there was nothing to be done with them except wait till it was time for them to leave and go out into the world – and God help the world, is all I can say.

There were about thirty of them, sometimes more, some-times less. The youngest would have been seven, the oldest seventeen, maybe eighteen. Needless to say, the older ones were the hardest to handle. Their hides were so toughened that beatings didn't work on them any more, unless you sent them to Brother Harkins, which I did only when all else failed. Harkins was a tough bastard, a real sadist, I have to say it. He was brought up in an orphanage himself, so you'd think he'd have a bit of sympathy, but instead it only left him with a grudge, and of course he took it out on the lads – he used a hurley one time on Connors the tinker, who couldn't have been more than nine or ten.

The tinkers were the hardiest of the lot, though, they could survive anything. But young Connors damn near died when they let Harkins at him. Connors's father and two of his uncles came to the school, but Brother Muldoon, the head man, sent them about their business. Muldoon wouldn't brook any nonsense like that, from parents or relatives or anyone else. We were a law unto ourselves, over there. Oh, yes, a law unto ourselves, and we applied it with rigour.

If the Connors boy had died, he wouldn't have been the first. There'd been two or three that were 'lost' – that was the common euphemism. The lost boys of Carricklea Reformatory and Industrial School. I never asked for details. That kind of thing wasn't discussed.

The place had started out as an army barracks, and it looked it, a big gaunt granite barn of a thing perched on a rock above the sea. Don't ask me why they needed a barracks out there, in the middle of nowhere – not even in the middle, on the edge of nowhere, more like. There was the bay on one side, and a bog on the other, stretching all the way to Nephin, the second-highest mountain in Connacht. The lads had rechristened it the 'Effin mountain. They gave everything a nickname. Mine was Tom-tit. I didn't care, they could call me what they liked.

Sometimes I miss the place, believe it or not. There were certain evenings, especially in summer, that were so lovely I'd get a lump in my throat just to look around me, the sea like a mirror of polished gold and the smoke-blue mountain rising up in the distance, and the whole landscape flat and still, like a backdrop in a play. But I wouldn't want to return there. Oh, no. My name for it, though I'd never say it to the boys, was

Siberia. We were all inmates, the boys, the Brothers and me, inmates of the prison house of Carricklea.

We'd been warned against making favourites among the boys. A Redemptorist priest, name of Brady, I remember him well, used to come twice a year and give us a talking-to – the Brothers and me, not the boys – and that was his hottest topic. 'To make a favourite, dear brothers in Christ, is to make an occasion of sin,' he'd say, leaning over the edge of the pulpit in the little basement chapel, glaring down at us, his horn-rimmed glasses flashing. When he really got going, on sins of the flesh and the fires of Hell and all the rest of it, little splotches of foam, like cuckoo spit, would gather at the corners of his mouth. I never liked him, with his creepy smile, and he didn't like me, either, that was plain. You can take it from me, that fellow knew a thing or two about the sins of the flesh.

But I should have listened to him, I know I should. I was the chaplain there, the only priest in the place – the Brothers resented me for it – and I had a special responsibility to set a good example. And I tried. I really did try. I'm no theologian, certainly I'm not, but what I could never understand was how God, having created us, should expect us to act differently to the way he'd made us. Not one of the great conundrums, like Free Will and Transubstantiation, I'll grant you. All the same, it's a question I've wrestled with all my life, all my life as a priest, that is.

His nickname was Ginger. Hardly original, given that mop of rusty curls that no comb could tame. He was nine, when he came to Carricklea. He'd been in a place in Wexford, a proper orphanage, I think it was, but they couldn't handle him, so they said, and offloaded him on us. He wasn't the worst, by any means. Half wild, yes, like all of them, couldn't read or write and didn't even know how to wash himself. I took him on as my special project, with the aim of civilising him. I taught him to read. I was proud of that. Yes, Ginger was my special lad. It never occurred to me this might be what Brady, the Redemptorist, meant by 'making favourites'. I still don't believe I was doing harm. Oh, some of it was sinful, I don't deny it. But as an old priest I knew years ago in the seminary used to say, that's what God is there for, to forgive us our sins.

Anyway, where there's love, how can there be sin? Didn't Jesus himself command us to love one another?

Ginger was a fine lad, as I saw when we'd managed to scrape the dirt off him and get his hair cut. Big, even then, and not what you'd call graceful, but there must have been something about him that led me to single him out. Maybe it was that he was a loner, like me. I believe he preferred horses to human beings. There was a Connemara pony that he used to ride around on, bareback. The pony was so small, and saw-backed, too, that Ginger used to have to hold his feet up to keep them from dragging on the ground. He was devoted to that animal, though, and the feeling was mutual. It was a pleasure to see the two of them trotting along the bog roads, the big red-headed boy and the little pony with its yellow mane floating on the breeze.

Ginger, I have to admit, had a savage side to him, though he tried to keep it under control when I was around. To be with him was like being in a cage with a wild animal that had been tranquillised, and the tranquilliser was wearing off. So keep in mind, through what follows, that I was always just that little bit afraid of him. But fear is a fine spice, sometimes, isn't it? – some of you will know what I mean.

I made enquiries about him. It was never easy to find out the backgrounds of the poor waifs that had the misfortune to end up at Carricklea. His mother, so I was told, was a respectable girl, or she had a respectable job, anyway, as an assistant in a hardware store in that town where she lived in County Wexford. As usual, no one was saying who the father was. All I learned was that he was well-to-do, and well known in the place, and that when she got in the family way he paid her to take herself off to England and stay there. It was the old story, a decent working-class girl preyed on by a rich seducer and ending up alone in a back street in some soot-begrimed city in the Midlands – or the wastelands, more like – of England. And they'd have the nerve to call *me* a sinner!

How did it happen that I got banished to Siberia? It was all on account of what started out as a bit of a lark. I was a young seminarian, and got a chance to go to Rome one summer, with three or four others. We'd been chosen, along with a dozen or so groups from various seminaries around the country, to have the honour of an audience with Pope Pius himself. I liked Rome. No – God, I loved it. I'd never been out of Ireland before, and then there I was, in Italy! The sunlight, the food, the wine, the fresh mornings on the Pincian Hill or the soft nights in the shadow of the Colosseum. Nothing could have prepared me for what they call the *dolce far niente* of Italian life, even though the war wasn't long over and the city was a shambles and seemed to be inhabited entirely by crippled soldiers, prostitutes and blackmarketeers. Fellows like me, 'the boys in black', as we used to call ourselves, we were innocents abroad, in a wicked world.

I met up with a young fellow called Domenico – what better name for a trainee priest? – who took a shine to me and showed me around the city. He used to call me *bel ragazzo*, and tease me for not having a word of Italian, even though his English wasn't as fluent as he thought it was. He was a little fellow, with dark smooth skin and oiled black curls tumbling over his forehead. And those eyes – I'd always thought the description 'laughing eyes' was just a form of words until I met Domenico. Years later I saw a reproduction of a painting, by Caravaggio, I think it was, with a figure in the background that was the dead spit of my Roman pal. Domenico. Ah, yes.

We went all over the city together, to the Vatican, of course, and the Pantheon, and the Forum, and the Villa Medici – oh, everywhere that was worth seeing. Domenico could have been a professional guide, so knowledgeable was he and so eager to show me round. It wasn't all sightseeing, either. He took me to cafes and restaurants off the tourist trail, where we ate real Italian food, not those 'feelthy, *feelthy*' pasta dishes, as Domenico used to say, that they palmed people off with, at disgraceful prices, in the big popular places around the Spanish Steps and on the Via Veneto.

I remember clearly a little bar we went to one afternoon that Domenico said was more than a hundred and fifty years old, with chipped mirrors and a black-and-white tiled floor, and little high round tables of green marble that you stood at. We each had a glass of Frascati wine, crisp and almost colourless, and a plate of Parmesan cheese between us, that was all, but the occasion was one of the high moments of my life.

I'd never known such – such bliss, before or since. Isn't that strange? Just a glass of wine and a bit of cheese, and I was in heaven.

Then I made a mistake. One night, Domenico and I dressed up in civvies and he took me to a dive in a back street in Trastevere, across the river. The place was crowded and filled with smoke – in those days the Italians smoked nothing but American cigarettes, when they could afford them, Camel and Lucky Strike, they were all the rage – and there was a smell of drains and sweat and garlic. I drank too much Chianti, and ended up in a room somewhere at the back with a dirty mattress on the floor, and a kid who couldn't have been more than eleven or twelve, though he certainly was no innocent, young though he was. Anyway, there was a police raid – they were looking for a foreigner who had killed a girl – and the next thing I knew I was in a police station, with no Domenico anywhere about to help me, trying to explain that I was a clerical student, from Ireland, and that I certainly hadn't killed any girl. They wouldn't believe me, because I was in mufti, with no dog collar. By then I had sobered up, I can tell you.

Eventually a priest came down from the Irish College, a big Kerryman with a red face, who vouched for me and got me out, after a couple of hours of non-stop talking. He brought me back to the convent near the Circo Massimo where I had been staying. In my innocence I thought that would be the end of it, but of course I was sent home in disgrace – I never got to see the Pope, though I pretended I had, I'm ashamed to say – and was called up to the Archbishop's palace in Dublin to be given a going-over by John Charles in person.

The worst of it was, he let me know, that not only had I gone on a skite and got drunk and made a spectacle of myself in front of a crowd of Italians – His Grace didn't have much time for foreigners – but that the Italian police, half of whom were communists, had caught me in a 'compromising position', a full newspaper report of which had to be suppressed by officials at the highest levels of the Vatican. All this His Grace told me, those thin lips of his white with fury. He laid it on hot and heavy, and I left the palace with my ears burning. I was only a young seminarian, remember, and still terrified of anybody in authority, and there was nobody more authoritative than His Grace the Archbishop.

Mind you, I've learned a thing or two since then. For instance, I've heard rumours about McQuaid himself that make me wonder if it was righteous anger that got him so hot under the collar that day, or something else, such as envy, for instance. But enough of that, I'm not here to spread scandal.

So, anyway, it was Siberia, for me.

At this point, I have to make a confession. Ginger, even before he was cleaned up, or especially before he was, reminded me of the street urchin I was caught with that night in Trastevere. It wasn't that there was the slightest physical resemblance between the two of them, except for a sort of slack, sulky look around the mouth that they both had. All the same, the minute I saw Ginger I was reminded of that night in Rome, in that dirty back room in that place on the far side of the Tiber.

I'll say this much, and I don't care whether you believe me or not, but I'd never have dreamed of getting into bed with him, with Ginger. Never, may God strike me dead this minute. I had too many memories of the nights when I was little and my father would come to my room, with a bag of Fruit Drops or Liquorice Allsorts in the top pocket of his pyjamas, and make me swear not to tell anyone – 'It's just between you and me, Tommy lad, isn't that right? Just between you and me and the wall.' He didn't come every night, and I know it will sound strange, but the nights when he didn't were almost worse than the ones when he did. It was the anticipation, you see, the anticipation and the fright. I'd lie there, hour after hour, afraid to let myself fall asleep, listening for the sound of him tiptoeing across the landing. You know the way a wedge of light falls into a bedroom from outside when the door opens? I've never been able to see that without getting a shiver down my spine.

Anyway, I won't keep on about it, only to say that's why I would never get into Ginger's bed. I couldn't think of him lying there in the dark, the way I used to, holding on to the sheet as if it was the edge of a cliff, with a terrible river raging below me, or a forest on fire. No, I couldn't have done that to him.

I'll tell you the way it was, and I hope you will believe me, for it's the truth.

We had to discipline the lads, and we had to do it ourselves, otherwise there was no alternative but to send them to Harkins, and I certainly wasn't going to let Harkins anywhere near my Ginger. I've no doubt a few of the Brothers got a kick out of beating the poor chaps, with a cane or a leather strap or, sometimes, with their bare fists. It was the way things were done – rough justice for all. And as I've said already, we were all inmates in that place.

I remember there was one young Brother, name of Morrison, I think it was, who for a whole year after he came to Carricklea refused to hit the boys at all. He was a pacifist, I suppose you'd say, and was very strict in his opposition to corporal punishment – sweet Jesus, I was about to write *capital* punishment! We had taken in a pair of tinker twins that year, the Maughans, terrible bruisers, the two of them. One of them, Mikey, had lost an eye at some point in the past, and that was about the only way you could tell him apart from his brother, Jamesy. Mikey was the worst of the two – oh, a terrible fellow, unmanageable altogether. A day came when he got on Brother Morrison's nerves so badly that Morrison lost his rag completely and dragged him out of carpentry class into the corridor and beat the living daylights out of him, in the process nearly knocking out his one remaining eye. The door of the carpentry room was a good two inches thick, made of solid oak – they knew how to build, those Victorians – but they said you could hear the thumps of Morrison's fists on Mikey's face, and poor Mikey's grunts, as clear as if the two of them were in the room.

That evening, in what was called the Commons, where the Brothers used to get together for a well-deserved drink after teatime, poor Morrison, looking very ashamed of himself, came creeping in, and what did the others do but start up a solemn handclap. 'Welcome to your senses, since you've come to them at last,' one of them said to him – Harkins, I imagine – and they all gathered round him, raising their glasses in a toast and slapping him on the back. I suppose it was understandable, in a way. We had to stick together, and keep the likes of the Maughan twins in check, otherwise there'd have been anarchy.

I wasn't there that evening, I'm glad to say. Would I have joined in congratulating the lapsed pacifist? I hope not, but honestly, I'm not sure. Weren't we all brainwashed the same way?

Anyhow, end of digression.

The thing is, I had to give Ginger the odd wallop, for he was no angel, that's for sure – how could he have been, given all he'd seen and suffered in his short life so far? Misfortune, which should teach us to be decent to one another, makes brutes of us instead. That, at least, has been my experience.

I wonder if I should stop here. I wonder if I have the stomach to go on. But I owe it to Ginger, and to myself, to tell the thing the way it happened. Without confession there's no absolution. Mind you, as I've said, I don't think of myself as a great sinner, though I know that's for the good Lord to judge.

The trouble was, Ginger, when you hit him, looked so – I don't know. So vulnerable, so small – so fragile, you might say, though he was the size of a bull calf and was anything but delicate. All the same, anyone with half a heart would have had to take pity on him, and comfort him, after a beating. You see, a boy who has been hurt is so appealing, that's the thing. The way Ginger would cringe, and try to turn away and lift up one shoulder to shield himself, the way those slack, swollen-looking lips of his would tremble, the way the tears would stand up in his eyes – above all, the way he would try to seem not to mind when I hit him, the way he'd try to be brave, and manly – all that was, well, I can only say it was irresistible. And then of course I'd have to take him in my arms and put my hands on him, because I wanted to make

275

the pain stop, wanted to make him feel better. But afterwards I'd get annoyed, not to say angry, because he had looked that way and had made me do what I did, and I'd have to beat him again, to try to make him stop being the way he was, and then he'd hunch himself up again, with his arms over his head, to protect himself, and try so hard not to cry, and all the rest of it, that the whole thing would start up again, and would go on, until the two of us were exhausted, and it would be over, until the next time.

I hope you see the point I'm trying to make here. It was an endless circle – first the box on the ear or the smack across the face, then the flinching and the cringing and the unshed tears, so that I'd have to grab him and hold him to me again – a circle I couldn't break, I couldn't. It wasn't my fault. I know it wasn't.

It happened the first time one day in June, on the Feast of Corpus Christi. I've always loved a procession. From my earliest childhood, the sight of a line of Legion of Mary girls all in white walking solemnly along and strewing rose petals in front of them from a basket, and the boys slow-marching behind them, in their short-sleeved white surplices and long black cassocks, all that never failed to move me, almost to tears, and sometimes, even, I would cry. I never feel nearer to God than when I see a choir of children and hear them singing '*Tantum Ergo*' or 'Sweet Heart of Jesus Fount of Love and Mercy'. Of course, I shouldn't need that kind of thing to support me in my faith, and I don't need it, really. It's just that there's something deeply affecting in the sight of a solemn ceremony of the Church enacted by children, with all their childish awkwardness and innocence. I never minded when

276

the girls giggled or the boys nudged each other and sniggered. Who would mind such things, except maybe Harkins and his like? I saw, in this harmless irreverence, a proof of the gravity of the mystery that was being celebrated, the mystery of God made flesh and offering up that flesh to insult and torture and torment, so that death would be undone and we, God's children, could go on to live forever in the afterlife.

Does that make sense? It does to me.

It was beautiful weather on the feast day that year, the sun shining in a heat haze over the sea and the air shimmering above the bog, and the mountain – the 'Effin mountain! – so clear I thought I could make out the sheep grazing on its slopes. There was a choir of girls from the towns and villages round about – we had to keep an especially vigilant eye on the older boys that day, I can tell you – and our fellows as well, all scrubbed and clean and on their best behaviour.

The procession started at the school gate and went down by a boreen to the seashore and then back up again through a meadow and over to the stone church on the headland – they say that church dates back to the twelfth century – where Mass was said by me and the local parish priest, and Communion was distributed, and then we all processed back to the school, where a big trestle table was set up on a grassy space at the side, with tea and sandwiches laid out, and lemonade was served, and biscuits and cakes. Ginger and another sturdy young fellow, I can't remember his name, carried the banner with the image of the Sacred Heart on it, and two tassels trailing from the lower corners right and left and held up by two girls from the Junior Infants class at the Loreto Convent over by the lake, and me walking behind with the lovely weight of the aspergillum in my hand – I love that word, aspergillum – sprinkling holy water right and left. It was so affecting, that day, hearing the children's voices wavering in the breeze coming in from the bay, and smelling the scent of the rose petals the Loreto girls were strewing, and looking up into the blue sky and seeing the little white puffs of cloud sailing steadily inland.

I hope it won't seem blasphemous if I say that I think what happened in the vestry, when the procession was over and the girls had gone home and our boys were dismantling the trestle table and clearing away the leftover food – there wasn't much of that, needless to say – was in a way a continuation of the rite we had all just finished celebrating. There was only Ginger and me in the vestry. We could hear the sounds above us of the last of the clearing up being done, and of Father Blake, the parish priest, driving away in his Hillman Minx, but down here, in the basement, all was dreamily quiet and tranquil. Ginger had pulled his surplice over his head – he was wearing only shorts and a string vest underneath it – and I put my hands on his shoulders and made him look up at me. He just stood there, with his face raised, his eyes wide open, and it seemed to me he knew what I was going to do, knew I was going to lean down and kiss him, and pull up his vest, and put a hand inside his cassock, and down into his shorts, and then make him turn around, so that his back was to me.

How am I supposed to describe the anguished tenderness I felt for him, there in the afternoon light of the vestry, amid the smells of the sacred vestments, of candle grease, of Communion wafers? How am I to say how beautiful is the sight of a boy bending over, on trembling legs, his face pressed into a rackful of vestments and his two hands lifted, clutching the heavy embroidered cloth, making little whimpering sounds and jerking and shaking from head to toe as I pounded myself against him, pounded and pounded, my eyes fixed on the back of his neck and my hands around his chest, caressing him, holding him upright, holding him against me, this warm pale shivering creature who for those few moments was mine, was mine alone – was *me*. Who, I say, who could adequately describe what that was like?

Don't tell me you know about a thing until you've done it. And don't tell me that, having done it, you won't want to do it again. Don't point your finger at me and call me names and say that God will punish me. So few of us know what it's like – more than you'd think, but few, all the same – we who live in the secret, enchanted world, where everything is forbidden and yet sometimes, on some rare and magical occasions, everything is allowed.

How long did we get to spend, Ginger and I, in our private paradise? Not even a year, but I can't complain. Paradise for me, certainly, but what about him? He cried afterwards, every time – he was only nine – but I got used to it. And I'm convinced I helped him. He needed to be loved, whether he knew it or not. How many of us, at that young age, could have said what was good for us, what was right for us? Ginger must have had some sense of pride at having been picked out and made my special one. That must have been a source of pleasure for him. I have to believe that, and I do.

There were plenty of other candidates I could have chosen. Word must have got around, at certain levels anyway, about

Ginger and me. As the summer wore on and gave way to autumn, I began to notice that I had accumulated, without any effort on my part, a little band of – what will I call them? Acolytes?

In every institution there's an unofficial hierarchy. It's natural – even the choirs of angels are ranked in strict order, from your poor old workaday guardian angel at the bottom, all the way up to the six-winged seraphim, the burning ones, who serve the Lord God directly. Carricklea wasn't the holy realm of Heaven, however, and the pecking order was fixed on the basis of physical courage, ruthlessness and sheer cunning.

In my time, the boss among the boys was a little blond-headed tyke by the name of Richie Roche, who can't have been more than thirteen. He ran the place like a mafia boss, dishing out favours and punishments through a network of henchmen whose wages were paid in cigarettes, Mars bars and dirty pictures – God knows where *they* came from. All this was known to the authorities, even to Brother Muldoon, the head man, but nothing was ever done about it, for the simple reason that the system worked. Richie kept order in the place, and order and a peaceful life was what everyone wanted, not only the Brothers and the boys, but the grocers and the newsagents and the sweet-shop owners who supplied the school, and who made a handsome profit from the system. I sometimes wonder if in fact Richie and Brother Muldoon were in cahoots – it wouldn't surprise me one bit if it was the case. The Lord, and his ministering seraphim, work in ways unknown to us ordinary mortals.

Anyway, below the level of Richie and his band of hoodlums there was a group of half a dozen or so unfortunate poor creatures who crept about like mice, devoting all their energies to not being noticed and thus avoiding the worst of the bullying that went on. These were the ones I noticed had taken a shine to me, smiling at me in the corridors, and offering to run errands for me, and working harder than anyone else in the Apologetics class that I conducted on Saturday mornings. I hate to say it, but they were complete little tarts, and of course I would have nothing to do with them, except the odd time when an opportunity arose that was too good not to take advantage of. There was one little doe-eyed fellow I cornered now and then in the boiler room, and gave him what for up against the hot-water pipes, just to teach him that if you're constantly asking for it, sooner or later you're going to get it, and you may not like it as much as you thought you would.

But mostly I left the mice alone, for didn't I have Ginger?

He wasn't always as compliant as I expected him to be – after all, if I had him, didn't he have me? – and on a couple of occasions I had to call in Richie to persuade him to mend his ways. Oh, I wouldn't speak to Richie directly, you understand, but there were ways of getting the message to him. He was a clever little hoodlum, was our Richie, and knew which side his bread was buttered on. He also knew exactly how far he could go, and when to stop. He and his gang never hurt Ginger too badly, and those couple of times when they gave him a hiding on my behalf they let him off fairly lightly. But I can tell you, when he came back to me afterwards he was a much chastened fellow. Those were the occasions when I treated him with particular tenderness, massaging his bruises, and going easy on him, in our sessions in the vestry.

Speaking of which, I often wonder what it was about the vestry that made it the chosen place for Ginger and me to have our little get-togethers? There must have been something about the vestments that attracted me. The care I had to lavish on making sure we didn't damage them or leave stains on them! Imagine if at the altar one day I had turned around with a big grey stain on the back of my chasuble.

Oh, yes, there's another thing I have to confess. The first time, that day of the Corpus Christi procession, I used an altar candle on Ginger. There was a box of them beside me, and I just grabbed one up in my hand. I can only say in my defence that it was my first time, too, and I didn't really know what to do, and I suppose I was afraid, as well, that I might hurt myself, or even do myself damage. But it wasn't right, and I only did it the once, with the candle.

Ah, but I've made myself sad, thinking back over those lovely old times. I should go over there, to Carricklea, on a visit, one of these days. The school is still there, busier than ever – they've nearly a hundred boys now, I'm told – and you never know what I might chance on. Ginger can't have been unique, after all. The trouble is, I've lost my taste for the younger ones – must be the effect of getting on myself, for I'll be thirty-six next birthday – and anyway I've a new friend, now. A new favourite, as that Redemptorist would say.

I don't know whether it's God or the Devil who sets up co-incidences, but who would ever have predicted I'd end up in Ballyglass? I suppose Ginger thought, when he saw me in the town the first time, that I'd arranged it myself, but how could I have known he'd be here? I don't know how I even recognised him, for he's nothing like he was in the old days. I could see from the way he gaped at me – he's turned into a complete dolt, I'm sorry to say – that he knew me, straight away, but I had the presence of mind to pretend I didn't remember him at all. It's for the best, all round, I'm sure. I wouldn't want him telling stories to the Osbornes, and certainly not to one of them in particular.

To make a favourite, dear brothers in Christ, is to make an occasion of sin.

WINTER, 1957

24

The heater in the Land Rover wasn't working – Matty Moran, who was supposed to have a way with machines, had been meant to fix it, but hadn't – and Lettie complained of the cold, and wanted to go back to the house to fetch a blanket. Dominic, who was driving, said he wouldn't wait for her if she did.

As Strafford was getting into the back seat, he was surprised to see Lettie climbing in at the opposite door. He wished she would sit beside her brother, in the front seat. He didn't feel up to dealing with Lettie just now.

It wasn't snowing, but a hard frost had set in, as Colonel Osborne had predicted, and as they lurched and skidded down the drive they heard the ice crunching under the wheels.

'Where's the party that you're going to?' Strafford asked.

'At the Jeffersons', outside Camolin,' Dominic answered, without turning his head. 'I don't know why we're going, it's bound to be awful.'

'Julian Jefferson is his bestest friend,' Lettie confided to Strafford, in a stage whisper. 'They're just *inseparable*, my dear.'

Dominic kept his eyes fixed on the road ahead, swerving to avoid lumps of dirtied ice that had fallen into the ruts. Trees loomed in the headlights like frozen dervishes.

'O Jesus, Mary and Joseph, but I'm so *cooold*!' Lettie whined, putting on an exaggerated brogue. 'Sure it's perished we'll be, out here stravaging on the wild roads in such a night of shnow and frosht, *ochone ochone!*'

Her hip was pressed against Strafford's, whether by accident or intentionally he didn't know. The former, he hoped. Lettie frightened him, a little.

'I can walk from the crossroads, and you can go straight on,' he said to Dominic. By the green glow from the dashboard he saw the young man's eyes in the driving mirror swivel to meet his own. Why is it, he wondered, that people always seem so sinister when they look at you in the mirror like that? It was like being spied at through a letter box.

'Wouldn't hear of it, old boy!' Lettie said, now impersonating her father again. 'What if you were to get frostbite? We'd find you stretched out on the side of the road here when we're coming home. You'd be like Father Tom-Tom, only all over white instead of black, like the negative of a photograph.' Now she put on a cockney accent. 'Your Honour, I wuz proceeding in the direction of the town of Ballyglass, when I spotted wot at first I took to be a snowman—'

'For God's sake, Lettie, do shut up,' Dominic said.

Lettie nudged Strafford in the ribs. 'I believe our Dom-Dom is nervous,' she said, again in a loud whisper. 'Must be the thought of seeing little Julie Jefferson.' She leaned forward and tapped her brother on the shoulder. 'Did you get him a Christmas pressie, Dom-Dom? Let me guess. A manicure set? A bottle of *Evening in Paris*? A volume of Oscar Wilde's witticisms bound in green silk? Come on, brothereen, do say.'

But Dominic said nothing, only drew his head deeper into the collar of his car coat, and drove on.

Presently they arrived outside the Sheaf of Barley. There

was a Christmas candle burning in one of the downstairs windows, but otherwise the place was dark. It was Christmas Eve, everyone had homes to go to. Almost everyone.

Lettie kissed Strafford on the cheek and squeezed his hand. Her lemur eyes shone in the dim light from the dashboard. 'Will you be all on your own?' she asked. 'What about that busty barmaid, what's-her-name? – the one with the red hair. Maybe she could be persuaded to keep you company. Mind you, don't stay up too long, Father Christmas might get impatient and go on to somewhere else.'

'Enjoy the party,' Strafford said.

Dominic had turned all the way round in his seat. 'Did your colleague turn up?' he asked.

'No.'

'Gone AWOL, has he?' Lettie asked. 'Is that the fellow with the odd-shaped head?'

'Yes,' Strafford said. He had opened the door and was stepping down on to the snow. 'I fear he's dead.'

He swung the door shut behind him and climbed the snowy bank to the pub. Lettie rolled down her window and called out something, but he pretended not to hear.

Reck let him in. He had a glass of whiskey in his hand, and a crown made of red tissue paper sat askew on his large round head. '*Love and joy come to you, and to you your wassail too!*' he sang, in a deep bass. 'Mistress Claus and I are indulging in a little Christmas cheer in the snug – will you join us, Inspector?'

Strafford thanked him and said no, that he was tired and would go to bed.

'To bed, to bed?' Reck cried in mock dismay. 'But it's Christmas Eve, sir!'

'Yes, I know. I think I may be coming down with a cold.'

He was halfway up the stairs when Mrs Reck appeared in the doorway below. She too was wearing a paper hat. She asked if he wouldn't change his mind and come and have a drink, and he told the lie again about a cold coming on. Then he hurried on up the stairs and slipped into the sanctuary of his room.

There was no hot-water bottle in his bed.

When he was hanging up his coat on a hook in the back of the door, something crackled in one of the pockets. It was a piece of paper, a page torn from a lined notebook. Some words were scrawled across it in capital letters. He held the paper under the light of the bedside lamp.

ASK DOMINIC ABOUT THE
SHELBOURNE HOTEL

He gazed at this message for a long time. Then he got undressed and climbed into bed, shivering. A moment later he sat up again and reread the note. He didn't know what it might mean, but he thought he could guess who had written it.

Once more he lay down, and switched off the lamp. If only, he thought, if only there were a switch with which to turn off one's mind.

The curtains were open, and gradually the room became suffused with the grey-blue glimmer of starlight. He closed his eyes.

Later, when he thought he was asleep, he discovered he hadn't been when a hand touched his shoulder, making him jump. He had not heard the door opening. He struggled up in a tangle of bedclothes and switched on the lamp.

'Ssh,' Peggy whispered. 'I've come to give you your Christmas box.' He was never to forget her laugh, a sardonic, mischievous gurgle. 'I don't suppose you got me a present, did you? No, I thought not. Ah well.'

She wore a green jumper and a white blouse and a heavy tweed skirt, but her feet were bare. She began to take off her clothes.

'What are you doing?' he asked.

She had struggled out of her jumper and was unbuttoning her blouse, and now she paused. 'What does it look like I'm doing? Do you want me to stop?'

'No, no. It's just—'

'It's just what?'

'Well, it's Christmas Eve. Why aren't you at home, with your family?'

'Because I'm here, with you. Have you an objection to that? No? Then move over – I'm perished with the cold.'

He squirmed back against the wall and she lay down in the warm spot he had vacated in the middle of the bed. 'Feck it,' she said, 'how did I manage to forget the hot-water bottle! Your feet are freezing.' She held his face between her hands and kissed him. The taste of her lipstick reminded him of the penny sweets of his childhood. 'Now you'll think I'm a tart,' she said. 'In fact, I've never done this before – I mean, I've never got into bed with a paying guest.'

'Peggy, what age are you?'

'I told you, I'm twenty-one.'

'I don't believe you.'

'All right. I'm nineteen, going on twenty. But I'm not, you know—'

'You're not what?'

'A *virgin* – God, you're slow!'

'I'm sorry.'

'That's all right,' she said.

The feel of the girl's body against him caused a catch in his throat. For a terrible, panic-stricken moment he was afraid he might be about to cry. What was the matter with him? He thought of Jenkins.

They lay face to face, he on his right side, she on her left. She snuggled closer to him, letting one of her breasts loll on his forearm. 'I'm glad you're slow on the uptake,' she said. 'Not like that fellow Harbison. Jesus, he never gives up. By the way, he was looking for you earlier. Something about a horse.'

'Oh, Lord.'

'Don't worry, he's gone.'

'Gone? Where did he go?'

'I don't know. Home, I suppose, if he has one. He left a note for you, Mrs Reck said. Anyway, no matter about him, we're well rid of him.'

For a moment Strafford was confused, thinking of the note he had found in the pocket of his coat. That couldn't be the one that Harbison had left. But then what—? Oh, to hell with it. He would think about it in the morning.

Peggy leaned into his embrace, twining both her legs around one of his. 'Ow!' she squeaked. 'You've terrible sharp toenails, do you know that? And you could do with a haircut, too. What you need is somebody to look after you.' She chuckled. 'Don't look at me like that, I'm not offering to marry you.'

They heard a church bell chiming far off across the fields.

'Mrs R. must have taken a shine to you,' Peggy said.

'Why is that?'

'She told me to give you fresh sheets. Usually I just iron the ones that are on the bed, and change them once a week, no matter how many dirty old buggers have slept on them.'

He laughed. The down on her arms was as soft as her breath.

'Oh, Peggy,' he said.

She was trembling.

'Listen,' she whispered, 'have you one of those things? – you know what I mean.'

'What things?'

'Jesus, you really are hopeless! A Frenchie – a French letter!'

'Oh. I'm afraid not. I'm sorry.'

Condoms were illegal in Ireland, and even if they hadn't been he wouldn't have had one. Cheerfully accommodating girls of the likes of Peggy were a rarity, or they were in his life, anyway.

'Then you needn't think you're going to stick that thing in me.' She pressed his leg more closely between her own. 'Don't worry, there's more than one way to skin a cat.' She kissed him again, laughing into his mouth.

Later they switched on the lamp, and Peggy put on her jumper and they sat cross-legged side by side on the bed with the blankets draped over their shoulders – 'We sure did skin that poor old cat,' Peggy said with a happy sigh – and played jackstones, using pearls from Peggy's necklace, the thread of which had snapped at some point during their improvised exertions. She had to teach Strafford the rules of the game. 'We start with onesies,' she said. 'You throw up all five stones –

imagine the pearls are stones – and catch as many of them on the back of your hand as you can. Then you throw up a single stone and pick the others up one by one – see? When you've got all five of them in your fist you win that round, and then we go on to twosies.' But the fake pearls were no good because they kept rolling off the backs of their hands, and in the end they gave up the game and lay down again side by side.

'You know they play jackstones in Mongolia?' Peggy said. '—Or is it Tibet. Somewhere like that, anyway. I read it in a magazine. Amazing, isn't it, to think of children playing the same game here that they do there, all that distance away.' She hummed a tune under her breath. 'I'd love to go some- where like that,' she said, 'to India, or China. Somewhere really far away.'

'Perhaps you will, one day.'

'Oh, yes. In the meantime, keep an eye out for flying pigs.'

They were silent for a while, then Strafford turned on his side and gazed at her profile. She had the beginnings of a chubby little double chin.

'Thank you,' he said.

'For what?'

He leaned forward and kissed her shoulder, dipping his lips into its milky sheen. 'For – this.'

'Ah, well, I couldn't leave you on your own, on Christmas Eve, now, could I.' She paused. 'Your friend that's missing – have you known him long?'

'Jenkins?' He turned over on his back again and gazed up at the shadowed ceiling. 'Not long, no. And I wouldn't say he was my friend, exactly. We work together.'

Now it was she who turned to look at him.

'You're a lonely fellow,' she said.

He glanced at her in surprise. 'Lonely? Why do you say that?'

'Because it's true, I can see it in your face.' With a finger-tip she traced the outline of his nose, his lips, his chin. 'You should have someone of your own. You're not bad-looking, you know, even if you are a bit on the bony side. And you should cut those toenails. But I like the way your hair falls over your forehead. It makes you look like a little boy. Stop tapping your nails against your teeth, though. That would set a girl's own teeth on edge.'

She was, as he soon discovered, a snorer. He didn't mind. She rested heavily against him, twitching and murmuring in her sleep. He turned off the lamp and lay for a long time gazing out at the blue-black night and the sky crowded with stars. He had been living in the city for so long he had forgotten what the night sky was like out here in the country. He had forgotten about the silence, too, which was louder, somehow, than the city's night-time hum.

The weather forecast had said the snow was gone for good, but that there would be frost and ice for some days yet, before the thaw set in.

A white Christmas.

In the middle of the night Peggy sat up with a start, mumbling urgently. Strafford touched her shoulder and she lay down again.

'I didn't know where I was,' she said sleepily. She ran her fingertips over his face again, barely touching him. A blind man's touch. 'You're nice,' she said. 'You're a nice man.'

He sighed. That was what Marguerite used to tell him,

fondly, but not without a certain wistfulness – niceness was not exactly an exciting quality in a man. But that was long before the night she flung the wine at him. By then she had discovered a side to him that wasn't nice at all.

Peggy sat up again and switched on the lamp. There were little pads of baby fat in the folds of her armpits. He admired the soft gleam of lamplight across her bare back. He too sat up. She was putting on her blouse.

'And now,' she said, 'I have to go back to my own cold bed.'

He kissed the nape of her neck, which made her shiver.

'May I come with you?' he asked.

She looked at him over her shoulder. 'Certainly not,' she said, and laughed. 'Are you joking? I've taken enough of a risk, for one night.' She was in the middle of pulling on her jumper, and now she stopped, and stared at him through the neck-hole. 'Holy God,' she said, 'I've just realised, I don't even know your name!'

'My name?'

'Your Christian name.'

'Oh,' he said. 'No, you don't, do you.'

'Well, are you going to tell me what it is, or not?'

'It's St John.'

'Sinjun?' she said. 'What sort of a name is that?'

'It's spelled Saint John, but pronounced Sinjun.'

'Why?'

He shrugged. 'I don't know. Tradition.'

'Oh, that's right,' Peggy said archly. 'The Prods are great ones for the tradition.'

She had to stand up to pull on her skirt. 'Give us a hug,' she said, 'before I go to that bloody fridge of a room.'

After a while he said, 'Archbishop McQuaid told me Protestantism isn't a religion at all.'

'Then what is it, if it's not?'

'A reaction against a religion. According to the Archbishop.'

She laughed. 'Oh, that would be old Chilly-Chops, all
right!'

'Chilly-Chops?'

'It's what I call him. He always looks as if he'd been left out
all night in the cold, with that grey face he has, and the little
beady eyes. How did you come to be talking to him, anyway?'

'He sent out a summons for me – he has a house outside
Gorey – to tell me the Church expected every man, me especially, to do his duty.'

'To do his duty and say nothing about what really happened to Father Tom, is that it?'

'How wise you are, Peggy.'

'A girl has to keep tabs on the likes of His Holiness John
Charles, that's for sure. I don't want to end up a slave in a
laundry somewhere, working my hands to the bone and the
nuns shouting at me.' She pushed him away, not untenderly.
'Now I'm off, Christmas Eve or no Christmas Eve.'

She stood up, adjusting her skirt and running her hands
through her hair.

'It was a lovely Christmas present,' Strafford said. He was
lying on his side, with a hand under his cheek. She leaned
down and kissed him on the forehead.

'Next time, make sure to bring a Frenchie with you,'
she said, 'and who knows what you might get from Father
Christmas.'

25

In the morning he rose late. Mrs Reck, sleepy, in a woollen dressing gown and fluffy pink slippers, wished him a happy Christmas, and made his breakfast for him. He was hungry, and ate two boiled eggs and four slices of toast.

He thought of Jenkins. A crystal of icy dread had formed inside him, that no toast or tea or Christmas cheer, or even sweet Peggy's attentions, could melt.

Through the window he saw that the clouds were gone. How strange the sky looked, scoured clean and of a powdery blueness, naked – no, nude, after days of being wrapped in layers of dirty cotton.

He would call Sergeant Radford. They would have to organise another search party. It wouldn't be easy to get the men out again, on Christmas morning.

Barney the dog came waddling out of the kitchen. Seeing Strafford, it stopped. It was wearing, tilted over its left ear, a cone-shaped party hat made of crimson cardboard sprinkled with fake frost, and held precariously in place with an elastic string under its throat. Dog and man gazed at each other, the dog clearly daring the man to laugh.

When Strafford had finished his breakfast, Mrs Reck set down a shapeless parcel by his plate, wrapped in tissue paper and tied with twine. Inside was a pair of grey woollen gloves.

'Happy Christmas,' she said. 'I hope they fit you. I knitted them myself for His Majesty Mr Reck, but the bloody man won't wear them.'

Strafford thanked her, and said he was sorry that he had nothing to give her in return. She blushed.

'Oh, I nearly forgot,' she said, 'Mr Harbison left this for you.' She fished in the pocket of her apron. 'Here you are.'

She handed him a cork beer mat, advertising Bass ale. On the back was written, in pencil, in a childish hand, *Tell Osborne Im prepared to give 100 guineas for that horse. F. Harbison.* Strafford shook his head. He had not even seen Father Tom's horse, but he knew he would never forget it.

There was no sign of Peggy. When he asked after her, Mrs Reck said she had gone home – 'It is Christmas Day, in case you'd forgotten' – and gave him what, to his consternation, he thought was a knowing look. Had she heard Peggy creeping back to her room in the small hours?

He put on his hat and coat and his new, hand-knitted woollen gloves.

The door locks of the Morris Minor were frozen, and he had to go back and get a jug of hot water from the bar to pour over them, saving half of it for the ice on the windscreen. He was weary of this seemingly endless winter.

Once more the engine, to his renewed surprise, started on the first try.

It was only then that he remembered the other note, the one that had been left last night in the pocket of his overcoat. He didn't need to go back for it. He remembered what it said.

All was silent at Ballyglass House. Only Mrs Duffy was about. She told him Colonel Osborne had gone to church, that Mrs Osborne was 'lying down', and that Lettie was asleep.

'And Dominic?'

'I believe he's gone out with the dog.'

'Do you know which direction he went in?'

'Down by the Long Meadow, I'd say. That's where he usually goes.' Strafford could see she was itching to know why he had developed so sudden an interest in the son of the house. 'Go right, and through the wicket gate, and follow the path.'

'Thank you,' he said. He caught faintly the smell of roasting turkey. 'Oh, and tell Mr Duffy I wish him a happy Christmas, will you?'

He borrowed the wellington boots and the big black coat he had worn yesterday, and stepped out into the sparkling, windless morning. The air was clear and cuttingly cold, and struck into his lungs like the blade of a knife. In the silence he heard the sound of a snow-laden branch breaking somewhere far off in the woods.

Beyond the wicket gate the path curved downwards along a snow-covered slope. There was ice, and he had to go carefully, taking mincing little steps and holding his arms out from his sides for balance, like a tightrope walker. At the bottom of the slope the way became easier. The snow here was criss-crossed by animal tracks. Colonel Osborne had said that foxes were a plague this year. There were bird prints too, crisp as hieroglyphs cut in stone.

Here was what must be the Long Meadow, blanketed with snow. He spotted a robin on a fence. His talisman. His familiar.

Before he saw the dog, he heard its deep-throated bark. Then it came into view, trotting along briskly with its head down, sniffing in the hedgerow. Strafford stopped beneath an ancient, leafless elm, and waited. When Dominic saw him, he stopped, too. He was wearing his checked overcoat and his Tyrolean hat with the feather in the brim. His shepherd's crook was in his hand. The two men stood, twenty yards apart, regarding each other in the clear, tense air. Now the dog too saw Strafford, and stopped and peered at him, its nostrils twitching. For some moments they made a tableau, the three of them, the two men and the dog. Then Dominic came forward.

'Hello,' he said warily. 'What are you doing out here?'

'Looking for you,' Strafford answered.

The dog was sniffing delicately at Strafford's boots, puzzled by their familiarity.

'You were looking for me?' the young man said, surprised. 'Why?'

'It's time we had a talk.'

Dominic thought about this, then squinted up at the sky. 'Lovely day,' he said.

'Yes.'

'I'm going to the house.'

'I'll walk with you.'

Dominic nodded. He was still looking away. The dog glanced from one of them to the other and whined impatiently. The two men still stood together, an ill-assorted pair.

'What did you want to talk to me about, exactly?' Dominic asked, tapping the tip of his shepherd's crook on the icy ground at his feet.

'Let's go, shall we?' Strafford said.

'First tell me what you have to say.'

The dog whined again, and sat down grumpily on its haunches. Strafford twitched his shoulders under the weight of his borrowed coat. It was still damp from yesterday's snow.

'My feet are cold,' he said. 'I really think we should make a move.'

Dominic shrugged, and the dog sprang up eagerly, grinning, and showing a floppy pink tongue.

They set off and walked along by the side of the meadow.

'Any news of your colleague, what's-his-name?' the young man asked.

'Jenkins? No, there's no news of him.'

'It's very strange, his just vanishing like that. Do you think something happened to him?'

Strafford wasn't paying attention. He walked on in silence for a while, then spoke. 'I know about the Shelbourne Hotel,' he said, keeping his eye on the snowy pathway ahead of them. Dominic's step didn't falter, but the blood drained from his face, and he looked for a moment as if he were about to cry. 'Do you want to tell me about it?' Strafford said softly.

'I thought you said you knew?'

'I do,' Strafford lied, 'but I'd like to hear your version.'

A rabbit hopped out of a patch of brambles at the side of the path, saw the trio of menacing creatures approaching, and turned and dived back into the bush, the patch of white on its tail bobbing. The dog shot away in pursuit.

After a few paces Dominic stopped abruptly and turned to the detective.

'*How* do you know?' he asked suspiciously.

'Someone wrote me a note,' Strafford said, stopping too and turning back to face the young man.

'What sort of a note?'

'Just a scribble. No signature. It didn't go into details.'

'Lettie,' Dominic said, stabbing the shepherd's crook into the ground with angry force.

'Why would you think it was Lettie?'

'Because I told her, about meeting him at the hotel.' He laughed bitterly. 'That will teach me to confide in her, the bitch.'

The dog returned from its fruitless chase. It stood between the two men, again looking from one of them to the other, puzzled and uneasy.

'Tell me what happened,' Strafford said.

They walked on, the dog trotting ahead. They could see the house from here. The sunlight glinted on a wireless aerial sticking up beside one of the chimneys.

'We were in Dublin because Lettie was starting at Alex,' Dominic said. 'Alexandra College, you know – boarding school. Daddy had to make a fuss, of course, to mark' – he mimicked his father's voice – 'the great event in his daughter's young life, don't you know.' He gave a bitter little laugh. 'So he took us, the four of us, Mummy as well, to stay at the Shelbourne. It was awful. Lettie was getting all the attention, and I was jealous.'

'What age were you?' Strafford asked.

'Oh, ten, I suppose. Ten or eleven. They got Lettie installed, and that night my parents went to dinner at Jammet's, and left me at the hotel. I couldn't sleep, and went downstairs. The place was crowded – there was something going on, the Horse Show, or something like that – and no one took any notice of me, despite the late hour.' He stopped, and Strafford heard him swallow. At each step he stabbed the shepherd's crook at the pathway. He wouldn't meet Strafford's eye. 'I didn't notice him, at first. He was sitting on his own in the lobby, at one of the corner tables, out of the lamplight. He was often at our house in those days, for the Keelmore hunt. But even when I did spot him I didn't recognise him, I suppose because I hadn't seen him in an ordinary suit before, and without his collar. He caught my eye and smiled, and put a finger to his lips, as if we were already conspirators. Then he beckoned me over. I remember what he said to me – "Don't tell any-one," he said, "but I'm here in disguise." Meaning he was in mufti. He was staying at the hotel, I don't know why. I think he often stayed there. He invited me to sit down, and asked if I would like to eat something. I was tongue-tied, of course, but he called over a waiter and ordered me an ice cream sun-dae with chocolate sauce. Funny, the details one remembers. I was shy, but pleased, too. Being there made me feel – I don't know – it made me feel grown-up, I suppose. Grown-up and sophisticated, to be sitting in a busy hotel, late at night.'

They had come to the slope below the wicket gate. They stopped, Dominic looking up at the house, frowning and bit-ing his lip, and Strafford looking at him.

'So what happened?' Strafford asked.

'Well, we sat there, him drinking whiskey and I with my ice cream. I had the impression he'd been there a long time, wait-ing. Maybe he knew we were staying there, but he couldn't have known I would come down. He asked me where my par-ents were, and when I told him, he seemed surprised, I mean surprised that they would have left me on my own. I hadn't thought it was a strange thing for them to do, but suddenly it seemed very – very romantic, you know? I mean like in a novel, or a film. I felt like David Copperfield, or Pip, in *Great Expectations*. My head was spinning. I was just a child. I didn't understand anything.'

They had come to the wicket gate. Dominic was about to open it, but Strafford put a hand on his arm and said, 'Let's walk back a bit the way we came. There's some heat in that sun, we won't freeze.'

The ashen-faced young man looked at once miserable and excited, and kept jiggling the shepherd's crook in his hand and gnawing at his lip. He seemed almost to have forgotten Strafford's presence. In his mind he was back there, in the lobby of the Shelbourne Hotel, with Father Tom in his elegant suit and tie, the two of them together, like men of the world.

'Then he asked me to come up to his room. He said he had something to show me, a book or something – I can't remember.'

'And you went.'

'Yes. I went.'

Strafford understood at last. It was the one thing that hadn't occurred to him, the one piece of the jigsaw he had missed, and yet how obvious it was. He could see it, he could play it out in his head, like a film, as the young man had said. He could even hear the dialogue. *Finish up that ice cream. Good man. This way – here's the stairs. I'm on the first floor. Here we are – come on in. And here's the book. Sit down beside me on the bed and we can look at it together. Are you not tired, so late at night? What time did your parents say they'd be back? Are you in the same room as they are? No? A room to yourself, eh? Maybe I'll come along and see you there, later. Neither of us*

306

is sleepy, I think, are we? Don't say a word to your parents, though – it will be our secret. I used to love staying up and talking to my friends late at night, when I was your age. What number is your room? All right. Why don't you take the book and run along there now, and I'll come later. Three taps, I'll give – tap, tap, tap – so you'll know it's me.

They walked slowly back down the sloping path. The dog kept pace with them, still looking up questioningly at them and frowning, wondering why they were behaving so strangely, why there was such tension between them.

There was that robin again, with its little bright bead of an eye.

'And then, when you came home, you saw him again?' Strafford asked.

'What?' The young man stopped and gazed at him, blinking. He had again that swollen, tremulous look, the look of a child about to burst into tears.

'When he was staying here, at the house, he would come to your room, as he did in the hotel?'

'Yes.'

'And you stayed – you stayed friends, ever since?'

'Yes.'

They walked on.

'It always seemed so innocent, in a way,' the young man went on. 'Like the games children play – mummies and daddies, doctor and patient – you know? And there was the same kind of excitement, the same sense of doing something that was forbidden and all the more thrilling because of that. And in fact, we did play games. He would put on his priest's outfit, and I'd be the altar boy, or a child receiving Communion. And then, the thing itself, well, it was never more than hands, his hands, my hands, sometimes our mouths. I'd never let him do more than that. He was very gentle and considerate. He never made demands, never tried to force me to do things I didn't want to do. He said it couldn't be wrong if there was love, that God himself was love – I never paid much attention when he started on about that kind of thing, about God, and love, and forgiveness. There was a word he used, *agape*. It's Greek. I'd never heard it before. It means something like brotherly love, only more than that. I think he was trying to persuade himself, as well as me, that we weren't really doing anything wrong. "Oh, you're just a little boy," he'd say, "*my* little boy." But I knew what we were doing, and I didn't care.' He paused. 'You can't imagine what a relief it is to hear myself saying these things out loud. Do you know what I mean?'

They had come to the bare elm tree where they had stood together a little while ago, and now they stopped again. The dog ran in a circle around them, whining impatiently.

'Did you see him, on Tuesday night? The night that he died?'

'Yes. He came to my room. He had pictures to show me, photographs.'

'What kind of photographs?'

'Of children. He used to have new ones all the time, we often looked at them together. I don't know where he got them.' The young man paused. His expression by now was one of anguished suffering. 'He was making sure that I was still – that I was still interested in that kind of thing. There's a sort of solidarity, you know. A sort of comfort, in knowing that others are – are the same as you are.'

'And when he left you, to go back to his own room,' Strafford said, 'you must have heard something. You must have heard him cry out.'

'I didn't – really, I didn't. I was asleep. He always stayed until I fell asleep. "You need someone to watch over you," he'd say. Like the song, you know? Anyway, my room is at the other end of the corridor.'

They were silent. Strafford looked steadily into the young man's eyes. 'Do you know who did it, Dominic? Do you know who killed him?'

'No, I don't,' the young man said, returning look for look, unblinking. 'Do you?'

Strafford glanced aside, tapping a fingernail against his teeth. 'Yes, I think I do.'

'But you're not going to tell me.'

'No.'

They turned and walked back again towards the house, each of them lost in his own thoughts. They arrived at the wicket gate once more. The young man said, 'Can I tell you something? I'm not sorry that he's gone. It's terrible, isn't it? But I'm not, I'm not sorry. It's like being addicted to something and then waking up one morning and finding the drug or whatever has been taken away and yet the craving isn't there any more.' He opened the gate and they went through. 'Will this mean I'll have to talk to other people? Will there be solicitors and things?'

'If there's a trial, yes, I think you'll have to testify.'

'Couldn't you just – couldn't you just not say anything? My father—'

They came to the crest of the slope and stopped. They

could hear, faintly, the sound of the telephone ringing in the house.

'I'll try to keep you out of the worst of it,' Strafford said. 'I can't promise anything. It will be up to the courts.'

The young man nodded.

'I'm going to give up medicine,' he said. 'I'm not cut out to be a doctor.'

'What will you do?'

'I don't know. I'd like to travel. I have some money, from my mother. I want to see Greece, the islands. Maybe I *will* become a beachcomber. That's a life that would suit me.' He looked down, and scuffed the snow with the toe of his boot. 'I suppose you're disgusted?'

'No. It's not part of my job to pass judgement. I just investigate. That's my only duty.'

'Very convenient,' the young man said, with a bitter smile.

'Yes, I suppose it is.'

Now Dominic turned to him pleadingly. 'Are you sure you can't just – you know – keep silent? What good will it do for all this to come out, all the things I've told you? He'll still be dead.'

'It's not as simple as that, I'm afraid.' He paused. 'Those photographs,' he said quietly, looking away. 'The ones he brought for you to look at. You're not interested in that kind of thing any more, are you?'

Before the young man could reply, Mrs Duffy appeared on the front steps and called out to him.

'Inspector! Come quick! There's someone on the phone, looking for you.'

Strafford strode off across the snow-covered gravel and followed the housekeeper into the hall. She pulled back the black velvet curtain and handed him the receiver.

'Hello? Strafford here.'

'Your man, Jenkins,' Sergeant Radford said. 'He's been found. I'm sorry.'

'Where?

'The Raven Point.'

26

After Radford had hung up, Strafford called Hackett's office at the Pearse Street barracks, but he wasn't there. When he tried his home number, the phone was engaged – off the hook, probably. Even Hackett took Christmas Day off. Strafford called Pearse Street again, and told the desk sergeant to send a squad car out to Hackett's house with news of Jenkins's death.

Colonel Osborne had just returned from church. He offered Strafford a drink. He smelled of hair pomade and eau de cologne. Strafford asked for a whiskey, but only held it in his hand and forgot to drink it. His brain was numb.

'Another death!' the Colonel exclaimed, shaking his head. 'I tell you, you should round up those tinkers over at Murrintown. Did I see you with Dominic, by the way? Lettie, of course, still hasn't made an appearance. And you missed Hafner, he just left. That man, such devotion to duty! How many doctors do you know would make a house call on Christmas Day? Stay to lunch, will you? Turkey and ham, all the trimmings. Mrs Duffy comes into her own at Christmastime.'

Strafford got the car going and was at the Sheaf of Barley by noon. There was the smell of turkey here, too.

'Joe told me what happened,' Mrs Reck said. 'I'm so sorry. And in our van, too!'

Her husband, she said, had gone out to the Raven Point. He had taken her car, and brought Matty Moran with him, for company. 'Poor Joe, he's very upset. He's feeling very guilty over not reporting the van missing.'

'It doesn't matter,' Strafford said. 'I saw it on the road, yesterday.'

'What, our van?'

Yes, he had seen the van, and had seen who was driving it. He knew now without doubt who it was had done the priest to death. And he guessed the reason why. Father Lawless had been chaplain at Carricklea industrial school.

He went up to his room and lay on the bed. It was cold, and he kept on the big black borrowed coat. It was almost dried out by now. He would hold on to it for the moment, and be glad of it. It would be cold at Raven Point.

The bed smelled of Peggy. He turned on his side and put a hand under his cheek. A wedge of cold sunlight was shining in at the window. He hadn't been responsible for Jenkins. Jenkins should have been able to look after himself.

He had asked Radford, who was out at the scene, to come in and pick him up here at the Sheaf. Now all he could do was wait. He buried his face in the pillow and breathed in Peggy's scent. He felt something small and hard pressing against a rib. It was a pearl. They played jackstones in Mongolia, he thought – or was it Tibet?

Radford arrived in the battered Wolseley. He looked no better than he had the previous day. His eyelids were swollen, and the whites of his eyes were a liverish yellow, and bloodshot, too. He made to put a hand on Strafford's arm but then drew back. 'I'm sorry,' he said. Strafford nodded, forcing a smile. He felt empty.

Radford drove at speed over roads sparkling with frost, but

still it took them more than an hour to reach the Raven Point. They had left the Wexford road at a crossroads in some small village and set out across the marshlands. It was flat and featureless terrain, with frozen bog holes and ponds fringed with stands of dried sedge. Curlews rose out of the heather, sending up their desolate cry. The sun seemed impossibly shrunken, a flat gold coin nailed to the sky low down at the side. The winter day had begun already to decline.

They saw the parked ambulance and the black squad car from a long way off. Two Guards were there, in their peaked caps and blue serge overcoats.

Sergeant Radford drew the car to a stop, and he and Strafford sat motionless, gazing before them through the windscreen. Then they got out. The sea was off to their left, and they heard the soft pounding of waves.

Reck's van was stopped a little way off the road, leaning at an angle, the front wheel on the passenger side sunk to the axle in the marshy ground. The two Guards saluted. One of them was the desk man Strafford had tangled with at the barracks in Ballyglass. What was his name? Fenton? No, Stenson. He had been smoking a cigarette but now he threw it away. The other was a big stolid fair-haired fellow, who stood off to one side and said nothing.

The ambulance driver sat on the running board of his vehicle, smoking a cigarette. He looked cold – everyone looked cold – and fed up. Reck and Matty Moran had been here and gone.

Strafford approached the van.

'It was found by two fellows out shooting duck,' Radford said behind him.

'Where's Jenkins?'

'In the back.'

Strafford sighed, and turned to Stenson. 'Let me have a look.'

But it was Radford who came forward and pulled open the van's rear door. It shuddered on its hinges.

Jenkins lay on his side in a huddle behind the driver's seat, half covered by a jute sack. There was blood in his hair.

'He took it full on the crown of the head,' Radford said. 'A hammer, or something blunt, anyway. Three blows, maybe four.'

Strafford stood with his hands buried in the pockets of the borrowed greatcoat, impassive and silent. Then he asked, 'Any sign of Fonsey?'

'Fonsey?' Radford said, frowning.

'Yes. I saw him, with the van. He was driving.'

The two Guards looked at Radford. He gave his head a shake, as if to dislodge something from an ear.

'So,' he said. 'Fonsey.'

Strafford turned. 'There was no sign of him?' He shrugged. 'There wouldn't be, of course,' he said, addressing himself. 'He'd be long gone.'

'There were no tracks leading back to the road,' Garda Stenson said.

'Did you look in the other direction?' Strafford asked.

'There's only the sea out there,' Stenson replied.

Strafford looked at Radford. He was thinking of the drowned son. Young men walking into the sea. Radford didn't return his look.

'Cover him up,' Strafford said to no one in particular. He

turned to the ambulance driver. 'Where did you come from?'

'Wexford,' the driver said. He was a thick-set fellow with heavy black eyebrows.

'If you take him, you'll have to bring him to Dublin. Can you do that?'

The driver looked at Radford, and then at Stenson, and shook his head. 'I was told to bring him to the County Hospital.'

Radford put a hand on Strafford's shoulder. 'Let him do that, and leave the body in the ambulance until your people can collect it.'

Strafford turned again to Stenson. 'You had a good look round?'

'Myself and Garda Coffey here made an initial investigation of the interior of the van' – he was rehearsing for his day in court – 'and located various items, but none of them were connected with the fatality.'

'How do you know?'

Stenson slid his eyes in Sergeant Radford's direction, then turned back to Strafford. He began to say something, but Radford cut him off.

'There's no sign of a weapon,' he said to Strafford, 'and not much blood, either. He was killed someplace else and driven here.'

Strafford nodded. He moved past the others. He smelt the smoke on Stenson's breath.

There was a sort of track, and he walked along it, the frozen mud crunching under his tread. He kept going, and after a little way the track petered out, giving on to a narrow stony beach littered with seaweed. The tideline was fringed with ice.

He stood for a minute gazing over the sullen, waveless water. He could hear the curlews crying behind him. There was a strong smell of salt and iodine. He might have been standing at the edge of the world.

He turned and walked back. 'Let's go,' he said to Radford.

The old car bumped along the track, its shock absorbers groaning. The ice on the bog holes on either side shone like mercury in the last of the sunlight.

'This is where your son was found, isn't it?' Strafford said.

'Yes,' Radford answered. 'He was washed up here.'

'Did Fonsey know him?'

'I suppose they'd have seen each other about the town, or when Larry was at Ballyglass House.' Larry. Strafford remembered Radford saying his son didn't allow his parents to call him by that name. Radford read his mind. 'It's how I think of him, God knows why. He's Larry, now.'

'What about the priest? You said your son knew him well?'

Radford waited a beat before replying. He was moving his palms back and forth on the rim of the steering wheel.

'That priest,' he said at last, 'was a cancer. He deserved what he got.'

Strafford thought about this for a while. 'Why didn't you report him?' he asked. 'Everybody seems to have known what he was up to.'

Radford gave a hard little laugh.

'Report him to who? Maybe you haven't heard – you don't "report" a priest. The clergy are untouchable.' He did that ugly laugh again. 'Hasn't anybody reported that to you?'

'Even when they're a cancer, and preying on the young?'

Radford sighed.

'The most that could have been done,' he said, 'would have been to get him transferred. That's all the Church ever does, when one of theirs lands in trouble. Then he'd just get up to his old tricks somewhere else.'

Strafford folded his arms and leaned back in the seat. 'Fonsey,' he said, 'and your son, and the boy up at the House.'

'Young Osborne?' he said, then nodded. 'Of course. That was why the priest was up there all the time.'

Strafford looked out of the window at the passing landscape. After a long silence Radford asked, 'How did you know it was Fonsey?'

'I told you, I saw him in Reck's van. But I knew already, I think. Fonsey was at Carricklea, and so was the priest.'

They came to the end of the marshlands and bumped up an incline and turned on to the main road.

'Where do you want to go to?' Radford asked.

'We'd better have a look at Fonsey's place. He might even be there.'

They travelled the rest of the way to Ballyglass in silence. Then Strafford gave directions. They parked at the spot where Jeremiah Reck had stopped to offer Strafford a lift.

They got out of the car.

'We go down this way,' Strafford said. 'It's steep, mind your footing.'

There was blood in the snow again outside Fonsey's caravan, but this time it wasn't rabbit's blood. There was a hatchet, too, with blood and hair on the blunt back of the blade.

Strafford looked about, shaking his head. 'Who was it said they'd scoured these woods?'

The door of the caravan was unlocked. They went inside.

Strafford, the taller of the two, had to duck his head going through the doorway. More blood here, a lot of it. Jenkins's blood.

'Fonsey must have surprised him,' Strafford said. 'Had he found something?'

'This, maybe.'

Radford used his handkerchief to pick up a knife with a long blade worn thin by years of sharpening. 'Flensing knife,' he said. 'Butchers use them.' He put the knife back on the Formica table hinged to the wall. Then he said, 'Jesus, what's that?'

On the floor under the table there was a smashed cut-glass tumbler, out of which had spilled what looked like a fistful of rotten meat, bruised and blackened and purple in places. Radford squatted on his heels and probed at the sticky mess. 'Jesus,' he said again, more quietly still.

They both knew what it was they were looking at.

Radford took a deep breath.

'This is what Jenkins found,' he said, 'this, and the knife. And then Fonsey arrived.' He got to his feet with a grunt and studied the blood on the floor, on the walls. 'Looks like your case is solved, all right.'

'You think so?'

'Don't you?'

'I suppose, yes. But how did Fonsey get into the house?'

'We'll ask him, when we find him.'

'When we find him,' Strafford said. 'Yes. When we find him.'

They made their way up the icy hillside, among the silver birches. In places the going was so slippery they had to haul themselves hand over hand from tree to tree. When they got to the road they stood to rest for a moment, breathing heavily. Then Radford turned away and leaned forward with his hands braced on his knees and vomited on to the ground. He straightened up again, wiping his mouth. 'Sorry,' he said. He cleared his throat and took in a long gulp of air. 'What do you want to do now?' he asked.

'Drive me back to the Sheaf of Barley, will you? I have to phone Dublin.'

He called Hackett at home and got through this time. They spoke of Jenkins. There was not much to say.

'The newspapers have been on to me,' Hackett said.

'About Jenkins?'

'Someone told them he'd gone missing.' Stenson, Strafford thought. 'And I told them to bugger off – I'd advise you to do the same.'

Then Strafford told him of what he and Sergeant Radford had found in the caravan.

'God almighty!' Hackett said hoarsely. 'I'm just after getting up from my Christmas dinner.' He paused. 'The poor fellow's tackle, balls and all, in a whiskey glass? That was a nice Yuletide present for you to stumble on. What about the young fellow, what's he called, Fonsey Welch – any news of him?'

'My guess is he's dead, too.'

'Christ, we've a bloodbath on our hands. I'm coming down – they're sending a squad car for me now.'

'I'll meet you at Ballyglass House.'

'Right. And Strafford—'

'Yes?'

'Merry Christmas.'

Next day, Fonsey's body was found washed up on the beach at the Raven Point. There was ice in his hair. His eyes were open, the eyelids frozen. Strafford thought of the barn owl that had flown at him out of the snowy darkness that night on the road, of its flat white face and wide-spread wings, and of its eyes, too.

CODA

SUMMER, 1967

He didn't recognise her, at first, when he caught sight of her crossing the hotel lobby.

It was – what? – ten years and more since he had seen her last. She wore a flowered summer frock that didn't suit her. It was too short, showing off too much of her slightly bowed legs. She had straightened her hair. From a stark white central parting it hung down on either side of her face, and was turned up at the ends in what he thought was called a 'kick'. Her sandals were of a shiny shade of electric blue and cross-laced halfway up her calves. Ancient Greece was the fashion of the moment. A big canvas satchel was slung over her shoulder, and a pair of enormous black-framed sunglasses were pushed up into her hair, movie-star style.

He knew her by her walk, a more graceful version of her father's rolling military slouch.

His first instinct was to dodge behind a potted palm that stood to one side of the revolving main door. What would he say to her? What would they say to each other? But how ridiculous it would be if she spotted him crouching behind a plant. He hesitated, and then it was too late. She saw him, and stopped.

He had been wandering aimlessly about the hotel for a good half-hour, unable to find a place to settle. The Horse-shoe Bar was loud with braying politicians, and the air of genteel melancholy in the lounge was less than welcoming. He had booked a table for a solitary dinner. It was still early, however, and the restaurant was deserted, and he didn't care to think of himself sitting there alone, in the midst of all that glass and silver and starched white linen.

The early summer evening outside was a blaze of smoky gold sunlight, and he could hear the blackbirds whistling in the trees across the road, behind the black iron railings of St Stephen's Green. The soft loveliness of the light, the birds' passionate warbling, the busy coming and going of guests and the smell of cigar smoke and women's perfume, all this only served to depress him. He thought of cancelling the table and going home, but couldn't face the prospect of an empty house, and sardines on toast. And so, with his hands sunk in his trouser pockets, he ambled listlessly here and there, from the lounge to the bar, from the bar to the restaurant – where still not a single table was occupied – until he caught sight of her, and the past rushed forward and stopped him in his tracks.

'Oh Lor',' she said, doing her cockney voice, 'it's you!'

Why should they both be so surprised, to meet like this? What was more surprising was that their paths hadn't crossed before now. Dublin was a small city.

'How are you?' he asked. They hadn't shaken hands. 'You look—'

'Older?'

'That wasn't what I was going to say. You were a girl, last time I saw you.'

'Yes, I suppose I was, though I didn't feel particularly girl-ish. How many years is it?'

'Ten years. More.'

'That long? My, doesn't time fly.'

While they spoke her gaze flitted over him, a slight smile playing at the corners of her mouth. She still found him faintly laughable, he could see. He didn't mind.

'You haven't changed in the slightest,' she said. 'What age are you now?'

'Oh, immensely old. Forty-something. I can't remember.'

'And I'm twenty-eight – I know you're too much the gentleman to ask. I'm getting married tomorrow.'

'Are you? Congratulations.'

'Hmm. Buy me a drink – have you time? – and we'll raise a toast to me and my lucky bridegroom.'

The Horseshoe Bar was still crowded, and the lounge was still gloomy despite the late sunlight pouring in at the three tall windows. They went to the long, narrow saloon on the hotel's Kildare Street side. Only a few of the tables here were occupied. They sat on stools at the bar. She lit a cigarette – Churchman's, he noted – and asked for a gin and tonic. He ordered a tomato juice with ice and a dash of Worcester sauce.

'You're still not a drinker?'

'Yes,' he said. 'Still practically a virgin.'

'You used to drink Daddy's whiskey.'

'Out of politeness.'

'Yes, you were always polite. Infuriatingly so.' He recalled seeing her reflected in the glass of the French window upstairs at Ballyglass House, her glimmering pale nakedness. He realised, it came to him just now, that he had been a little in love with her, while imagining it was her stepmother he desired. He knew himself hardly at all, in those days. Was it any different, now?

'You know what they call that in New York?' the young woman said, pointing with her cigarette at his glass. 'A Virgin Mary. Isn't that clever? A Virgin Mary for an almost virgin.'

She studied herself idly in the mirror behind the bar.

'Do you know New York well?' he asked.

'No. I've never been there.' She lifted her chin and blew a stream of smoke over his head. 'I changed my name, by the way,' she said.

'Oh? To what?'

'Laura. I always wanted to be called Laura.'

'So – Lettie no longer.'

'That's right. Lettie is gone.'

She recrossed her legs, and tapped her cigarette on the rim of a heavy glass ashtray that the barman had set before her. Strafford couldn't get used to her new, stark hairstyle.

'Who are you marrying?' he asked, taking a sip of his drink. It tasted of nothing much. He recalled the stylised portrait of Jesus and his Sacred Heart hanging on the wall in Archbishop McQuaid's parlour. The arid air of sanctity. The silver-grey light beyond the window.

'I'm marrying a man called Waldron,' Lettie-Laura said. 'Jimmy Waldron. We've known each other for yonks. He locked us both in a lavatory once and put his hand up my knickers. I can't have been more than ten or eleven. Then, years later, I kneed him in the balls one evening at a party – he got sick all over the floor. That's as sound a basis for marriage as any, wouldn't you say? Mind you, he insists he can't re-member either occasion, says I must have made it all up. Men have wonderfully defective memories, have you noticed?' She darted her cigarette at the ashtray again. Her bright-scarlet lipstick was slightly smudged at one side of her mouth. 'And what about you? Still single?'

'No, I'm married. Her name is Marguerite. We knew each other for a long time too, like you and your chap. In fact, we went out together for years, broke up, then got together again. No children, before you ask.'

'I wasn't going to. Children are such a bore – I hope Jimmy won't expect me to have any of the little blighters. If he does, he's in for a disappointment.'

He took another half-hearted sip from his glass. He really didn't like the taste of tomato juice, but when it came with ice cubes and a paring of celery it at least looked like a real drink.

'How are things at home?' he asked. 'Are you still living at Ballyglass?'

'No, I have a place up here now. I've been working in an art gallery.'

'I didn't know you were interested in art.'

'I'm not. It's just a job. That's why I'm getting married, so Jimmy the groper of little girls can take me away from all this.'

'I can see you're very much in love.'

She shrugged. 'Oh, Jimmy is all right. He makes me laugh, sometimes, especially when he thinks he's being serious. He has a nice house, on Waterloo Road – his parents died and left him well off, thank God. Being poor wouldn't suit me at all. Oh, look, I seem to have finished my drink. Can I have another?'

He signalled to the barman. In the lounge, someone had started to play on the piano a soupy version of 'Falling in Love Again'.

'Listen to that,' Strafford said. 'It's your song.'

'Oh, yes, from my Dietrich phase.' The barman brought her drink. She stirred it pensively with her index finger, then put the finger into her mouth and sucked it. 'Yes, Jimmy is all right,' she said. 'Though I feel sorry for him, having to put up with me for the rest of his life' – she glanced at Strafford slyly from under her eyelashes – 'if he lives that long.'

She lit another cigarette. It was her third.

'And the family,' he asked, 'how are they?'

'Oh, much the same. Daddy's gone a bit gaga, I think, but then how would you know? The White Mouse still thinks she's a vamp. She spends most of her time in bed, tended by the Kraut – I don't know what she'd do without her regular course of injections. Poor old Kraut, how has he put up with her, all this time? I suppose he has to have his injections, too.' She looked at Strafford speculatively for a long moment, leaning her head to one side. 'You thought she might have killed my mother, didn't you.'

He smiled. 'The possibility crossed my mind.'

'I suppose it's a detective's job, to suspect everybody of everything. And who knows, maybe you were right? – maybe Miss Mouse did give Mummy a shove. I wouldn't put it past her, though I don't think she'd have had the nerve.' Strafford was about to reply to this but she stopped him, tapping a finger rapidly on the back of his hand. 'But listen,' she said, 'you'll never believe what Dom-Dom went and did. He converted! Yes, turned Catholic. And – wait for it – now he's a priest. What do you think of that?'

Strafford was surprised not to be surprised. There was a certain, dreadful symmetry to the thing.

'Where does he – I'm not sure what the word is. Practise? Officiate?'

'He's in one of those ghastly schools in Connemara, looking after the souls of a band of juvenile delinquents. I must say, it was the last thing I expected of him.' She looked into her glass, and her voice became deliberately flat. 'Of course, he and that priest were very close, for a while.'

'Yes, like Laurence Radford,' Strafford said, watching her. She had gone very still, and now she put her finger into the glass again and stirred it slowly round and round in what remained of her drink.

'I wonder why they put lemon in,' she said. 'I used to take my gin neat, you know. I always had a naggin of Gordon's in my gymslip pocket.' Now she glanced at him sidelong. 'I really was a naughty girl, in those days.'

'The Radford boy,' Strafford persisted, '—his father told me you were sweet on him.'

She lifted the glass and drained it, leaning her head far back. 'I was in love with him,' she said simply. 'Can you be in love at – what was I? Sixteen? Seventeen? It felt like love. But of course I was wasting my time. I didn't know how things were, you see. I didn't know about Father Tom-Tom and his wiles.' She paused. The cigarette she held in her fingers had an inch of ash suspended from it. She seemed not to notice. 'And then my Laurence went and did himself in – not that he was ever mine, of course, except in my schoolgirl fantasies. I cried for a week, poor sap that I was.'

'Two deaths, within a year,' Strafford said, 'your Laurence, and then Fonsey Walsh.'

'Oh, Fonsey did the right thing,' she said. 'Poor Caliban,

he would have had an awful time in prison.' Suddenly she pushed her glass away. 'Listen, it's hateful in here – all this mahogany – shall we go out, maybe take a little stroll in the Green? It's early still. Are you meeting someone? – is wifey on her way?'

'No, she's – she's not here.' In fact, he and Marguerite were separated, perhaps permanently, he wasn't sure. After it had happened – no wine on the wall this time – he had found, to his surprise and faint shame, that he didn't mind very much. 'What about you? Will you be meeting your fiancé?'

'No, this is his stag night, God help us. He's staying at the Kildare Street Club, round the corner – God help them. He's quite the puker, still, especially when he drinks.'

She stepped down from the stool and shouldered her canvas bag. They went out into the sunlight, and crossed the road and passed through the big corner gate into the Green. The evening was still warm. Courting couples lay on the grass. At the pond a small boy and his mother were feeding crusts of bread to the ducks. A tramp was stretched full length on a bench, fast asleep. The sky above the trees had turned to indigo. They skirted the flower beds. People were sitting on the granite parapet of the fountain, others were slumped in deckchairs, as if stunned after the day's long heat. A man in shirt-sleeves and braces wore a handkerchief on his head, knotted at all four corners, to protect his bald scalp from the sun's dying rays.

'Are you still a detective?' Lettie asked – Strafford couldn't think of her as Laura.

'Yes – just about.' She looked at him questioningly. 'I was very nearly kicked out of the Force,' he said. 'I gave the story to an English newspaper, after Fonsey was found.'

'I know. The *Sunday Express*, wasn't it? Daddy was very disappointed in you' – she put on her father's voice – '*Damned fellow, thought I could trust him, then look what he goes and does.*'

Strafford smiled, biting his lip. 'The Archbishop was disappointed too,' he said. 'Tried to get me transferred to the Blasket Islands, or somewhere equally congenial.'

'What happened?'

'My boss dragged his heels, and here I am, still pounding the beat.' With four stiff fingers, he pushed a lock of hair away from his forehead.

'I quite fancied you, you know,' Lettie said. 'I knew I hadn't a chance, of course – you were too busy pining after the White Mouse.'

A pale little girl went past, bowling a hoop, with a little boy running behind her, crying.

'Were you there, when they found Fonsey?' Lettie asked.

'No.'

'Why did he kill that detective? – what was his name?'

'Jenkins.'

'That's right.' They had stopped, and she was watching the play of water in the fountain. 'Why did Fonsey kill him?'

'You know why,' Strafford said.

'Do I?' Still she kept her eyes turned away from him. 'Look at all those tiny rainbows the spray makes.' Now she turned to him. 'How would I know?' she asked.

'Because you know everything there is to be known, about that time, about all that happened. Don't you?'

She held his gaze for a moment, then turned abruptly and walked on. He watched her go, then followed. The bandstand

333

was ahead of them. In two or three paces he caught up with her. She had slipped the canvas bag from her shoulder and was swinging it at her side now.

'Everyone said he got what he deserved,' she said.

'The priest?'

'Of course the bloody priest!' she snapped. 'Who else did you think I meant? – Fonsey?' She shook her head. 'Daddy, the poor booby, was the only one who was taken in by Father Tom, with all his talk about horses, and hunting, and the rest of it.' She swung the bag more rapidly at her side. 'You know it was him who drove Laurence Radford to kill himself? Did you know that?'

'I knew, yes.'

'Oh, of course,' she said with bitter sarcasm, 'you knew it all, didn't you. But you didn't. It was all guesses, most of them wrong.'

'Yes, you're right. When I look back, I seem to myself to have been like someone in a theatre watching a play and understanding only a fraction of the plot.'

She stopped abruptly on the path and turned to him. 'What would you do,' she asked, 'if you found out who really killed that priest? It wasn't Fonsey, you know that, don't you? Fonsey cut him, in that awful way, and lit a candle by his head, God knows why, but he didn't kill him.'

She was gazing at him, motionless, not blinking.

'Then who did kill him, Lettie?'

'Laura.'

'Who killed him, Laura? Are you going to tell me?'

'You didn't answer my question. What would you do, if you knew the truth?'

'You don't think I do know?' he asked, almost teasingly. She said nothing, only fixed him still with that unblinking stare. He looked away from her, over the tops of the trees. A full moon, transparent as tissue paper, hung at a crooked angle at the tip of a distant spire, making him think vaguely of the East. 'I don't know what I'd do,' he said. 'Nothing, probably.' He looked at the toecaps of his shoes. 'How did Fonsey get into the house? That was the thing I kept asking myself. Did he have a key, or did someone let him in? What do you think, Lettie?'

'I told you,' she said coldly, 'my name is Laura.'

'Sorry – Laura. But tell me, did someone come down and let him in, and creep up the stairs with him and wait for Father Tom to come out of – to come out of wherever he was?'

She turned and walked on again. 'What does it matter?' she said over her shoulder. Again he followed, and again caught up with her.

'You knew about Dominic, didn't you,' he said. '—You knew about him and Father Tom.'

'I wish you'd stop calling him that – Father Tom! Jesus! You know he invented that name for himself? "Call me Tom, for the Lord's sake!" he used to say, with that fake heartiness, grinning, and slapping people on the back. I'm glad he's dead. I'm glad I—' She broke off.

'What are you glad you did?' He put a hand lightly on her shoulder. 'Tell me,' he said, in almost a whisper. 'Tell me. I know you're right, I know Fonsey didn't kill him. Maybe he meant to, and his nerve failed – he didn't like killing things, not in cold blood. Tell me.'

335

She looked down at his hand. 'Oh, are you going to arrest me?' She raised her eyes and smiled into his face. 'What do you want me to tell you, that you don't know already?'

'You could tell me how a person can sleep at night, a person, for instance, who grabbed the knife from Fonsey and ran up behind the priest and drove the blade into his neck and let him stagger down the stairs and into the library and fall on the floor there and bleed to death. Could you sleep, Lettie – Laura – if you'd killed a man like that, no matter how much he deserved to die?'

She opened her eyes very wide, leaning a little way back from him, still smiling.

'How would I know?' she asked lightly, with a little laugh. 'You remember what a sound sleeper I was, in those days. I still am.'

Then she hitched her bag on her shoulder again, and turned and walked away, back towards the hotel. He watched her until she had crossed the little hump-backed bridge over the duck pond and disappeared into the shadows on the far side, under the trees.

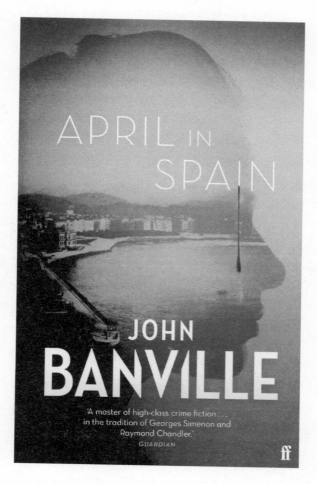

APRIL IN SPAIN

JOHN BANVILLE

'A master of high-class crime fiction . . .
in the tradition of Georges Simenon and
Raymond Chandler.'
GUARDIAN

ff

Read on for the first chapters of the new
Detective Inspector Strafford novel
available now

faber

LONDON

1

Terry Tice liked killing people. It was as simple as that. Maybe liked wasn't the right word. Nowadays he was paid to do it, and well paid. But money was never the motive, not really. Then what was? He had given a lot of thought to this question, on and off, over the years. He wasn't a looney, and it wasn't a sex thing, or anything sick like that – he was no psycho.

The best answer he could come up with was that it was a matter of making things tidy, of putting things in their right place. The people he was hired to kill had got in the way of something, some project or other, and had to be removed in order for business to proceed smoothly. Either that, or they were superfluous, which was just as good a reason for them to be disposed of.

Needless to say, he had nothing personal against any of his targets – which is how he thought of them, since 'victim' would sound as if he was to blame – except insofar as they were *clutter*. Yes, it gave him a real sense of satisfaction to make things neat and shipshape.

Shipshape, that was the word. After all, he had been in the British navy, for a while, at the end of the war. He was too young to enlist, but he had lied about his age and was taken on, and 'saw action', as the fruity-voiced high-ups liked to say, hunting German submarines in the North Atlantic. Life at sea was boring, however, and boredom was one of the things Terry just couldn't put up with. Besides, he was prone to sea-sickness. A sailor who was seasick all the time, that would be a fine thing. So as soon as the chance came, he got out and transferred to the army.

He served for a few months in North Africa, propped on his elbows in wadis, fighting off the flies and taking potshots at Rommel's famous Afrika Korps whenever they put up their big square heads, while off on the horizon the tanks buzzed like beetles, spitting fire at each other day and night. After that he did a spell in Burma, where he got the chance to kill a lot of little yellow fellows, and had a fine old time.

In Africa, he had caught a nasty dose of the clap – though was there such a thing as a nice dose of the clap? – and in Burma he contracted an even nastier case of malaria. If it wasn't one thing it was another. Life – a mug's game.

The end of the war was a shock for Private Tice. In peace-time, he didn't know what to do with himself, and drifted from place to place around London, and from job to job. He had no family, that he knew of – he had been brought up, or dragged up, more like, in an Irish orphanage – and didn't keep in touch with his mates from the old days in the desert or on the ocean wave. There weren't that many of them, any-way. None, in fact, if the truth were told.

For a while he had a serious go at the girls, but it wasn't a success. Most of the ones he picked up turned out to be on the game – he must give off a particular scent or something, since the brassers fairly flocked to him; it was a thing he noticed. Of course, it was against his principles to pay for it, and anyway *it* wasn't much to write home about, in his opinion.

There was one who latched on to him who wasn't a tart. She was a hot little redhead, halfway respectable – she had an office job in the Morris motor car factory up near Oxford, though she was cockney to the bone. He didn't drive a car, himself, so he only saw her if he went up on the train, or when she came down to the Smoke the odd weekend for a bit of fun among the bright lights.

Sapphire, she said her name was. Ooh-la-la. In the Dog and Bone one night he had a rummage in her handbag, just out of curiosity, while she was off powdering her nose, and came across an old ration book and found out her real name was Doris – Doris Huggett, from over Stepney way. That was the same night he realised, when he took a close look at it, that her hair was dyed. He should have known, it was that bright, with that fake metallic shine, like the shine on the curve of a brand-new Morris Oxford mudguard.

Doris-alias-Sapphire didn't last much longer than any of the others. In a place in Soho on New Year's Eve she had a couple of Babychams too many and turned away and spluttered with laughter at some remark he had made. He couldn't see anything funny in what he'd said. Drunk though she was, he took her out the lane behind the club and gave her a few smacks to teach her manners. Next morning, she rang up screaming, and threatening to have him done for assault and battery, but nothing came of it.

That was a thing he wouldn't stand for, being disrespected and made fun of. He had just linked in with an East End outfit, and was doing some profitable robbing and the like. He had to get out, though, after knifing one of the younger blokes in the crew for mimicking his Irish accent – the Irish accent, it should be said, that he hadn't known he had, until then.

He was handy with a knife, and with shooters – he'd been in the army, after all – and was pretty nifty with his fists, too, when the need arose, even if he was a bantamweight. One of the Kray twins, Ronnie, it was, took him on for a while as an enforcer, but his low stature was against him. That was why he liked Burma, despite the heat and the fever and all the rest of it – the fellows he'd been sent to kill down there were his own size or smaller.

It wasn't easy making a living on Civvy Street, and he was getting desperate, he didn't mind admitting it, when Percy Antrobus came sashaying into his life.

Percy was – well, it was hard to say what Percy was, exactly. Heavy, pasty-faced, with a woman's hips, and bruise-coloured pouches under his eyes and a fat lower lip that sagged and turned a glistening shade of dark purple when he'd had a few. Brandy-and-port was his tipple, though he started the day with what he called a *coupe*, which as Terry discovered was just the French word for a glass of champagne. Percy took his champers ice-cold. He had a swizzle stick that was made of real gold. When Terry asked him what it was for, Percy looked at him in that way he did when he was pretending to be shocked, his eyes big and round as pennies and his mouth pursed into a crimped little circle that looked less like a mouth than a you-know-what, and said, 'Dear boy, surely you wouldn't think of drinking champagne before noon *with bubbles in it*?'

That was Percy.

And you had to give it to him, he it was who saw Terry's potential, and introduced him to his true vocation.

Funny, the way it turned out, that his first paid-for target should be, of all people, Percy's old Ma. She had a few bob in the bank, quite a few, in fact, and was threatening to cut Percy out of her will, on account of something he'd done or hadn't done. Percy, at his wits' end, had decided the only thing for it was to have her done over before she had time to ring up her solicitor – a 'complete stinker', who had it in for Percy, according to the man himself – and order him to bring her the aforementioned document so she could strike from it the name of her only son, the said Percival.

Terry had come across Percy for the first time one foggy November night in the King's Head in Putney. Afterwards it occurred to him that it hadn't been a chance encounter at all, and that Percy had picked him out deliberately, as a lad likely to help him in the matter of his inheritance. When, coming up to closing time, Percy started telling him about his problem with 'the Mater' – he really did talk like that – and how he intended to go about solving it, Terry thought he was joking.

But it was no joke.

When they were saying goodnight outside the pub, their breath rising up in big dense puffs through the already dense pea-souper fog, Percy stuck two tenners into Terry's breast pocket and suggested they meet in the same place at the same time the next night. Terry was in two minds whether to go, but go he did. When Percy saw him coming in the door he gave him a big smile, and treated him to a pint of pale and a dish of jellied eels, and whispered in his ear that he'd pay him a hundred pounds sterling to put a bullet in the old girl's noggin.

A hundred quid! Terry had never expected to see that much money all in the one fist.

Two days later he shot Mrs Antrobus in Kensington High Street, in broad daylight, grabbing her bag to make it look like a common or garden snatch job done by some panicky kid. Percy had supplied the pistol – 'Absolutely untraceable, laddie, I assure you' – and arranged for it to be got rid of afterwards. This was how Terry discovered just how well connected the fat old poofter was. Untraceable heaters didn't grow on trees.

Next morning the papers ran a big story on the old girl's death, accompanied by 'an artist's impression' of 'the brutal killer'. Terrible likeness.

A few days after the funeral, Terry was treated by his new friend to a slap-up lunch at the Ritz. Terry was uneasy about them being seen together in such a public place, especially after the sudden demise of 'the Mater', but Percy gave him a slow wink and said it was all right, that he often came here with 'handsome young chaps such as yourself'.

When lunch was over, Terry's head was spinning from the wine and the stink of the cigars that Percy smoked, which he did even during the meal. They ambled down St James's Street and dropped into the premises of John Lobb, Bootmaker. There Terry was measured for a pair of brogues – he would have preferred something sharper, but when he took delivery of the shoes a couple of weeks later and tried them on, he felt like a lord. He managed to get a look at the bill, and was glad it was on Percy's account. Percy also bought him a dark-grey titfer at Locks the Hatters, just a few doors up from Lobb's.

'A young man in your line of work can't afford to look the part,' Percy said, in his plummy, chairman-of-the-board voice, and sniggered. It took Terry a second or two to get the twist of it. Wit, that was.

'What line of work would that be, exactly, Mr Antrobus?' Terry enquired, putting on the innocent act.

And Percy only smiled, and tried to pinch young Terry's neat little backside.

Terry still wore the Lobb shoes on occasion, especially when he was missing Percy, although that wasn't very often. They had aged nicely, the brogues, and fitted more snugly with each wearing. The grey hat had got badly rained on – at the races at Ascot, as it happened, to which top-hatted Percy had taken him, for a special treat – but Terry didn't mind as he had never got the hang of wearing it. He thought it made him look like a spiv, not the gentleman Percy had meant to turn him into. Poor old Percy.

He'd had to go, Percy did, in the end, eyes wide with surprise and his mouth shaped into that little puckered pink hole. Went down with a bump and a muffled rumble, like a sack of potatoes.

DONOSTIA

2

There was a narrow entrance to the bay, so that the water, once inside, fanned out in the shape of an enormous seashell. In fact, the bay was named La Concha, the Spanish word for shell. Because of that bottleneck channel and the long curve of the beach, the waves didn't run along at a bias, as they did on beaches at home. Instead, there was just one immensely long wave that broke with a single, muffled crash, from the point of the Old Town over to the right, all the way along to the headland far off on the left, where there was a funicular railway that, all day long, inched its laborious way up and down the side of a hill. When Quirke woke at night, with the window open beside the bed, it was as if there were a big, friendly animal asleep and softly breathing out there in the darkness.

All this fascinated him, and he spent a lot of time sitting in front of the window just looking out at the view, his mind a blank. 'You look at the sea as other men would look at a woman,' his wife said with amusement.

It was she, Evelyn, who had suggested San Sebastián, and before he could think up a convincing objection, she had written off for a brochure to the Hotel de Londres y de Inglaterra. 'Honestly,' he scoffed, 'the names they give to these establishments!' Evelyn ignored him. But when he saw the place he had to admit it was impressive, sitting smack in the middle of the seafront facing the bay, a solid, handsome edifice.

'That's "The London and England Hotel", right?' he said, reading the name on the brochure. 'Why can't we stay at a Spanish one?'

'It is Spanish, as you very well know,' his wife replied. 'It's the finest hotel in the city. I stayed there once, when the war was on. It was very good. I'm sure it still is.'

'Look at the prices,' he grumbled. He knew better than to ask how she had come to be in San Sebastián in wartime. Questions like that were *verboten*. 'And this is not even the high season,' he added.

It was spring, she said, the best season of all, and they were going to Spain on a holiday, even if she had to handcuff him and push him up the steps and on to the aeroplane.

'Northern Spain is southern Ireland,' she said. 'It rains all the time, everywhere is green, and everyone is Catholic. You will love it.'

'Will they have Irish wine?'

'Ha ha. You are so funny.'

She turned away and he smacked her on the bottom, with just enough force to make it wobble in the wonderful way that it did.

Strange, he thought, that the same passion was still there between them, the same erotic thrill. It should have been embarrassing, but it wasn't. They were middle-aged, they had made a late marriage – a second one for both of them – and, so far, they still couldn't get enough of each other. It was absurd, he would say, and 'Oh, *ja, ja*, ziss is zertainly zo!' Evelyn would agree, putting on her exaggerated, Herr Doktor Freud accent to make him laugh, while at the same time guiding his hands on to her broad, uncorseted, wobbly bum, and kissing

354

him on the lips in that light, peculiarly chaste fashion that never failed to set his blood sizzling.

It was a mystery to him that not only had she married him, but had stuck with him, too, and showed no signs of letting go. Her steadfastness was the very thing that made him nervous, however, and sometimes, in the early morning especially, he would rear up in a panic to check that she was there beside him in bed, that she hadn't given up on the whole project and slipped away in the night. But no, there she was, his large, soft-eyed, mystifying wife, as loving and lightsome as ever, in her always slightly amused, slightly distracted way.

His wife. He, Quirke, had a wife. Yes, the notion of it never failed to surprise him. He had been married before, but never like this; no, never like this.

And now here they were, in Spain, on holiday.

She had been right about the weather – it was raining when they arrived. She didn't care, and neither, really, did he, though he wouldn't say so.

About the greenness of the place she was also right, and about the Catholicism – there was a sense of staid piety that could have been Irish. It certainly wasn't the Spain that old Spanish hands wrote about, with scorching dust, and hot-eyed señoritas stamping the low square heels of their clunky black shoes, and *hidalgos* – was that the word? – in skin-tight trousers fighting each other with knives, and everybody shouting *Viva España!* and *No pasarán!* and plunging swords between the shoulder blades of lumbering, bloodied and bewildered bulls.

All the same, however much the place might seem like home, Quirke still resented being on holiday. It was like, he said, being in a drying-out hospital. He had been in more than one such place, in his day, and knew what he was talking about.

'You love to be miserable,' Evelyn told him, giving one of her soft, low laughs. 'It's your version of being happy.'

His wife was a professional psychiatrist, and regarded his many fears and phobias with benign amusement. Most of what he claimed to be the matter with him she diagnosed as play-acting, or 'performative defence', as she put it – a barrier erected by an overgrown child against a world that, despite his distrust of it, meant him no harm.

'The world treats us all equally,' she said.

'Mistreats, you mean,' he countered darkly.

She had once compared him to Eeyore, but since he had never heard of Pooh's mournful friend – A. A. Milne was not an author who would have figured in Quirke's blighted child-hood – the gibe fell flat.

'You have no problems,' she would say gaily. 'You have me, instead.' Then he would smack her on the backside again, hard, and she would turn and shimmy into his arms and bite him on the earlobe, just as hard.

Become a Faber Member and discover the best in the arts and literature

Sign up to the Faber Members programme and enjoy specially curated events, tailored discounts and exclusive previews of our forthcoming publications from the best novelists, poets, playwrights, thinkers, musicians and artists.

Join Faber Members for free at faber.co.uk

faber
members